Innocent Girls

A SAKURA BIANCHI THRILLER

Paul McDonald

Copyright

This is a work of fiction. Any references to real people, living or dead, actual events, businesses, organisations and localities are intended only to give the novel a sense of reality and authenticity. All names, characters and incidents are either the product of the author's imagination or are used fictitiously, and their resemblance, if any, to real-life counterparts is entirely coincidental.

Content warning: The following story includes graphic scenes of death and violence, including sexual abuse and torture. It depicts issues that may be sensitive for some readers.

Please read with care.

Day six since the abduction

1

Sakura sat in the rear seat of the sedan provided by her grandfather, Hirutu. He was the oyabun (leader) of the Hirutu yakuza. The car had been stolen three weeks earlier, and tonight, the registration plates had been replaced with those from another vehicle. These precautions were necessary to avoid detection from the police and the Hidetada yakuza family, who were the most prominent human trafficking syndicate in Japan.

Tonight, they were visiting a baishun yado (brothel) to begin searching for a young girl who had been abducted six days earlier to be forced into prostitution. They didn't know exactly where she was being held, but they suspected the Hidetada yakuza was involved, and they knew this baishun yado was connected to them.

Two of her grandfather's most trusted and senior men sat in the front seat. Tatsuo Ishikawa was driving and of average height for a Japanese man but very powerful and trained daily. He had broad shoulders, a thick neck, and a powerful chest. Despite being in his early sixties, he was still a formidable warrior, and many younger men would think twice before confronting him. Tatsuo means 'Dragon Man' in Japanese. So, when Sakura first met him at her grandfather's home, she thought it a fitting name as his body was covered entirely in colourful yakuza-style tattoos, except for his head, neck, and hands.

In the front passenger seat sat Takeo Kobayashi. He was big for a Japanese man, standing over 200 centimetres tall and weighing 105kg, all muscle. He had a scar running from his right ear lobe to just below his jaw, an old wound from a knife fight with two older men when he was only 14. Takeo means 'Warrior' in Japanese; it was also a very fitting name.

Yakuza have an unwritten code; not to interfere with another family's business, as this creates tension and conflict. Twenty-three years ago, the Hidetada yakuza decided they would control all of Tokyo's prostitution assets and went to war with other yakuza clans involved in prostitution. The battle had raged for six months, and at its conclusion, one hundred and fifty men had lost their lives. The police force obtained significant budget increases to halt the conflict and prevent the death of innocent bystanders. Three hundred baishun yados had been shut down, and revenues for all yakuza clans dropped dramatically as clients stopped buying services. Over four hundred yakuza were arrested and imprisoned. It had taken a decade for the businesses to be re-established and profitable.

Sakura's grandfather remembered the war well, as his businesses were also targeted. It was important that tonight his team not be identified as Hirutu family yakuza. He did not want Hidetada to know they were searching for the girl, and he did not want to start another conflict.

Sakura activated Bluetooth on her phone and connected it to the car's audio system. She played the audio message her grandfather had provided as they left his house. It described the layout of the baishun yado they would visit tonight. The audio recording had been obtained through blackmail, a common tactic used by the yakuza. They had obtained a video of an important man in compromising positions with a woman who was part of their yakuza family. They had asked her to seduce the man and record it without the man's knowledge. Once she understood why they needed the video, she was happy to help in the investigation. They also had a video of the man entering and leaving the baishun yado they were visiting tonight. They had threatened to provide this footage to his wife, who was unaware of his nocturnal activities. The audio played through the car speakers, the voice that of a distressed man.

"The door is protected by two video cameras monitored by guards in an office on the first floor. Both guards carry handguns and knives. Two heavy latches secure the thick door; it would be difficult to breach it forcefully. The door opens into a small vestibule, and stairs lead to the first floor. Halfway up the stairs, there is a small landing where the stairs change direction and lead up to the first floor in the opposite direction. A corridor runs to the end of the building. All the rooms are accessed on the right side of the corridor. There are two bedrooms; a third room is where the guards are stationed, and the fourth is a small bathroom with a shower. When a client arrives, one guard will go downstairs to let them in, take the cash and lead them to one of the two rooms depending on the type of woman the man has requested. They are warned not to injure the girls, or there will be serious consequences. These men are big, ugly, and professional thugs."

The audio finished, and the three-person team discussed their strategy while nearing their destination. The baishun yado was in an older area of Tokyo which consisted of traditional buildings from the 1900s. Paper lanterns hung from most of the wooden shop fronts. All the shops were small, just two levels, and made from timber. Some were painted, others had allowed the timber to be exposed to the elements, and the wood had turned a grey silver over time. The signage on the buildings was brightly painted or used lighting to advertise their names. The original homes and shops had been converted into restaurants and geisha bars, interspersed with several high-end baishun yados.

They drove slowly past their destination. Sakura looked at the building, checked it to the photo on her phone, and was satisfied it was the correct business. Tatsuo drove for another block and then parked the car.

2

Sakura took hold of her tsurgi sword and her tantō (a short, bladed sword), pulled the mask of the ninja hood down to hide her face, just her eyes showing, and then stepped out of the car. Once outside, she stored the swords in their sayas (scabbards), which had been sewn into the back of her outfit, only the sword hilts showing. Then, together the three of them walked to the baishun yado.

They passed by a karaoke bar, and music drifted outside with the sounds of a drunken crowd. The night air was calm and crisp; there was a rumble of thunder in the distance, a storm was threatening. The street was poorly lit as the local businesses had resisted the council's initiative to install street lighting. Instead, they preferred the illumination from their establishments, retaining this ancient town's cultural aspects. Unfortunately, this resulted in pockets of darkness lingering at the fringes of the light.

Walking towards the baishun yado, they were startled by a deep meow. A black cat emerged from the darkness, walked directly across their path, raised its tail, and sprayed them, a tomcat's act of defiance. Sakura wasn't superstitious or religious. She learned about the world's reality at the young age of ten when during a home invasion, she was sexually assaulted, left for dead, and orphaned. Regardless, she couldn't help but think the cat's appearance was an ominous symbol.

They studied the baishun yado; they could see the two cameras on either side of the door, providing a view of anyone standing there. However, by staying close to the wall, they could remain out of the camera's range. So Sakura and Takeo took positions on either side of the door directly under the cameras.

Tatsuo walked towards the door, his head slightly down. He wore a wide-brimmed kasa (hat) to hide his face from the camera as he knocked on the door. When they heard the door bolt being withdrawn, Sakura and Takeo used their tantō to sever the camera wires, thus terminating the external camera feed. A large, bald man answered the door. He was younger and taller than Tatsuo, so he didn't detect any threat. Instead, he barked, "Who are you? Do you have an appointment?" Tatsuo did a slight, respectful bow, and as he straightened, he smashed his right fist into the man's lower jaw with a vicious uppercut. The man fell backwards, like a felled tree.

Immediately, Sakura stepped over him and fled up the first flight of steps. The steps were narrow, just wide enough for one person, typical in these older dwellings where space was at a premium. Her leather slippers were silent on the steps as she carefully placed each foot close to the walls on each tread to eliminate any boards squeaking. She moved swiftly, stopping when she reached the small platform where the next set of steps turned 180 degrees to climb up to the first level. She chose this landing to launch her attack; she would be hidden from anyone coming down the steps. Taking a deep breath, she calmed her mind and reached behind her shoulder, slowly drawing her tsurgi from its saya.

In her heightened state of awareness, she could hear a faint 'ting', the note the sword made when it was released from the saya. Then, a man yelled in Japanese, "Hey mother fucker, are you ok?" When there was no response, she could hear footsteps, moving quickly but not running. She also heard 'shush chunk', the sound of an automatic weapon chambering a round. This confirmed that the second guard was armed. Sakura waited silently, the tsurgi held tightly in both hands above her and to the right of her head, hardly breathing, as still as a statue.

First, she saw the barrel and then recognised the Beretta 92FS, a favoured weapon of the yakuza. When the hand and forearm holding the gun started to round the corner, she struck downwards in a smooth continuous diagonal stroke from above her right shoulder to her left thigh, stopping the motion when the sword was level with her left hip. This stroke is known as the Kesi Giri. She had practised this sword stroke daily during her ten years of training at the Sohei Temple. She had targeted the radio-carpal joint, where the wrist joins the radius and the ulna, the two primary forearm bones. Only ligaments and cartilage hold this area together. The blade of her tsurgi severed the hand from the arm smoothly and without any loss of momentum.

The hand dropped to the ground, still holding the Beretta. The man screamed and continued around the platform, blood streaming from his arm stump. Sakura stepped quickly to face her opponent; he was a heavily tattooed yakuza mobster. His face was white from shock, and his mouth opened wide as he screamed in pain. The screaming halted quickly as Sakura struck again, attacking the neck, the sword crossing from left to right, removing the head cleanly. A spray of arterial blood arced across the walls in the shape of a rainbow as the guard tumbled to the stairs headless, sliding downwards towards the front door.

Sakura removed a plastic bag from a concealed pocket in her outfit, placed the head inside, pulled the ties closed, and then attached it to a ring on the belt she wore around her waist. Next, she wiped the blade on her victim's shirt, removing most of the blood. Then, taking a silk cloth from her trousers, she wiped the blade clean before returning it to its saya.

She could see Takeo had secured cable ties to the wrists and ankles of the guard whom Tatsuo had knocked out earlier. He placed a hood over the man's head, then effortlessly hoisted the large guard onto his shoulder and walked outside to deposit him in the trunk of their car.

Sakura turned and climbed the steps to the first floor; shoji doors accessed the small four rooms. She opened the first shoji door to see a man in his 40s hastily put on his trousers. He turned when he heard the door slide open. Sakura scanned the room. There was a western-style bed, and a naked girl lay on her back, her right wrist handcuffed to the headboard and her left ankle handcuffed to the footboard. Her eyes were opened but glassy, indicating she was heavily sedated. Sakura could feel her anger growing, a deep burning sensation in her stomach.

The man tried to push past her, but she struck him hard with a roundhouse kick to the head, striking him in the temple. He dropped to the floor unconscious. The skull's temple, or 'Pterion Bone', is located above the ear and is the joining point for four skull plates; this area is thin and fragile. Behind the Pterion bone is a major cranial artery called the middle meningeal artery. If this artery is severed, the skull cavity fills with blood causing severe pain; death can occur within hours. Sakura knew her kick was fatal; she had felt the skull shatter through her thin leather slippers. He would die without immediate medical attention. Yet, she felt no remorse; he deserved it.

She turned, left the room, and opened the second room door. An older man and a woman in her twenties were lying under a sheet, anxiously looking at Sakura as she entered the room.

Sakura spoke quietly in Japanese. "Are you here by force or by choice?"

The woman bowed her head and said, "Choice."

Sakura walked to the bed and yelled at the man, "Get up now!"

He quickly got out of bed. He was naked, hairy, and fat. He stood trembling, covering his genitals with both hands. Sakura struck him with a punch to the jaw, and he spun around and fell to the floor face down, unconscious. She drew her tsurgi sword, then drove it into the back of the man's neck, the blade slicing between the C3 and C4 vertebrae, severing his spinal cord. He would die in three minutes because his body no longer communicated with his brain. His breathing had already stopped.

"Now, give me the names of the people who run this operation."

The girl said, "They will kill me."

Sakura said, "If you don't tell me, I will kill you! They will never know; he won't tell them." Sakura pointed at the man lying on the floor to emphasise the point. The girl talked for several minutes providing information that Sakura recorded on her phone. Sakura had planned to kill the prostitute; however, after listening to her story, she felt empathetic towards her and decided to let her live. She was wearing her hood and mask so the woman would not be able to identify her but would know she was a woman.

Sakura said, "Listen to me very carefully; the men who own this baishun yado will want to know who did this. I want you to tell them you were in the room with a client when you heard men yelling, 'Where do you keep the money?' Tell them your client got nervous; he tried to flee when two men entered the room; they killed him and raped you. Then, they took the girl from the room next door. Can you be convincing?"

"Yes, of course I can; I must lie daily."

Sakura walked into the third room, it was separated into two areas: a dining area and the security office. The dining area had a small table, two chairs, and a bar fridge. The security side held three monitors; two were blacked out, probably the cameras they had disabled earlier. The third monitor showed the corridor, and she could see the bloodstained wall at the end of the hall. There didn't appear to be any other cameras, and the security system was basic; no live feeds were going off-premises. Sakura accessed the control panel, searched backwards through the video to when she entered the corridor and deleted all the footage that contained images of her. Then she powered down the remaining camera.

There was an iPhone on the table. She picked it up; it could prove helpful. However, it was locked and required facial recognition. She removed the head from its bag and pointed it toward the iPhone; it took a few attempts before the phone opened. Entering the phone's settings, she reset the phone to open with a 6-digit PIN 111111. There was a locked drawer under the table supporting the security monitors. Sakura returned to the corridor and searched the dead guard's pockets until she found the key. The drawer contained JPY 2 million, the day's takings. She pocketed the money. She wanted this to look like a robbery gone wrong.

She walked into the fourth room, the bathroom, which contained a small shower and toilet, and was surprisingly clean, with fresh towels for the clients to use when they had finished. No one was hiding in there; it was empty. Returning to the first room, she spoke softly to the young, sedated girl. "Can you hear me?" There was no reaction. She opened her lock-pick kit and selected a tool suitable to remove the handcuffs. Fifteen seconds later, the girl was free, the handcuffs no match for Sakura's lock-picking skills. As Takeo walked into the room, Sakura wrapped the bed sheet around the young girl to provide her with some warmth and privacy. He gently lifted the girl onto his shoulder and took her to their car.

3

Tatsuo drove away from the baishun yado, one guard secured in the trunk of the car, the other headless and lying inside the baishun yado, with another two of the baishun yado customers killed or dying in the rooms. The young girl was sleeping, her head resting against Sakura's shoulder. Sakura told Tatsuo, "Drive to the nearest hospital; this girl requires immediate medical care." Then she lightly slapped the girl's face, trying to revive her from this drug-induced stupor.

"What is your name?"

"Akahana", the girl whispered.

"Do you know who did this to you?"

"Let me sleep," the young girl said, her eyes rolling back into her head as she lost consciousness.

When they arrived at the hospital, Sakura went inside, collected a wheelchair, and then returned to the car to collect the girl. She pushed the wheelchair to the admissions desk and said, "I have just rescued this young girl from a human trafficking operation. She has been raped multiple times and drugged for several days. She requires treatment." As Sakura spoke, she watched the colour drain from the nurse's face. When she had finished, the nurse handed her an admission form and asked if she could fill in her details so the police could interview her. Sakura smiled, turned, and left the hospital. She had no time to complete forms or talk to the police; she needed to interview the mobster stored in the trunk of their car.

While Sakura was in the hospital, Tatsuo called a member of their yakuza family. Earlier that day, Hirutu had provided him with several yakuza contacts; each contact could offer a particular service depending on the requirements. When the man answered, Tatsuo said, "I need a quiet place to conduct an interview."

"Where are you?"

"Shinjuku"

"Ok, I will meet you at the Takahata on Riverview Drive. Do you know it?"

"Yes, we will be there in 15 minutes."

"Ok, I will see you soon."

4

The Takahata is a large Japanese restaurant catering to wealthy Japanese businessmen. Fine dining, fine sake, and fine geishas are their trademarks for entertaining their clientele. Tatsuo exited the car and walked towards the restaurant entrance, where a solidly built Japanese man stood smoking a cigarette. He was wearing an expensive tailor-made suit that accentuated his physique. Tatsuo discreetly provided the secret hand signal indicating he was a member of the Hotato Family. All yakuza who worked for Hirutu knew this signal; the punishment for disclosing this hand signal to non-Hirutu yakuza was death, including immediate family. For forty years, this secret had been maintained, serving the family well, especially at times like this when it was essential to confirm the validity of a fellow family member. The man acknowledged with the correct hand signal response and introduced himself as Kai.

"Drive down the laneway on the left, and at the rear of this building is garage access. I will open the door for you. Enter and park in space nine." Tatsuo bowed, thanked Kai, and went back to the car. He smiled at the irony because nine is considered an unlucky number in Japan. It is pronounced 'ku', the same pronunciation as agony or torture. Very fitting for what was to become of the mobster in the trunk of their car.

After parking the car, they followed Kai as he walked towards a heavy steel door. He used a large key to unlock the three 'Hinaka' deadbolts which secured the door. Hinaka deadbolts are Japan's most robust and challenging to lockpick or force. The opened door revealed a windowless room, approximately 5 metres square and heavily soundproofed, judging by the material affixed to the walls. The floor sloped gently on all sides towards a large square metal grate in the centre of the room. On top of the grate was a heavy steel chair with metal wrist restraints connected to the chair's arms, metal ankle restraints on the front legs, and a metal neck restraint attached to the chair's high back. Five comfortable chairs were spaced around a large wooden table on which three different size boxes sat. Kai said, "The boxes contain various interviewing tools depending on your preference." He pointed to the rear wall, "Over there is the refrigerator. It contains chilled drinks, water, sodas as well as beer. Feel free to help yourself. The room is completely soundproofed, and the walls and door are designed as a 'Faraday Cage'. Electronic signals cannot enter or leave this room. When you are finished, or if you require anything, please use the buzzer on the wall. This will notify me. Until then, the room will be locked, preventing entry or egress."

Tatsuo and Takeo left to collect the hooded mobster from the car trunk, carrying him back to the room. They said goodbye to Kai, and he closed and bolted the door. Once the man was seated in the chair, they pulled their masks down from their hoods, exposing only their eyes. It was important that this man not see their faces. Tatsuo stood behind the man, removed his hood, then wrapped his strong arms around his neck and held him tight. "We will remove your restraints now and sit you in this chair for a nice discussion. I will break your neck if you attempt to escape or fight back. Do you understand?"

"Yes," said the man. He had lost much of his bravado since he had challenged Tatsuo at the door of the baishun yado.

Takeo cut the plastic cable ties from his legs and used the chair's metal restraints to secure his legs tightly against the chair. The design of the restraints was state-of-the-art. They had an adjustment wheel that enabled them to be tightened by incremental amounts for a tight fit. Next, he cut the cable ties restraining his arms and secured them tightly against the chair arm using the adjustment mechanism. Finally, Tatsuo attached the neck restraint, and they stood back to admire the ingenuity of the chair's design.

Whilst the men were securing their captive, Sakura had started to open the boxes on the desk to understand what they contained. The first box she opened contained several electronic components, a transformer with a dial enabling it to be set to different voltages or amps to deliver an electric charge. It came with several additional accessories; alligator clips for attaching it to fingers, toes, tongue, and nipples. In addition, there was a long thin tube that could be inserted into a male or female urethra and a metal plug designed for either the vagina or rectum. Of course, she wasn't expecting to use any of these.

The second box held items for delivering burns to a body. A small blowtorch and six butane cartridges, A branding iron in the shape of a heart that could be heated and pressed onto the flesh. There were two retraction devices, one which could be inserted into the mouth to force it open and another that looked like it could be used to keep an eye open.

The third box held a vast array of cutting instruments, saws, bolt cutters, different-shaped knives and hooks. They were all made from surgical steel and shone in the fluorescent light. If they had been used before, they had been thoroughly cleaned. Sakura left this box open; she knew Tatsuo was proficient at conducting interrogations and could extract information from even the most hardened criminals. She knew his preference for creating pain would be the instruments in box number three.

The table had storage underneath, and Sakura opened one of the doors to peer inside. There were rows of containers with labels on them describing the contents. She scanned the first row: diluted vinegar, industrial strength vinegar, hydrochloric acid, sulphuric acid. She grabbed the container with diluted vinegar and placed it on the table.

Tatsuo asked the man, "What is your name?"

"Yoshihara," the bald man said.

"Well, Yoshihara, listen very carefully to me. An important man has lost his niece; her name is Honoka Kondo. We believe members of your human trafficking organisation have abducted her. If you wish to live past this night, you will tell us the information we require to find Honoka. We want to know where she may be kept and the names of men who could help us find her."

"I know nothing; the man you killed at the baishun yado was the contact for our supplier. Every few weeks, they come to collect the girls and replace them with new girls. Our clientele prefers variety, so the girls are moved around frequently."

Tatsuo had heard stories like this before; interrogations usually began this way, so a form of persuasion was necessary. Sakura decided to turn up the heat a bit, the bald man looked way too comfortable for her liking. She removed the severed head from the bag attached to her belt and placed it in his lap, the lifeless eyes looking up at him. Instantly she could see the fear growing in his features.

"Perhaps you would like to join a similar fate as this man?"

Yoshihara's face had gone deathly pale; he said, "You are asking me to betray my family. What you ask is my death sentence. The organisation has many tentacles. Each tentacle's knowledge is limited to their business; this ensures that if one tentacle is exposed, the others will remain operating. Please, I don't have any information to tell you. I am the lowest rung and don't understand how this business works. I only open the door and protect the girls from aggressive customers."

Sakura returned the severed head to its bag, it's new home.

Tatsuo had been over at the table, collecting instruments, and had returned. Using a sharp knife, he pushed it through the man's trousers just below his hip and cut through the thin fabric to his ankle. Next, he opened the trouser leg and folded it back into the man's lap, Yoshihara's leg now completely exposed. Tatsuo held a medical scalpel up in one hand; in the other, he held a hooked instrument.

"Last chance to provide answers before I begin."

"I can't tell you anything!" yelled Yoshihara.

Tatsuo used the scalpel to open a deep 10-centimetre cut into the side of the man's leg, starting just above and behind the knee joint. The man screamed! Tatsuo pushed the hooked instrument into the man's leg (it was similar to a crochet hook), and he dug around inside the leg, searching for something. When he pulled it out, Sakura could see he had captured a white rope-like structure 3mm in diameter. As he pulled it outside the leg, Yoshihara gave a blood-curdling scream, and then he fainted from the pain.

Tatsuo left the nerve in the hook dangling from the man's leg. He explained what he was doing. "This is the common peroneal nerve, a sub-branch of the sciatica nerve, and runs from above the knee to the foot. Its purpose is to control the foot's movement. I have stretched and relocated it from the facia it normally slides within, but it's still connected. The pain he feels from this action is excruciating, orders of magnitude worse than the most painful sciatica pain. He will awaken soon; the pain will be agonising until I release the nerve and let it return to its position. What I'm doing will most likely result in permanent nerve injury. His gait will be affected, and he will probably have constant pain for the rest of his life."

Tatsuo was correct; in a minute or so, Yoshihara regained consciousness and started screaming, "Stop it! Please, stop the pain!" Tatsuo released the nerve, and it sprang back into the wound. Yoshihara stopped screaming. Sakura bent over him, staring into his eyes, her eyes the only feature visible under her mask. Then she removed his phone from his pocket, held it to his face, and unlocked it. She reset the phone to open with the PIN '111111' as before, as this combination was easy to remember.

In a drawer of the table was a large A3 writing pad with a thick cardboard back providing rigidity and a large black marker pen. During interrogations, the hands were targeted to persuade a subject to reveal the information required. It was common to remove fingernails, which may seem superficial; however, it is excruciating. Often a finger or two is donated to the interviewee. Similarly, the mouth is another structure that can undergo damage; the tongue is usually removed, the tonsils and epiglottis burnt, or the back of the throat branded. All these combined can make it challenging to obtain the information when the victim is ready. A black marker can be held in an injured hand allowing the person to write a name, phone number, or even an address on the large paper and be legible. Sakura used the black marker to write the number 2 on the rear of the phone she had taken from Yoshihara.

Then she wrote the number 1 on the phone she had taken from the guard she had killed at the baishun yado.

Sakura handed Tatsuo the container that held the diluted vinegar.

"Now Yoshihara, let's try again. Who do you report to?"

"Benji was the contact; you killed him; I don't know anyone." Tatsuo poured the vinegar into Yoshihara's wound, resulting in a blood-curdling scream not dissimilar to the howl of a cow being slain in an abattoir.

Sakura opened the contacts on his phone, selected Favourites and said, "Who is Sara? Should I call her?"

"No, please don't; she is my wife."

"Well, what about Akari?"

Yoshihara started to sob, "My daughter."

"Perhaps we should call her and arrange for her to come here and meet you."

Yoshihara was no longer sobbing; he was crying uncontrollably. Sakura and her team knew that success in an interrogation often required leverage, and threatening a man's family was a powerful tactic.

"Yoshihara, if you don't tell me the name of your boss or who is the next man in the chain of command, we will need to gather your family here to persuade you."

Yoshihara broke down, howling, "I don't know!" Then he emptied his stomach contents over the front of him. Some made it into the steel drain.

Unfortunately, he didn't have any helpful information for them. So, they would need to try another approach.

<u>5</u>

Tatsuo applied antibacterial powder to Yoshihara's leg and secured it with a clean bandage. While removing the chair restraints, Sakura pushed the button to summon Kai. They replaced the hood on Yoshihara's head and cable-tied his wrists behind him. When Kai opened the door, they thanked him for providing the premises and returned to their car. They returned Yoshihara to the car trunk and then drove ten minutes to a small reserve by the Meguro River Walk.

After removing Yoshihara from the car trunk, Tatsuo carried him to a bench and let him sit, the hood still over his head. "Yoshihara, you need to go to the hospital for treatment. Whom do you want me to call to provide directions to find you?"

"Tenjin."

"Is he a work contact?"

"Yes, he used to work at our baishun yado, but he was promoted. He should still be awake, and he will come and collect me. Thank you."

Sakura searched the contacts; there was only one Tenjin, no surname. Finally, she nodded at Tatsuo, who reached down, lifted Yoshihara by the shoulders, hoisted him over his head and threw him into the river. The river was three to four metres deep at this point. They watched as he struggled to stay afloat, but with his hands secured behind his back and the hood tightened around his neck, it was only a short time before he started to sink and start his journey towards Tokyo Bay.

Sakura unhooked the bag from her belt containing the other guard's head, swung it over her head twice, and then released it. It sailed over the railing and 15 metres out into the river. Tatsuo clapped his hands together loudly, "Bravo! Bravo! Good throw, little one." They silently walked back to the car and started driving back to her grandfather's house. It had been a long night. They agreed to meet at 8:00 am in her grandfather's study.

***

Sakura was lying in bed, her mind racing, ideas cascading in and out like a swirling pool in a raging stream; sleep was impossible. Four men are dead, and the young girl, Akahana, is in hospital. However, they had a potential lead, 'Tenjin', a prostitute's statement, and two phones that may provide other leads. They had made good progress today, but was it enough to rescue Honoka?

Day 7 since the abduction

<u>6</u>

Sakura entered her grandfather's study and was surprised by its transformation. Last week they decided they would need room to conduct meetings and store information, a 'war room'. Her grandfather had offered his study as it was large enough to accommodate ten people easily.

An attractive woman was sitting on one of two comfortable-looking couches on the western side of the room. They were positioned each side of a long rectangle-shaped table. The woman stood and walked towards Sakura, her hand outstretched.

Sakura took her hand, noticing the calluses on her fingertips, and they shook hands, each woman with a powerful grip.

"My name is Megumi; I work for your grandfather and will provide your team with Tech Support."

"I am Sakura; it's nice to meet you."

"There is coffee and tea over there on the counter if you want a drink."

"No, thank you. Did you do all this?"

"Well, yes, I was responsible for the design and requirements. My team installed the furniture and equipment. I'm hoping it will be suitable for your purpose."

"It's amazing! How were you able to do this in just a week?"

The conversation was interrupted when Tatsuo and Takeo entered the room. They exchanged introductions with Megumi, and whilst the pleasantries were underway, Sakura studied her. It was apparent she was not intimidated by these men, nor did she behave subserviently.

Her hair was black, straight, styled in a ponytail, and held in place by a decorative hairpin, constructed from polished and lacquered sandalwood. An intricate design at one end and two rows of precious stones running along its length. A master artisan could have only made it.

She wore a yellow polo-neck sweater, tight white Gucci jeans, and a Gucci belt. On her feet, she wore Italian-made leather boots that covered her calves. Interesting! Sakura wondered, who is this woman?

She could see her eyes sparkled with intelligence, and her skin glowed; her only make-up was lip gloss and some pink eye shadow. She didn't expect to have their own 'Tech Support'; she hadn't realised her grandfather had technicians in his employment.

Sakura's gaze searched the room, studying the new equipment. In the middle of the room was a completely transparent, thin-panel screen; it must have been over 120cm in width. It stood upon a thin metallic stand, its futuristic design defying physics. Studying it further, she could see icons displayed along the bottom of the screen, most likely the user interface. Towards the eastern wall was a sizeable industrial-style desk with storage drawers, ergonomic chairs, four laptop computers and four large, curved monitors. Finally, in the northern corner of the room was a full-sized server rack with hundreds of blinking lights, all contained within a solid stainless-steel cage with four locking bolts securing the door. Sakura wasn't overly familiar with modern technology but knew enough to understand that this could serve a multi-floor office.

Hirutu entered the room, and everyone stood to meet him, bowing respectfully. He bowed back.

"Good morning, everyone, I hope you all slept well after your successful first assignment yesterday. I see you have met one of my most valued employees.

"I first met Megumi in March 2007. I was contacted by the Dean of Tokyo University, who suggested I meet a student he considered the most intelligent and innovative student ever to attend his university. He thought she was wasting her time attending the University and told me she could transform my business into a highly profitable, modern twenty-first-century business.

"We had dinner that night, and Megumi explained that she was developing an app for the newly released iPhone. I didn't understand what an app was or how an iPhone differed from my faithful Nokia. I was starting to wonder why I had invested my time meeting her and was considering leaving when she said something that got my attention. She explained that the app could send and receive messages that the authorities could not intercept. This is because the communication is encrypted in transmission and stored encrypted in the phone's memory. Therefore, if the police impounded a phone, they could not decrypt the message. Now that is interesting, I thought, and something I could utilise. That was the incarnation of the Ango-Ka app you are all familiar with.

"She explained that in ten years, it was foreseeable that every person would have the power of a computer in their phone. It sounded like a fairy tale to me, yet I could see from the gleam in her eyes and her passion that she saw this as the future and wanted to be a part of it. When I asked her what types of opportunities she could offer for my business, she talked about how the porn industry was driving the expansion of the Internet. She had my interest again, but I spoke too much. Megumi, please tell them what you have been involved with and how you have transformed my business empire."

Megumi faced the three of them and, in a powerful and confident voice, started. "The issues constraining growth in the porn industry were immediately removed with the introduction of the internet. Men no longer needed to visit a sex shop to purchase movies, they could watch porn from the comfort of their home, in their office, or their bed.

Most men found it difficult to walk into a baishun yado for fear of being seen. However, with the introduction of webcams, they could now interact with a woman. They could watch women of different ethnicities and body shapes and ask them to do whatever they desired with a simple payment.

I established a streaming service based on a subscription model. The customer pays a monthly fee of JPY2000, much less than the price of an X-Rated videotape or DVD, and they have access to millions of titles and webcam channels.

There are thousands of girls streaming from their homes, they pay JPY5000 a month and we provide them with access to our client base. We provide the payment system for a 30% fee from their earnings. It's a good deal for them, much better than prostituting, where they are limited to one customer at a time and still need to pay the baishun yado overhead. A good webcam girl can easily make JPY80,000 – JPY120,000 a night without the risk of disease or violence. We have 50 million subscribers growing at 4% a year."

Hirutu interrupted as Megumi paused for a moment. "I had exited the prostitution business years earlier when the yakuza prostitution war started; it wasn't worth the trouble. However, the yearly revenues from the streaming services were staggering and far surpassed the value that could be derived from prostitution. As a result, we have expanded the streaming service into all the Western nations, and now we are focusing on India and the Middle East. The 2021 profit was JPY$1.2 billion, achieved with just a small workforce. How many people are reporting to you now, Megumi?"

"I have three hundred employees; most of these are engineers. I leverage cloud-based services for all our infrastructure. We use Amazon Cloud Services and Microsoft Azure for all our computing requirements. They provide these services for a fraction of the cost of what it would be if we did it ourselves. These companies have destroyed the 'Barriers of Entry', providing serious computing power to the smallest businesses. Other revenue streams are from 'Denial of Service' attacks, Ransomware, or from breaching the security of international companies to steal intellectual property, as well as research and development information for on-sale to their competitors or a needy government."

"Thank you, Megumi. I think that's enough for the team just now. Why don't you explain how the 'war room' equipment operates?"

Megumi walked over to the large transparent screen in the centre of the room and said, "Please join me over here; space yourselves evenly on both sides of the screen." She touched an icon, and a colour picture of Honoka Kondo, the missing girl, was displayed in the middle of the screen. Using her index finger, she touched the image, then made it smaller and moved it to the top left corner. Three mouths hung open. This unique technology was so smooth, and it was like the picture was hovering in the air. Next, she touched a mapping icon, displaying a map of Tokyo. Touching the top right corner of the map with her index finger, she zoomed into the Shinjuku area. It was an unbelievably clear aerial view of the street they had visited last night. It wasn't in real-time; it was a satellite image; however, the detail was incredible; it was possible to determine the clothing worn by pedestrians.

She pointed at a building and drew a yellow circle around it with her finger. "This was the baishun yado you visited last night. Of course, we didn't expect the girl to be there, but it was our starting point, and now we have some valuable intelligence that I can use to further our searches. Sakura, can you unlock the phones you took from the two guards last night?"

Sakura did and said, "The code is 111111. We will also use this PIN for all the phones we secure in the future. Also, I have marked the back of a phone with where it was obtained so that we can keep track of them. The phone marked on the rear with '1' is from the headless guard, and phone '2' belonged to the man Yoshihara."

"Good. I will have my team download all the information from the phones, names, addresses, etc., and start building up a contacts map. We need a few more phones from different locations, or some loose tongues, to establish the most valuable connections. Now, let's discuss some housekeeping. I have agreed with Hirutu that the name for this operation is 'The Saviour'. I have updated the Ango-Ka app to provide secure access to the Saviour server. That's the server over there. Multiple industrial-strength firewalls protect it, and it is impossible to penetrate outside this room without the Ango-Ka app. So, I shouldn't need to tell you how important it is for you to protect these USBs with your life.

To help you, I have provided customised USBs. Takeo and Tatsuo, your USB integrates with this belt buckle." She held up a belt, and after pressing a barely perceivable recessed button on the reverse of the clip, a USB slid out from it, allowing it to be inserted into a laptop or iPhone. She said, "To return it to the belt, just push it in until it locks. Sakura, yours is hidden within this hair clip." She showed Sakura how to access the USB and return it to the hair clip.

Sakura said, "I have a recording from the prostitute at the baishun yado and a recording of Yoshihara's interrogation. I was planning on playing it to the team."

"Excellent. Over here at this desk are the laptops you can use for storing the information." Megumi plugged a cable between Sakura's phone and the laptop, opened the folder on the server named 'The Saviour', then created a folder called "Baishun yado 1", and copied the recordings from the phone to the folder. When the transfer had finished, she renamed the first audio file 'Prostitute' and the other audio file 'Yoshihara Guard'. She opened the 'Prostitute' file, which played over four small yet powerful Wi-Fi speakers; Sakura hadn't noticed these.

The team listened to Sakura's voice, "What's your name?"
"Yui."
"Have you seen this girl?"
There was a pause, and then Sakura said, "Yui looked at the photo of Honoka on my phone. Her response was to shake her head, so No."
Sakura's voice continued from the speakers. "Tell me about this place, the men, other places you work at, all you know."
Yui was sobbing, but she started, "This is the only work I can do. It provides adequate money to pay rent on a small apartment and buy food for my five-year-old son and my mother who also lives with us. You probably think I'm trash, but a single mother can't find well-paying work in Tokyo."
Sakura said, "I'm not here to judge you; I am looking for a young girl who has been abducted and is being forced into prostitution. I want to find her, and I want to punish the men responsible."
"I don't know any names. I receive a phone call around 3:00 pm. It's always a private number, and the caller tells me where I will work that night."

"Can you tell me the addresses of the baishun yados where you work?"

"Yes", nodded Yui, and then she provided Sakura with the addresses of five baishun yados, all in the Shinjuku and surrounding area.

"Anything else you can tell me?"

"They use heroin to keep the girls compliant. I became vulnerable after the birth of my son, and my boyfriend dumped me. It was this baishun yado where I became an addict. I had been looking for work all day. I had tried every bar and restaurant within three blocks and been rejected by all of them. No one was interested in a single mother with a baby. I was desperate. A man was leaving the baishun yado, and the guard offered me money to come in and see how it worked. I knew it was wrong, but once they gave me the heroin, calm overcame me, and I felt elated for the first time in months. The heroin made it easy to detach myself from work. I would leave my body for the customer to do as they wanted whilst I floated off to a better place. I worked from 9:00 pm to 6:00 am every day and was always home in time to look after my little boy. They used me every day. I had to do whatever they asked before they would provide me with a shot of heroin at the start and end of my shift. They have destroyed me with drugs, physically and mentally. The only positive is my mum and boy have food and shelter."

When the recording ended, Hirutu started clapping. "Well done, Sakura, that's five new leads. Last night proved to have been most valuable in progressing our investigation."

While the audio was playing, Megumi had been typing the addresses of the additional five baishun yados into the laptop. She was using an application that Sakura needed to become more familiar with. Then she pressed an icon labelled 'SEEK', and a blue hourglass appeared spinning on the screen. When the hourglass disappeared, a map was displayed. Next, Megumi selected an icon labelled 'PROJECT', and a map of Tokyo was displayed on the sizeable transparent screen.

The team moved to the centre of the room standing either side of the large screen. Six buildings were highlighted on the display. No, they weren't highlighted; they were pulsating. Sakura was amazed at the sophistication of this display. She had never seen this type of technology before. The buildings were positioned approximately three street blocks from each other. Megumi said, "These are the buildings Yui identified; the Hidetada yakuza are saturating this area with baishun yados."

Hirutu pointed at the pulsating building furthest from the baishun yado they had attacked last night. "We will assault this baishun yado tonight. We will use a freelance team for the attack. We understand the operation better now, so I don't want you three to be identified. I have the names of two men we can approach today and persuade them to assist us. Sakura, I will get you to recruit the men. Takeo, please convince our blackmailed associate to visit this baishun yado this morning. I want his description of the premises on an audio file on that laptop by 1:30 pm this afternoon, or the video will be sent to his wife. Then I want him to visit this baishun yado tomorrow." He pointed to a second building. "Same process, audio file received by 1:30 pm. After that, he can stop, as I'm sure we will have gotten Hidetada's attention by then."

Hirutu said, "Megumi, can you show the team the hypothetical organisation structure we believe we need to infiltrate to find Honoka?" Megumi closed the map of Tokyo and chose another icon. An image appeared on the display. It started as a small square and then expanded, flying outwards to fill most of the screen. Sakura's eyes widened; her respect for Megumi had increased exponentially since their first meeting just 30 minutes earlier; the animation and smoothness of the effect were very cool indeed.

Hirutu pointed at a photo at the top of the screen. "This is Tokugawa Hidetada, the oyabun of the Hidetada yakuza; he controls the human trafficking business. He has established an ingenuous decentralised, and autonomous structure for his operations. Using 'Chinese Walls', he has isolated each business, preventing infiltration. As a result, only a handful of people know the name of the person in charge of the next level." Below the photo of Tokugawa were five other pictures, each connected to Tokugawa with a line.

"These icons represent his other businesses: drugs, embezzlement, robbery, extortion and blackmail." Finally, he pointed at a computer's graphical image of a man. "This icon represents the people managing the human trafficking operations. Only Tokugawa knows who the head of this business is; none of the other businesses knows who runs the other areas. As a result, they never meet as a team. In this way, he can protect unwanted information flowing to the authorities."

He touched the icon, and the other yakuza businesses faded away, and a third layer of companies appeared. "We believe the next level is the processing centres, each residing in a different region of Japan. We're not sure how many, but perhaps as many as seven. They manage the acquisition, resource distribution and revenue collection. We need to leverage the information from the individual baishun yados to identify at least one of these processing centres." He pressed on one of the processing centres' icons, and another layer was displayed, showing ten more buildings. "We believe the girls are circulated through the various baishun yados associated with each centre. They manage these movements ensuring integrity for the other businesses if the authorities arrest any of these girls."

Megumi pointed back at the processing centres. "We need to find one of these next and I expect the guards' phones will provide us with a lead. Once we infiltrate this centre, I can access their computer system and find where Honoka Kondo is now. Any questions?"

Sakura looked around; Tatsuo and Takeo were blank-faced; she wasn't sure how much of the presentation they had understood. But she did; it was a hierarchical business with built-in barriers protecting itself. She could understand that Megumi was looking for connections, and based on their experience with Yoshihara, the guard they interrogated from the first baishun yado, it would be the phones and their data that were the key.

The room was filled with several beeps as each of the Saviour's phones indicated a notification had been received. Megumi looked at her phone and said, "This is timely; I have team members monitoring police scanners, rescue services and media coverage. They have found an interesting police transmission which they have sent to the server. You will need to use the Ango-Ka USB, to access the message on the server."

Sakura removed the USB from her hair clip and inserted it into her phone. An icon of an envelope with the Japanese character for 'A' changed from being ghosted out to solid. She selected it and listened to the message.

"Chief, it's Detective Kaiputo. I am on the banks of the Meguro River. A young boy fishing from the bank has caught a human head. The decapitation was done with a sharp instrument. It's clean cut. I have stored it in an evidence bag and will deliver it to the morgue for identification and forensics. The head is relatively undamaged; I don't think it has been in the water for long."

"Ok, bring it in, alert Missing Persons and write up your report."

So, the police found the head; Sakura wondered if the body had been located yet. Would the yakuza want to hide the murder at their baishun yado, or would they seek help from the police?

Hirutu said, "Tatsuo and Takeo, I want you to go to the hospital and retrieve Akahana. I have organised for a doctor to be here with us for the next few days. His name is Umi, and he has set up his intravenous equipment in guest room #3. Sakura, please join me on the balcony for tea, and I will brief you on today's assignment. Megumi, thank you for the briefing; please have your team commence their investigations into the data on the phones."

7

Sakura was in the driver's seat, and Takeo was in the passenger seat. Tatsuo and their doctor were sitting in the rear. Sakura slowed as they approached the hospital where they had left Akahana last night, the girl they had freed from the baishun yado. They needed to get her out before the baishun yado owners found her. Once a reward was posted for information leading to the girl's recovery, she would be located quickly. The yakuza have people everywhere, and the hospital would be no exception. Sakura wanted to rescue this girl from the traffickers, hoping they could obtain information from her to help them locate Honoka. First, though, they needed to release her from the Hospital.

Sakura found a spare parking space near the hospital entrance and parked the car. Dr Umi secured his identity card and access pass to his top pocket. He opened his medical bag and handed three items to Tatsuo, a pair of medical gloves, a thick dressing with cotton padding and a vile of ether.

"When you are ready to apply the anaesthetic, use the gloves to limit exposure. Empty half the contents of the ether onto the dressing pad. Do not breathe the fumes! Hold it tightly against the mouth and nose for 30 seconds. That will be adequate to disable an average-sized man for 20 minutes. The ambulance ramps are to the east of the building." He pointed towards the entrance.

"Got it," said Tatsuo, opening the car door and walking towards the ambulance ramp.

Takeo was wearing the hospital's orderly uniform. He said, "You are with me, Doc; let's go!"

Sakura watched them walk across the car park and into the hospital. Now all she had to do was wait.

She reflected on her conversation with her grandfather after this morning's briefing. She knew her grandfather was wealthy but did not know the extent until today. She arrived in Japan from Australia just two weeks ago and was discovering more about her grandfather and his business. For example, this morning, she asked him how he could quickly secure the different number plates. The question was prompted after she had witnessed one of the house servants replacing the plates on the car they had used last night.

He smiled and said, "Sakura, it is simple. One aspect of my business is protecting the shops and businesses under my area of control. I have loyal men who collect the money for me. Over the years, the revenue from that business has become less important to me due to the growth in the technology business. I have only remained in the industry for my men. Five years ago, I established superannuation accounts for all of them. They have no savings or other skills, so they would be unemployed if I exited this business. I deposit 50% of the protection money they obtain into their superannuation account, and the remaining 50% is their salary. Old age will catch up with them, and when they retire, I will surprise them with the little nest egg I have been building for them.

"When I want a car license plate, it only takes a call to one of these men. They pay a young street runner JPY1,000 to remove the license plates from a car parked at the Tokyo International long-term car park. It's generally weeks before the owners return and discover the missing plates. The street runner will pedal their bike to the airport, so they get exercise and money, and we get the license plates. If they get caught due to their young age, rarely are charges laid. It's a win-win for everyone."

8

Takeo and the doctor walked through the hospital entrance, and the automatic doors closed behind them. The temperature change was immediate, at least 10 degrees warmer inside than outside. The smell of disinfectant, bleach and sweat from human bodies doing double shifts assaulted Takeo's nasal passages. They entered an elevator, and the doctor pressed the button for level three.

Exiting the elevator, the doctor walked towards the nurse's station. Immediately, a young nurse asked how she could help them. "Which room is the girl, Akahana, in? Unfortunately, there was an abnormality in her blood analyses, so I need to conduct further tests."

"Room 3005."

"Thank you," responded Dr Umi.

Takeo followed the doctor into the room. The girl was deathly pale and sweating and on an intravenous drip. Takeo held her hand in his. It felt cold and lifeless, and he knew this young girl had endured more than her tiny body should ever have to deal with. The doctor lifted the patient chart from the end of the bed and started reading it.

"She should be ok to transport back to the house. We must take the saline drip with us; the other items attached to her can be removed." He disconnected her from the monitoring machines, removing the heart rate device from her index finger and the ECG electrodes from her chest.

He released the wheels on the bed and dragged the bed away from the wall. He pointed at the head of the bed and said, "You take that end" Together, they wheeled her past the nurse's station to the elevator. Dr Umi returned to the station, said something to the nurse that Takeo couldn't hear and then signed the paperwork she handed him.

He returned to the elevator, selected the button marked 'Ambulance Bay', and they descended four floors. The doors opened onto an underground concrete parking area where two ambulances were waiting. They heard the nearest ambulance start; then it moved towards them. Tatsuo jumped out of the driver's side door, wearing a paramedic uniform and opened the rear doors so they could roll Akahana into the ambulance. Inside, slumped against the front wall, was the near-naked driver whom Tatsuo had disabled. He was unharmed and would be ok when the anaesthetic wore off. The doctor disengaged the catches that locked the height of the bed, and it descended to its lowest point, making it easier for the girl to be transported. The bed was locked into the floor to prevent moving, and the intravenous drip was secured to the bed.

Dr Umi and Takeo remained with Akahana while Tatsuo closed the rear doors, entered the cabin and started the drive back to the house. He opened channel 22 on the ambulance CB and said, "Saviour 1, we have secured the merchandise and have commenced our journey."

"Copy that! I will follow on your six," replied Sakura.

When the ambulance passed Sakura's car, she slowly drove out from the parking place and stayed behind it.

Their plan assumed they would have 30 minutes minimum before the hospital was aware that the ambulance was missing. However, they couldn't drive the ambulance to the house because it had a GPS installed, and they did not want to disclose their location. Twenty minutes into the journey, the ambulance turned into a parking area for a local mall. Sakura drove up to the back of the ambulance, and they quickly unloaded Akahana, and the intravenous drip, into the rear seat, the doctor and Takeo on either side of her. Tatsuo sat in the front passenger seat, and Sakura drove off, leaving the ambulance driver sleeping in the rear of the ambulance.

"How does she look, Doc?"

"She will be okay; she is starting to regain consciousness. She is withdrawing from heroin. The chart indicates she is receiving 20 mg of methadone every 12 hours. I have a supply that will last a couple more days, but we may need your grandfather to secure more. I will reduce the dosage to 10 mg, and you should be able to interview her tomorrow morning."

"Good, we need to discover what this young lady knows. There may be hundreds of girls around Japan just like her. The men running this operation are evil; I am developing an extreme hatred of them, which will not be good for their future."

<u>9</u>

Takibi walked up to the bar to order their drinks whilst Daku located a suitable table. Takibi was thirsty and impatient; he didn't like to wait. Then, finally, the waitress came over. She was a young woman with purple hair tied into a bun on her head, held in place by a comb that looked like it was made from an abalone shell. She wore a black t-shirt, and the pub's name stretched across her chest. Takibi couldn't help but notice her full breasts, unusual for a Japanese woman.

She asked, "What will it be?"

"A pot of Oyuwari and two glasses, please." Oyuwari is a unique Japanese drink which combines 'Shochu', a strong spirit, in a teapot with hot water, usually six parts spirit to four parts of water.

Takibi handed his credit card to start a tab and carried the drinks to Daku, who was in a discussion with a man and a woman at a table. The couple looked worse for wear, the woman a drug addict judging by the track marks on her arm. The man was a sizeable Japanese man with protruding stomach, clearly a heavy drinker. Daku advised them that it was in their best interest to relinquish the table and move on.

The bar was trendy at noon, and the busy lunch trading session was underway. All the tables were occupied. The fat man was trying to impress his cheap date by resisting Daku's suggestions; however, when Takibi arrived at the table, he said, "Come on, babe, let's get out of this dump. I have some Johnny Walker Black Label scotch back at my apartment." They stood and left the bar. Takibi and Daku took charge of the table.

Takibi poured the strong drink into the two glasses, they clinked their glasses together, and Takibi said, "To our prosperous future!" Last night they had stolen a truck from a Zen petroleum service station when the driver had gone to pay for fuel. It was a small truck, just one tonne. They had driven it back to his house and broken the padlock securing the rear door. Inside, they found it contained delivery items destined for smaller shops. Amongst the soft drinks, biscuits, peanuts and candy were 60 cartons of cigarettes. The cigarettes were valued at JPY300,000. They should be able to sell them quickly for around JPY200,000. It had been a good night's wages for them. After unloading the most valuable goods, they drove the truck to the Shinjuku Takashimaya Shopping Mall's car park. It is an enormous car park by Tokyo standards and was empty at 9:00 pm when they had torched the truck. They had celebrated at Takibi's house with a few drinks and had agreed to meet at the Red Lion Den bar, their usual drinking place, at noon today.

A young man, maybe 16, entered the premises and approached their table. He looked at Takibi and said without hesitation, "An important lady is waiting for you in the conference room."

What the fuck, thought Takibi; this place has a conference room?

"Well, take us to your leader," he jokingly said.

"Follow me," said the young man as he turned and walked towards the rear of the bar. There was a single door with a sign, 'Employees Only'. He used a key to open it, stepped inside and gestured towards a table.

"Please sit."

Two vacant seats on their side of the table, seated across the table was a slender figure dressed in black their back towards them. So they sat and waited perhaps 15 seconds before the woman spun the chair around to face them. She was wearing a Ninja Yoroi, an outfit that consisted of a black jacket, black trousers, a black ninja hood with a face mask, only her dark brown eyes showed.

"Gentleman, I have a business proposition for you. Would you like to make some serious money for just an hour's work which may also include some pleasure?"

"Who are you?"

"My name is unimportant, but I can see you are anxious. All I want you to do is steal a few phones, and I will pay you handsomely for them."

"How much Yen?" asked Takibi.

"I will pay you JPY1 million for each phone. I want you to steal four phones over two nights. So, you each will make JPY2 million. It will be like taking candy from a baby. Are you interested?"

"Yes."

"Have either of you fired a Beretta 92FS?"

"Yes, I fought in the military," said Takibi.

"Good", replied Sakura.

She placed two small leather saps on the table. "You will need these. The saps contain two large ball bearings and are a formidable weapon when used to strike the forehead or back of the head."

Sakura knew she had their interest now, so she spent the next 30 minutes explaining the details.

Day 8 since the abduction

<u>10</u>

Takibi stood at the door of the baishun yado selected by the woman and knocked. As she had directed, they arrived at 2:00 am. Earlier that day, Daku had reserved two girls. A burly guard opened the door and asked their names; after confirming they had a booking, he let them enter the business.

"If you hurt either of these girls, there will be serious consequences, do you understand?" Then he pulled a pistol from behind his back, which he must have hidden in his waistband. He pointed the gun first at Takibi and then at Daku. "Do you understand?" The swiftness of the action had made the saliva in Daku's mouth dry, and he found it difficult to swallow. Both men nodded yes; Daku hadn't expected a gun to be pointed at him tonight, although the woman had told them the guards would probably be armed with a Beretta 92FS. The 92FS is a popular handgun for the Tokyo yakuza due to its compact size and superior stopping power as it is chambered with 9mm rounds and has a 15-capacity magazine.

"Up against the wall and turn around. I want to frisk you for weapons." While frisking, he placed his hand between Takibi's legs, checking for a weapon in his underpants.

Takibi lifted onto his toes and said, "Careful sport, I want to use that tonight." Both men had hidden the saps in their underwear as directed by the woman, hoping they would be mistaken for just a couple of well-hung men.

Once the guard was satisfied they were not carrying weapons, he asked for the money. Daku paid the amount he had agreed earlier in the day, and the guard escorted them up the stairs.

The building layout was exactly as the woman had described: a small dwelling with three bedrooms. The guard opened the first door and waited for Takibi to enter. Takibi looked towards the bed, centred in the small room. A young girl was naked, sobbing and shackled to the bedposts by her wrists and ankles, her womanhood exposed for all to see. Takibi was a hardened criminal, yet the smell in this room, a mixture of vomit, sweat, semen and despair, made his stomach lurch.

So far, the directions and advice the woman had given them were accurate. He wondered how she had planned this so thoroughly. The guard said to Daku, "Come with me; your girl is next door."

He escorted Daku to the next bedroom and opened the door. Daku walked into the room; it contained another young girl shackled to the bed. Before the guard closed the door, he asked, "What's the idea?"

The guard looked confused momentarily, then stepped into the room, "What?"

Takibi quickly bridged the distance between the two rooms, swung the leather sap as hard as possible, and heard the man's skull crack when it struck him. Daku captured the guard under the armpits as he fell towards him and lowered him to the floor whilst Takibi quickly removed the Beretta from the guard's waistband.

He pressed the magazine release, dropped it from the handle, and checked it to confirm it was loaded. He opened the slide, saw it was empty, slammed the magazine back in place, cycled the slide and heard the chunking sound of a round being chambered. He flicked off the safety and moved slowly down the corridor towards the fourth door, where the second guard should be stationed based on the woman's intel.

The guard was watching TV, leaning back in the chair, a beer in his hand, his feet resting on a small table, the chair's front legs off the floor. Takibi walked silently and slowly towards him. When he reached him, he tapped him gently on the side of the head with the gun barrel.

"Excuse me; I need your attention." The shock of the unexpected encounter caused the chair he was balanced on to fall backwards, and he landed on the floor, his legs pointing towards the ceiling.

Takibi contained a burst of laughter and maintained a menacing look. He pointed the gun at the unfortunate guard and said, "Where's the key to the money?"

"Do you know whom this baishun yado belongs to? Do you have a death wish?"

"Yeah, old man, I've heard all that before. Now remove your gun slowly using one finger, left hand." He held the gun out, and Takibi took it, storing it behind his back in his waistband.

"Now, unlock your phone and set a code '111111' to open it." The man obliged and handed him the phone. As directed by the woman, Takibi checked that the phone could be unlocked with the new code, then stowed it in his shirt pocket.

"Get tonight's takings for me before I shoot you!" The man smiled at him and didn't move. Takibi cycled the slide of the Beretta, and the unspent round flew out of the breech as another round was chambered, indicating the gun was loaded and he knew how to use it. The colour drained from the face of the man; he hadn't been in this situation before.

"Money!" he repeated, threatening the man with the gun again. Finally, he got up, opened a cupboard revealing a small safe, entered a four-digit code, and opened the door. Inside was a large bundle of notes.

"Now move over towards that wall and stand with your hands against the wall!" When the man did as he was told, Takibi hit him hard with the butt of the gun against the back of his head, and he fell to the ground unconscious. Takibi used the cable ties he had fashioned into handcuffs to restrain the unconscious guard's wrists behind his back and secured his ankles with a second cable tie.

The woman had told them they had two options: kill the men or ensure they couldn't alert authorities or their boss for three hours.

Takibi had killed men before, mostly in self-defence, but he didn't consider himself a killer. He thought this approach would fulfil his end of the bargain.

As he left the room, he removed a key ring hanging next to the door; he suspected this would unlock the girl's restraints. He walked into the third bedroom, where a woman was asleep or unconscious on the bed; she was unshackled, so she was probably another drug-driven prostitute.

The woman had told him they were to free the girls being held by force. If there was a prostitute in the baishun yado who was there by choice, they were welcome to use her as they desired. Takibi stared at the unconscious woman. He decided he would pass.

Walking back to the second room, he unlocked the girl's restraints and handed her a dressing gown hanging on a hook by the bed. He could see that Daku had similarly restrained the guard and asked, "Were you able to unlock the phone and reset it to unlock on '111111'?"

"Yes, I was able to unlock it with his fingerprint," then he handed Takibi the phone.

Daku said, "Please help this young girl downstairs while I free the other girl."

Once outside, they told the girls, "Walk towards the park", and pointed down the road. "It's only 50 meters. Wait on the seat, and someone will come to help you." Then, arm-in-arm, the two girls stumbled and staggered barefooted to what they hoped would be their freedom.

Turning towards 'River Reserve', the men walked towards the Tama River bridge. It was here that they would find the garbage bin with a black shopping bag inside. They were to put the phones in the bag. Inside the bag were two plain paper packages, each containing JPY1 million. Each package contained the payment for a phone.

Takibi placed the two phones in the bag and removed the two packages, handing one to Daku. They did a 'high five' and then turned for home. The woman had told them that if she were happy with their work tonight, there would be another job tomorrow. They walked back to their car, and Takibi drove home so they could have a drink and split the baishun yado takings between them. It had been a good night.

<u>11</u>

Sakura watched the two men leave, then walked towards the bin and removed the black shopping bag. She had told the men they could keep the gangsters' guns if they wanted. She wondered if they would, as that would be very foolish. She had also told them to keep the night's baishun yado takings; she didn't want it. Her prize was the information within these phones.

Opening one of the phones, she dialled 110, the emergency services number in Tokyo, and told the operator that an ambulance was required as two young women had been sexually assaulted. She waited nearby, watching the girls closely until the ambulance arrived.

She walked back to where she had parked her Ducati Monster motorcycle. As she neared the bike, she couldn't help but admire the beautiful red machine shining in the moonlight. First, she pulled her full-face helmet over her head. Then, in one fluid motion, she held the right-handle grip, inserted the key, lifted her left leg over the seat, righted the bike, toed the kickstand, and pushed the starter button. The big motorcycle immediately roared to life and settled into that distinctive note only a large displacement 90-degree V-Twin engine produces. She smiled, used her left big toe to select first gear, twisted the throttle and left a 7-metre black rubber strip as she headed home.

She was smiling under her helmet; perhaps the numbers in these phones would help provide contacts to progress their search for

Honoka. Then her smile transformed into a frown as she realised today was the eighth day since Honoka had been abducted. Sakura tried not to think about what had become of Honoka. That wouldn't help find her. She needed her mind to be clear, not muddled by emotion.

12

Sakura entered the 'war room' just before 8:00 am. She was tired; the last 36 hours had been exhausting, and her late night, early morning meant less than 4 hours of sleep. Nevertheless, the entire Saviour team was there, chatting and drinking coffee. She walked over to Megumi,

"These are the phones from the second baishun yado; the PINs are set to '111111' as requested."

"Great, I will get my team to start mapping the data on them to the other phones from baishun yado 1. You look tired, Sakura. Are you OK?"

"Yes, I feel exhausted. Today I have a much quieter day. I hope that Akahana is well enough to interview and hopefully provide more information."

Hirutu entered the room, "Good morning, Saviours; I hope you are all rested. In today's briefing, I arranged for us to call Hoshi Kondo, Honoka's father. But first, let's go around the room for any updates or questions."

Megumi started, "Thank you, Hirutu. My team has commenced the initial mapping of the data on the phones. Although we haven't discovered any pattern yet to identify relevant names, I expect we will progress once we have more phones to investigate. Yesterday, I placed a trace on the phone number belonging to Tenjin, which was provided by the guard from the first baishun yado. Tenjin is the man he requested we call to take him to the hospital.

She walked towards the transparent display in the centre of the room and selected an icon from the row at the bottom of the screen, which displayed a map of Tokyo. A yellow line overlaid the map, and four circles with time stamps were laid upon this line. Megumi pointed at the first circle.

"The phone was at this location during the morning and didn't move until 11:00 am. I suspect this is most likely his home. At 11:30 am, he visited this location for 15 minutes, at 12:30 pm, he visited this location for 18 minutes, then at 1:30 pm, he visited this location for 30 minutes."

Sakura was impressed that Megumi's team had the resources to triangulate and capture the phone's location. They must have bypassed the carrier's security systems to achieve this. Megumi pressed another icon on the screen, and an overlay flew from the top right-hand corner expanding over the map of Tokyo. It was the overlay she displayed yesterday of the six baishun yados. The one they visited and the other five from the addresses provided by the prostitute. "After the man left home, he visited these two baishun yados, Yui, the prostitute worked at these addresses. Then he went here." She pressed an icon, and the display changed to a Google Maps Street view. The property was an accountancy business.

Hirutu said, "Good work Megumi; I think we have found the 'bag man'!" The team looked confusedly at Hirutu, trying to understand what he meant. He continued, "The 'bag man' collects the takings from the baishun yado and delivers the money to the cleaners, who will wash it, turning it into legitimate cash takings. Following the money should lead us to a more senior person in the organisation. Who wants to provide the next update?"

Sakura spoke, "Early this morning, the freelance team robbed baishun yado 2. The operation went well; two more girls were freed and taken to the Hospital for medical treatment. I have given Megumi the two confiscated phones for analysing. The freelance team is prepared to attack baishun yado three tonight. I will provide them with the layout once I have obtained the audio file from Tatsuo."

Tatsuo said, "I will have the audio file for you by 1:30 pm today; I am driving our star baishun yado spy there at noon. He seems to be enjoying the work."

Dr Umi entered the 'war room', "Please excuse my interruption, Sir; I wanted you to know that the young girl Akahana is conscious and eating breakfast. Therefore, she should be capable of answering your questions today."

"Thank you, Umi. Sakura will join you shortly to question the girl; please leave now and ensure she is ready, say 9:30 am." Umi bowed towards the team and went back to care for the girl.

"Any other updates from the team?" When no one answered, Hirutu looked at his watch and nodded to Megumi, who sat down at a laptop, dialled a phone number and pointed at a microphone on the desk. Hirutu walked towards the microphone once the dial tone could be heard from the surround sound speakers.

"Hello?"

"Good morning, Hoshi. I have the Saviour team in the room with me. They are the primary people searching for your daughter. Can you update them on what has happened to date, please?"

"First, I would like to thank everyone involved who is looking for Honoka; we are concerned for her safety. She has been missing now for over a week. The Police have been actively searching for her, but they have over 200 girls missing in similar circumstances in the past six months. A team of friends have placed missing person posters all around the community. It's like she just vanished. There was a young girl, ten years old, who witnessed the abduction, but she couldn't provide any detail on the vehicle they took her in other than it was a van and white in colour. The police suspect she is no longer in Osaka and has probably been transported to Tokyo."

Hirutu asked, "Have you been contacted by anyone, perhaps asking for a ransom to return her?"

"No, we haven't been contacted."

Sakura said, "Mr Kondo, we are very sorry for your suffering, and I can tell you we will do everything in our power to find Honoka and return her to you. Furthermore, we will punish the men who have been holding her. You have my word on that!"

"Thank you, we need help; I have no idea what ordeal our beautiful daughter has been forced to endure."

They could hear crying at the end of the line. Takeo wiped his eyes with his hand; the team felt time pressure. The longer Honoka was missing, the less likely they would find her unharmed.

Hirutu spoke, "Hoshi, I think you and your family may also be in danger, especially if the yakuza discover we are looking for Honoka. I have a man coming to your home at 12:30 this afternoon; he will take you and your family to a safe house. Do you have passports for everyone?"

"Yes."

"Good, give him the passports; I will have new ones in fake names for you so you can leave the country. I will arrange all the details; you need to be ready at 12:30. You can take one suitcase each, and no phones or devices on which you can be tracked. From 12:30 today, you will be off the grid; you are not to leave any digital trail. Do you understand why this is important?"

"Yes."

"I want you to leave the house like you have embarked on a week's holiday. Do you have any pets?"

"Yes, we have a dog."

"Ok. Please ask your neighbour to feed the dog while you go to Niseko on a week's holiday. Give them dog food or money. I want them to be convinced you are on holiday in case anyone starts asking your neighbours questions.

Once we have your new passports, the man collecting you today will drive you to the international airport, and you will leave for Canada. Flights and accommodation arrangements will be made. He will also give you CAN$30,000, which you will need to divide evenly between the three of you to avoid the need to declare the cash. When we find Honoka, I will advise you and arrange for her to meet you in Canada. I will let you know when it's safe to return to Japan."

"Ok, we will be ready."

Sakura could hear the sadness in his voice. He sounded like a defeated man.

13

Sakura entered the guest room, now equipped as a hospital room, including a hospital bed, intravenous drip and medical equipment. The girl was resting, her eyes closed, Dr Umi sitting by her side. He leaned over and whispered into her ear. Her eyes fluttered open. He pushed a button on a control at the top of the bed. It started to elevate, allowing the girl to be in a sitting position.

"Good morning, Akahana; I hope you are feeling better. Are you able to speak to me? I have some questions?"

Akahana nodded and said, "Thank you for rescuing me from that horrible place. Dr Umi has told me a little about what has happened."

"Akahana, can you tell me how you came to be in that place?"

"I was on my way to school, walking on the footpath, when a van stopped ahead of me. A sliding door opened, and two men got out and grabbed me. They forced me inside the van and drove for about 30 minutes, delivering me to a large building. I had a hood on my head, so I couldn't see where I was. They took me to a room where other girls were being held. I stayed there for six days." Her voice started to croak as she began to cry.

Sakura held her hand and said, "I understand, Akahana. Take your time; can you describe the place?"

"They raped me daily, the men laughing about how they needed to train me for my new occupation! They injected me with heroin morning and evening. I would vomit, a man would clean me up, and then I would be raped again. Every day, new girls would arrive, and some would leave. It was a dreadful place. Finally, on the seventh day, they came for me and took me to the baishun yado where you found me. By then, I was hooked on the heroin; they could control me by withholding my fix. They would make me do things to them before I could get the heroin. I was living in Hell, with no escape, shackled to the bed, only released periodically to use the toilet and shower. The only food they provided was baby formula. They said I was fat and needed to lose weight; their customers didn't like fat girls. Every day I got physically weaker and developed a greater dependence on heroin. After three or four days, I didn't care anymore; my body was no longer mine; I just wanted to die."

Sakura opened her phone, selected the photo of Honoka and showed it to Akahana. "Have you seen this girl?"

"Yes, she arrived the day before I was sent to the baishun yado. She was crying, and I tried to comfort her. They had abducted her when she was on her way home from school. She said she had been restrained in a truck and transported here. It had taken many hours. She wasn't sure how long it had taken as they had already started to drug her. Three men each took turns to rape her during the journey."

"Can you tell me anything about the place they took you to? Was it one level, large, small?"

"It was a big building with many rooms. There were four of us in our room and at least six other rooms containing girls. I know because often, they would come for me to take me to another room to be raped. I could hear girls crying when I walked past the locked doors."

"Thank you, Akahana, you are a strong girl. Dr Umi will help you overcome the heroin addiction, and you can stay here to recover. When you are ready, advise Dr Umi, and you can contact your family.

Sakura left the room feeling very desperate. She needed to rescue Honoka soon. Over the past two days, she began to understand the type of animals they were dealing with. How many women had they destroyed? She could feel her anger rising. These men would suffer for what they had done.

14

Takeo was watching their recently recruited baishun yado spy as he finished recording his description for the layout of baishun yado 3. He replayed the recording to ensure the audio quality was okay. When the recording had finished, Takeo asked, "Anything else to add?" The man shook his head.

"Ok, get out of the car; you can leave. We won't be needing your services anymore. The video and photos we have of you will be destroyed."

Takeo doubted that the blackmail evidence would be destroyed. They may need this man's help again, but he should think he was in the clear now. He removed the small USB from his belt buckle and inserted it into his iPhone. He opened the Ango-Ka application and sent the audio recording to Sakura's phone. He looked at his watch. It was 1:20 pm; he was ahead of schedule. He started the car and drove back to Hirutu's home to report his progress.

Sakura's phone played a sound indicating she had a message. She could see it was from Takeo. She listened to the audio message and downloaded it to the Saviour Server. Next, she opened another messaging app that Megumi had developed on the PC. This app mimicked a phone, except it masked the origination number. She sent the audio file to Takibi; it would appear as a private number in his messages. He had provided her his mobile number, and she knew he would expect her message. They needed this information for their attack on the third baishun yado tonight.

****

Takibi and Daku were at their favourite bar having a drink when Takibi played the message. Once again, the woman had provided detailed instructions in an audio file from a man who must have staked out the baishun yado. So, that was how they were getting the detail.

She had told him to strike at 6:00 pm and that they were to kill the guards. She wanted to send a message to the yakuza. Takibi was uncomfortable knowing he needed to kill the guards, not because of remorse for the murdered men, he was more concerned with the repercussions for him and Daku. The yakuza did not take kindly to their businesses being robbed and even less so to their men being killed.

He had a burning sensation in his gut.
Fear?
Or indigestion?
He wasn't sure.
He was confident that tonight's job would be the last he did with this woman. He knew now he had made a deal with the devil.
She was a cold-blooded murderer.

15

Takibi and Daku left the baishun yado. They had the guns, the money, and the phones, and Daku had a young girl over his shoulder who was incapable of walking. Two other young girls were unsteady on their feet but could walk. They closed the door and walked towards the bus shed 70 metres from the baishun yado.

Daku felt nauseous. He had to shoot one of the guards, and it would be the first man he had ever killed. Takibi had told him they each had to kill a guard, that it is the criminal code and ensures each man has equal guilt and criminal sentence if convicted.

At the bus stop, he sat the unconscious girl on the bench and, as requested, dialled 110 to call an ambulance. After providing the directions and checking that the other two girls could look after the unconscious girl until the ambulance arrived, they left to leave the phones at the location they had been told. Then they headed back to their car in silence. Killing a man in cold blood leaves an empty feeling in a man's stomach.

Sakura watched the two men drive off then she retrieved the phones from the rubbish bin. She hoped the phones would reveal information to enable them to locate Honoka. She watched the young girls. It took 30 minutes for the ambulance to arrive. Once they were safe, she straddled her Ducati Monster, inserted the key and hit the starter. The bike started with a rumble from the exhaust pipes. The noise and vibration of the big motorcycle always thrilled her, bringing a smile to her face. It was impossible to describe the exhilaration from a big displacement V-Twin motor throbbing between your legs. It was something you needed to experience. She toed the bike into gear and roared away, returning to her grandfather's home.

When she got home, she looked at her watch. It was 8:30 pm, early enough. She decided to call Megumi, who answered on the first ring.

"I have two more phones from the third baishun yado. I can bring them to you if it's not too late. I am concerned that every day we lose, that young girl endures another day of horrors!"

"I'm still in the office, Sakura; please bring the phones, and I will start the analysis this evening. Hopefully, I will have answers for our 'war room' meeting tomorrow. I am messaging you the address now."

"See you soon," said Sakura. She opened the message and dropped the address into Google Maps. The directions indicated 30 minutes; Sakura knew she could do it in 20 minutes on her beloved Ducati.

Twenty-one minutes later, Sakura removed her helmet, placing it over the mirror of the left-hand grip and walked towards the building's elevator. Megumi's office was on the 10th floor. She selected the level and waited as the elevator ascended. Finally, she exited the elevator into a room that occupied the entire story; there were no internal walls, just external windows. It was a modern office with open-plan breakout areas outfitted with electronic whiteboards and comfortable chairs. Some areas had large screen monitors for connecting PCs or other streaming devices.

On the western side was an area with high-end luxurious furnishings. It was in this area that she could see Megumi walking towards her. Megumi hugged Sakura and said, "Welcome to my domain."

It was an unexpected act of emotion. Since the loss of her mother and the loss of her innocence ten years ago, Sakura has felt only two emotions - sorrow and revenge.

No, that wasn't entirely true; she had grown fond of her grandparents, Tatsuo and Takeo. She also had a daughter-like love towards the nurse who cared for her in Australia while she was recovering from her horrific injuries.

The embrace ended, and Sakura decided she had enjoyed it. She had only met Megumi yesterday, but she had to admit the older woman was remarkable, and she was also growing quite fond of her.

"Come over here," said Megumi as she returned to her office.
"After you called me, I messaged two of my team members. They are coming in to analyse the phones. They are night owls anyway, so I don't think it was too significant a burden for them. They know how important this work is, and any breakthrough they provide will be well rewarded from the bonus pool I retain for high achievers.
"Would you like a drink; I have Hendricks and Tonic if you are a gin fan?"
"Just a cup of tea, please; I am riding my bike."
Megumi walked to a commercial barista machine and asked, "Is Jasmine tea ok?"
"Sure, thank you."

Sakura could hear the machine start up and watched Megumi make herself a large glass of gin with tonic water. The drink cabinet was well-stocked, and high-end spirit brands sat on two backlit shelves. In addition, there was an ice-making machine, an assortment of crystal glasses and a substantial bar fridge which no doubt held expensive wines and champagnes.

She returned with Sakura's tea.
"Cheers."
Megumi drank deeply from the crystal glass and sighed, "That is lovely. Please come and sit over here." She led Sakura to a sparser area of the office, just two comfortable lounge chairs with a finely crafted table nestled between them.

Sakura placed her teacup on a stone coaster so as not to mark the fine wood of this delicate-looking table. It appeared to be made from sandalwood. Yes, Sakura was sure of it; she had detected the scent of sandalwood when she first sat down. However, she could not fathom what it would cost to find an artisan skilled and capable of constructing such a delicate and beautiful table.

Megumi noticed Sakura admiring the table.

"I imported it from India four years ago. It was once owned by Yashwantrao Holkar, who ruled the state of Indore from 1798 to 1811. His fifth wife commissioned its construction as a gift for their third wedding anniversary in 1805."

"It's beautiful, magnificent."

"It is my most prized table, its beauty brings me great pleasure, and I enjoy sitting at it, relaxing with a drink most days.

"I have good news, Sakura. The phone analysis has identified several names of interest. With the addition of these two phones, I'm confident we will be able to reduce the list to the key names."

Day 9 since the abduction

<u>16</u>

Hirutu entered the 'war room'. This was their third-morning session, and he hoped they would be closer to finding the abducted girl.

Yesterday, Sakura saved Akahana's interview to the Saviour Server and notified the team. Everyone confirmed they had listened to the audio file. Now they were all aware of the inhumane treatment of the abducted girls and the type of men they were chasing.

Hirutu started the meeting, "Morning Saviours, I think we have a breakthrough this morning. Let's start with Takeo."

Takeo walked to the centre of the room and faced the team. He was the largest and strongest person in the room; however, his discomfort was obvious. He was not accustomed to speaking in front of a group.

Finally, he cleared his throat and started.

"Yesterday, I staked out the location Megumi had tracked the 'Bag Man' to the previous day. Once again, he visited the business, arriving at 3:00 pm. It is an accountancy business named 'Ying and Yang Accounting'. He was there for 60 minutes, and then I followed him to his home."

Hirutu said, "Thank You, Takeo, that's great work. How do you suggest we gain entry to the business and access to the accountant? He could lead us to the next level of control."

"I think it would be relatively straightforward. After I finished following the bag man yesterday, I returned to the accountant's office and waited. He closed the office at 5:00 pm, leaving alone, so I suspect it's a single-man operation.

"He is a short, thin Japanese man, wears glasses, is middle-aged and balding. Conjure an image of a typical Japanese accountant, and you will have a close resemblance. He would be no match for any of us.

Let us strike tonight when he is about to leave; that will provide the entire night to obtain our desired information. However, I don't think it will take long to break this man."

"Team, your thoughts?" asked Hirutu. He looked at the team. They were all showing thumbs up.

"It's unanimous; tonight, it is. Megumi, please see if you can find any intelligence that may be useful for this evening."

"I will. Also, I have the data analysis from the six phones. I just received a message from my team. They have finished the mapping of the last two phones. To summarise, all six phones had Tenjin's number, so I am confident he is collecting takings from each of the baishun yados throughout the week. The phone trace has identified another nine baishun yados, so there are fifteen baishun yados in total in the Shinjuku region. He visits five baishun yados a day, so it takes him three days to visit all the baishun yados. After that, he has a day off and starts over again.

"Cross-checking the data against our other databases, I could identify customers with important positions in the police force and other official government roles. This may prove to be very useful in the future. Our best lead is to secure the accountant and understand how he cleans the money. Following the money should lead us to the next level."

Hirutu said, "Thank you, Megumi. Can you play the news media clip from Tokyo Broadcasting, please? Saviours, this was broadcast on this morning's 6:00 am news."

The news broadcast commenced on the large futuristic monitor. Jason Priestly reported, "Last night, two fishing vessels in Tokyo Bay were surprised when their prawn nets captured more than prawns. The

'Tokyo Star' captain radioed maritime services when the body of a man was emptied from their nets. Police have confirmed it to be a homicide as the man had a hood over his head, and his arms were secured behind his back by cable ties.

A second boat, the 'Jinzu', fishing in a different bay area, discovered a naked female body in its net. Police have confirmed this also to be a homicide but withhold further details." The broadcast ended.

Hirutu said, "I called the Chief of Police this morning at 7:00 am to ask for further details. He is a good friend of mine. He told me the autopsy on the woman was still to be undertaken, but she had been identified as Yui Shintaro. She was well known to the officers. She is 22 years of age, a heroin addict, and a career prostitute with links to the Hidetada yakuza family. She had significant injuries, consistent with being tortured. We can assume that Yui has told the yakuza everything she knew from the night you attacked the baishun yado. At a minimum, they will know that a female was present and trained in martial arts. Sakura, it's unlikely this will lead to them identifying you. However, it is their first crumb of information, and they are very good at assembling and interpreting crumbs."

A man knocked at the entrance door to the 'war room', gaining the room's attention. Sakura recognised him as the man who had provided them with the interview room at the Takahata restaurant.

Hirutu said, "Kai, welcome; please come in, and I will introduce you formally to the Saviours team." Kai bowed, entered the room and stood next to Hirutu.

"Tonight's operation to secure the accountant should be done without leaving any evidence that could lead back to us. I cannot stress how important it is that the Hidetada family do not discover that it is us attacking their businesses. We will use two vehicles tonight. The Saviours will be in the lead car, and you will be the advanced attack unit. Sakura, you will oversee tactics. I have asked Kai to join us tonight as well. He will drive the second car with Megumi and protect her if the yakuza have established an ambush. We need Megumi to extract the information from the accountant's computing system.

After you have secured the accountant, Kai and Tatsuo will take him to the interrogation cell at the Takahata restaurant for information extraction. Sakura and Takeo will return here after driving Megumi to her office so she can commence the analysis of the computer data. Any questions?"

The group was silent.

<u>17</u>

Hirutu was satisfied that today's 'war room' discussion was completed and said, "I have asked Kai to come here today because he is skilled in many different forms of martial arts, and I think you all need to train."

"Sakura, when did you last spar against an opponent?"

"At least four weeks, Grandfather. I welcome the opportunity to train."

"Excellent. Go and get into your fighting gear, and we will meet in the gym in 30 minutes.

"Tatsuo and Takeo, that includes you two as well; you are both looking soft and over the next few days, we will be coming up against more worthy opponents than the weaklings you encountered at the baishun yado. Moreover, as we get closer to the head of operations, you will encounter professional security guards and trained fighters. So, it will be good for you both to have some practice." The two men bowed towards Hirutu and, without responding, left the room to get changed.

"Megumi, there will be no need for you to get changed, I'm not expecting you to fight, but I think it's time we started to improve your fighting skills; it's been years since you did any formal fighting. I think Tatsuo will be an appropriate coach for you. I want you to stay and watch the event; I think you will enjoy it; I expect to see an incredible display of skills.

"Kai, do not be fooled by Sakura's diminutive form; she is a Sohei Warrior and will undoubtedly be a formidable opponent for you. Come, follow me; I will take you down to the gym so you can prepare."

The gym was situated on the first floor in the eastern wing. It was accessed by the corridor that ran parallel to the outside balcony. Kai was overwhelmed by the majesty of this home. It was enormous, and the furnishings were expensive. As he followed Hirutu, he passed three large doors, each opening onto the balcony overlooking the exquisite gardens. At the end of the corridor, Hirutu opened a large solid door that opened easily despite its size and apparent weight. Kai and Megumi followed Hirutu into the gym.

Kai saw that the gym was divided into four zones, the entire floor was covered with thick rubber matting. In one corner of the massive room a square fighting ring, approximately 5 metres by 5 metres enclosed by a 2-metre-high barrier of webbing. Once you were in the ring, you were confined to that area.

A selection of weapons adored the wall behind the fighting ring - wooden staffs, swords, and daggers. In addition to the wooden weapons, there were authentic weapons; a Nunchaku made from two lengths of hard polished wood connected by a 25cm chain. Two sets of Manikigusai, or Manriki, depending on which region of Japan you were from.

He had only fought against this weapon once and found it difficult to defend against when used in the hands of a trained warrior. The Manriki is a throwing chain traditionally used in feudal Japan. When thrown with a whipping motion of the wrist, it can injure or knock out opponents at a considerable distance. It was made from a 2-metre chain length, weighted at both ends with blocks of steel covered in spikes. The Manriki can be used as a self-defence weapon but also as an offensive weapon and was often used by ninjas.

Opposite the ring was a strength and weight area, the entire wall a mirror. It was equipped with a weight bench, dumbbells, an Olympic bar with a substantial selection of weight plates, ten or more kettlebells, a Smith machine and a pull-up frame for training the upper body. The last of the equipment was a treadmill and a rowing machine.

Hirutu pointed towards the other side of the room at a wooden structure that took up another corner. "You can get changed in there." Kai walked towards the room, carrying his gym bag. He saw that the fourth corner of the room held a Japanese shrine with burning incense. The area's purpose was probably for meditation. He was impressed with the apparent wealth of the Hirutu family.

He walked into the changing room and surveyed the area. It contained a hot tub, a sauna room, a toilet and a shower. He put his bag on the seat in the changing area and dressed in black shorts and a black t-shirt, both items made from Egyptian cotton. The material was light with excellent cooling ability. He replaced his shoes with soft leather slippers, which were tight fitting and provided him with total agility as well as protecting his feet.

He looked in the mirror, pleased with his appearance. He had a fine physique with sinewy strength, very few men had ever beaten him, and none had in the past three years.

Hirutu had warned him about Sakura but said nothing about the other two men. He wasn't concerned about Takeo; he was an older man; however, Tatsuo was much bigger and heavier than Kai; he may prove to be challenging. He sat down on the bench, took a deep breath then slowly released it. He repeated the deep breathing technique and felt his heartbeat settling. Closing his eyes, he meditated for 60 seconds which was more than adequate time to allow him to calm his mind. He was ready. He stood and strode confidently from the changing room and into the gym. He walked over to where Hirutu and Megumi were standing near the weapons wall.

"Kai, please select a wooden sword. I am going to have you spar against Sakura first. She should be here soon." Kai selected a wooden sword from the wall and did several practice strokes to assess its weight and to gain familiarity with the weapon. While it was wood and not steel, he knew it could still break a bone and bruise the skin. Furthermore, it appeared they would be fighting without any protection. Indeed, Hirutu hadn't suggested he should grab any, not even a helmet.

After several minutes, the other three joined them. Kai studied Sakura. She was dressed in loose-fitting black clothing, allowing the entire movement of all limbs. On her feet were a pair of soft leather shoes, similar to his footwear.

If trained correctly, the bones of the feet can harden to be as strong as steel. His toes were a weapon; the shoes purpose was to provide grip.

Sakura had tied her hair back, exposing her face and neck. He admired her Eurasian features. She was gorgeous. A slender and elegant neck supporting a beautifully chiselled face, the only blemish a small scar on her jaw.

"Sakura, you will fight with Kai first. Please select a wooden sword from the weapons wall." Sakura chose a slightly shorter-bladed weapon in comparison to Kai's. She had seen the weapon he had chosen, and by selecting this marginally smaller blade, she thought it would provide her with slightly more speed or at least enable her to match his pace.

Now that he was dressed to fight, she could see the strength of his body. She knew this would be a challenging bout. Her grandfather opened the door to the fighting ring, gesturing for Sakura and Kai to enter. Once inside, he secured it, preventing their egress.

"Combatants, remember this is a training session. I do not want to see any serious injuries. However, it must be physical for you to benefit, so I will not be angry if either of you suffers minor injuries. The bout will be timed for ten minutes. For you to win, the other must submit and accept their defeat. Otherwise, you will fight till the ten minutes are up, and it will be considered a draw. You will start and stop on the sound of the bell; please stand in opposite corners."

Hirutu walked towards the small desk at the side of the ring, sat down and pulled the chain connected to a 15 cm bell. DING! Sounded the bell, signalling the beginning of the bout.

Sakura studied Kai's stance. He was solidly built, and she knew his attacks would be quick and challenging to defend. Nevertheless, she readied herself to fight. Smiling at him, she removed her left hand from her sword and gestured for him to approach her, "Come on, Kai, let's see if you can defeat me; no man ever has!"

Kai would not be goaded. He stepped carefully towards her and positioned himself on her right side. He had determined she was right-handed, so he kept moving towards her right side, forcing her to keep turning towards him, the manoeuvre constraining her ability to strike with maximum power.

Sakura slashed down at him with surprising speed; he barely blocked her attack, which would have resulted in a muscle-bruising blow to his right thigh. He retaliated with a reverse strike to her left shoulder, which she could parry away easily. He stepped out, adopting a defensive stance, surprised at her strength and recognising she was well-trained.

Sakura lunged forward using her strong legs. Targeting his stomach, she drove her sword forward. Kai could spin away, avoiding the attack and struck hard at her blade, forcing it up and away from her body. He had expected the sword to fly from her hands as he had used all his strength, but Sakura had maintained her grip and instantly assumed an attacking stance.

They engaged again, Sakura striking at Kai; he deflected her blade and retaliated with an opposing strike which Sakura also deflected. The two warriors exchanged multiple attacks with ferocity, leaving the spectators' mouths agape. After several minutes of this incredible exchange, they parted, stepping back, leaving three metres of space between them.

Kai and Sakura were saturated with perspiration, both breathing heavily, sucking in the valuable oxygen needed to fuel their overloaded muscles from the exertion of the first five minutes of fighting. Sakura looked Kai in the eyes; she thought she was recovering quicker than him, perhaps providing a precious moment of advantage. She launched another attack.

She ran towards him, gripping her sword firmly, her hands positioned in front of her stomach, the blade vertical and pointing slightly towards Kai, protecting her face. She struck at his right shoulder; the blow was designed to be hard enough to dislodge his sword yet not injure him too severely. He pivoted to the left, deflecting her sword to his right so it missed his shoulder. She was surprised that he could move with such speed for his size and weight.

Although deflected, her blow retained its power; now, with no target to prevent its momentum, she was forced off balance, facing away from him, leaving her side unprotected and her head exposed.

He struck down at the top of her head with the pommel of his sword, using moderate force. Her legs buckled under the blow, and she fell to her knees, then collapsed forward, her forehead resting on the mat.

Sakura was shocked, her ears rang, and her head throbbed painfully from the blow. She had bitten her tongue and could taste the blood flowing into her mouth. Her eyes were moist, and her vision blurred. She knew this was the most brutal strike she had ever incurred in training, and this thought angered her. She slowly sat back on her heels, the effort making her nauseous.

Finally, she spat the blood from her mouth onto the mat. Then she looked up at Kai, her eyes menacing him as he said, "Do you submit?"

Kai felt guilt when he saw Sakura fall to the floor; he shouldn't have struck her so hard. She had fought bravely and skilfully up until that moment. He knew his blow would have removed the fight from most men, yet she had sat back on her heels, her eyes full of anger. He already knew the answer as he spoke the words asking for her submission. She would never submit.

Sakura stood unsteadily on rubbery legs and held her sword up high, ready to continue. Kai took two steps backwards and held his sword at a 45-degree angle towards her, his legs in a slight crouch. They began to circle each other slowly, Sakura using the time to recover from the brutal blow Kai had inflicted on her.

When her vision cleared, she closed the gap between them, letting loose a scream as she accelerated towards him, her sword raised high. She struck down hard, aiming at his head; she thought, let's see you dodge this.

As Kai raised his sword in a defensive position to protect his head, Sakura pressed down on the four corners of her left foot and struck him hard with the toes of her right foot, targeting his solar plexus. It was a perfect strike. She felt her toes penetrate the band of muscle protecting this vulnerable area. The solar plexus or 'celiac plexus' is a nerve bundle that, when hit with sufficient force, causes the nerves in the diaphragm to go into severe contraction resulting in complete exhalation of the lungs and a feeling of suffocation. After a powerful strike, the body sends warning signals to nearby organs, activating the entire sympathetic nervous system, resulting in a debilitating state of fear and inability to breathe.

Kai flew backwards into the webbing surrounding the fighting area and slid down onto his butt; his legs splayed out in front of him, his sword still in his right hand resting on the mat. He was gasping, his face pale as he tried to force air into his lungs, struggling to stop the spasms in his contracting diaphragm.

Sakura lowered her sword, resting the point on the mat, her chest pumped up, and a smile slowly appeared. She wiped the remaining blood from her mouth with her left hand. Then asked Kai, "Do you submit?" She doubted he could continue. She had never struck a man that ferociously in such a vulnerable area. He took another deep breath, his face regaining colour, placed his hand in front of him for support and stood. He raised his sword and readied himself, adopting a fighting stance.

Hirutu struck the bell. "Bravo, bravo," shouted the men. Megumi was clapping her hands violently; it had been a spectacle of exceptional skills, something she had never seen. She thought Sakura was superb. To take on Kai and almost beat him when he had a considerable size and weight advantage. She wished that she was strong like Sakura.

Hirutu had shared information with her about Sakura's background and the reason she returned from Australia ten years ago to train as a Sohei Warrior. He had told her that recently Sakura had travelled to Australia and killed the five men who had assaulted her and killed her mother. To have overcome such tragedy and avenged her mother was amazing. She was beginning to idolise the young woman.

Kai and Sakura left the ring, and Hirutu handed them both a towel and a water bottle. "That was an incredible spectacle of skill. Sakura, you fight well for someone who hasn't trained for four weeks. I want Kai to be your sparring partner and to do at least one hour's training each day until this mission is completed. Kai, you also fought well. Sakura is a killing machine, so to survive 10 minutes with her is a significant achievement. Now I would like you to have a few moments' rest, and if you can, I would like you to prepare for hand-to-hand combat with Takeo."

"Of course, Hirutu, it will be my pleasure to train with such a formidable opponent," Kai spoke with a confidence he didn't feel. Sakura had hurt him. He was pleased the bout had stopped when it had, another blow like the shot to his abdomen, and he doubted he could continue.

He took a few minutes to recover and studied Takeo, who had removed his shirt and was only wearing his fighting shorts, no shoes. He was massive, over 2 metres tall and at least 100kg, his body toned from years of training. He would have a significant weight advantage and a reach (arms and legs) of more than 20cm in comparison to Kai.

This advantage was unsettling, and he reflected on his fight with Sakura. He had a similar advantage over her, both in weight and height, yet she had almost beaten him. All he needed now was to harness equal courage to take on the much bigger man. He removed his t-shirt to remove a source of grip for Takeo.

Hirutu said, "Time to get into the ring, please, men." Once inside the ring, they faced off against each other in opposite corners, waiting for the starting bell. Kai was tired from the effort required to defend himself against Sakura. He knew this might be the longest ten minutes of his life. DING sounded the bell, and immediately Takeo launched himself at Kai.

The big man was swift. He leapt at Kai using his body as a spear, his legs leading, his body travelling at speed 1.5 metres above the mat. Nearing Kai, he kicked out with both legs striking him in the chest. It had happened so fast Kai couldn't avoid the massive legs; it was like being hit by a castle battering ram. He flew backwards at speed, halted by the ring's barrier of webbing which flexed, slowing his momentum, then propelled him forward.

He hit the mat face down, quickly rolled onto his back, then raised his legs to his chest, propelled them downwards and, using his strong abdominals, launched himself upright like a gymnast. He grunted; the effort had been painful, his abdominal muscles reminding him of the damage inflicted on them in the previous bout.

He adopted a defensive stance but was too slow. Takeo swept his legs out from under him, a savage hit to his left thigh, the force of the kick propelling his legs to his right side and his head to the left. He fell heavily onto his left shoulder. Before he could recover, Takeo was on him, his forearm around his throat, the weight of his body forcing Kai to bend over his legs, reducing his ability to counter.

The massive arm around his throat squeezed harder, he couldn't breathe, and his eyes started seeing stars. Just before he passed out, he struck hard with his right elbow, striking below the rib cage and at Takeo's liver. The liver is a vital organ, and a direct strike can cause debilitating pain; if the blow is significant, it can render the victim unconscious. Takeo's grip loosened, and Kai could roll free and get to his knees, sucking air into his lungs. He realised he was fortunate. He had been close to passing out and losing the bout. He studied Takeo. He could see he had hurt him, yet the big man recovered quickly and had already gotten to his feet. Kai stood, and they circled one another, each man searching for weakness and using the time to recover.

Kai struck first, a roundhouse kick to Takeo's left thigh. It was a brutal hit; the big man staggered but did not go down. Kai was in disbelief, he had hit him with all his strength, he knew now, it would be difficult to defeat this man.

They engaged again, using their fists to strike at vulnerable parts of the body, Kai targeting the kidneys and liver, Takeo striking at his abdomen and head. They went toe-to-toe for several minutes, and then they pulled away.

Megumi was watching the fight with her mouth agape. Both men had exchanged and taken heavy blows, yet neither looked as though they were ready to submit. She kept looking at Kai's body, which was finely honed. She was mesmerised by him. His solid calves and thighs, the bulge of his shapely glutes pressing against the material of his shorts. His strong arms, large biceps, chiselled pecs and a stunning six-pack, wow, what a stomach he had. His body was completely hairless, the perspiration making him shine. He was the perfect example of a man. She felt excited watching him; she had never seen a demonstration of such skills before.

She realised it was more than excitement; she was beginning to become aroused; he was very handsome. This surprised her; it had been years since she had been interested in a man. She had been driven to succeed in her career and had decided there was no time for men.

Her first love was as a teenager, and it had ended badly. She had been consumed with love; then suddenly, she was discarded because "he needed to move on", or so he had told her. This experience had hurt her; the bitterness of not being wanted had caused lasting pain for many years.

Kai saw an opportunity and lunged forward. Pressing his right foot firmly to the mat, he ducked under a right hook that may have taken his head off if it had connected. Using the leverage from his grounded right foot, he struck out with a powerful side kick, the heel on his left foot striking between the 9th and 10th floating rib on the right side of Takeo's body. This blow caused the liver to compress painfully, the resulting pressure wave over-stimulating the 'Vagus Nerve', which runs along the liver. Takeo collapsed to the floor like a rag doll, his body going into survival mode. The fight was over. Hirutu rang the bell, and Sakura entered the ring to check that Takeo was okay.

She got to her knees, held Takeo's head in her hands and turned it to face her. His eyes were open; he had a smile on his face. Then, looking up at her, he said softly, "I heard a bell; what a sweet sound it was; I don't want to fight this man any longer." Sakura bent down, kissed him on his forehead, then got up and scowled at Kai, ensuring he knew that she considered he had used excessive force to win the bout. Tatsuo held out his hand, which Takeo gripped, and the older man helped him to his feet.

Hirutu said, "Takeo, are you okay?"

"I'm good. I will be sore for a few days but no permanent damage. Kai is a courageous and highly skilled fighter. No man has hurt me as much as he has today. I respectfully decline to fight him again."

Hirutu laughed, "Yes, I can understand that. I was going to have Tatsuo show us what he can do; however, Kai has fought two worthy opponents today; it would be unfair for him to fight another bout."

Tatsuo was silently relieved. He was 60 years of age, and while very fit, he knew he was no match for this younger man. He would fight bravely, yet the outcome was inevitable. The man would beat him.

"Saviours, the real reason I asked Kai here today is because I think he would be a useful member of your team. Over the next few days, you will fight several battles, and an additional team member will be pivotal to your success.

So, whilst I endorse him, you will need to agree. For Kai to become Saviour 4 will require unanimous agreement by the team. Let's vote. Thumbs up, you agree; thumbs down, you disagree. Your decision will be final, and you will not be required to explain your reason for or against it. Now please, let me see your vote."

All three Saviours provided a thumbs up. Sakura was the first to speak, "Kai, welcome to our team. I know I speak for all of us when I say having such a skilful warrior will be beneficial to our success, and we welcome you as we would a brother."

Kai bowed towards the Saviours. "Thank you. I cannot remember a day when I have felt this honoured or this sore. You guys are badass, that's for sure! I will have bruises for a week or more to remind me of this initiation."

18

Hiroki had been orphaned at the age of three and fostered by Yoritomo Ito, a Hidetada yakuza general, to be nurtured and trained in the art of the samurai. Yoritomo was an important and busy man; regardless, he still provided his time to be a loving father to Hiroki, creating a powerful lifetime bond between them.

Hiroki's training had started immediately; by age twenty, he was one of Japan's most skilled warriors and assassins. Over the past three years, his name had become legendary, and the idea that Hiroki would be dispatched to settle a complaint resulted in most disputes or demands being resolved without conflict.

Hiroki lived by the samurai code, Bushido, which was the code of conduct for Japan's warrior classes in feudal Japan from the eighth century through to modern times. It guided the Japanese warriors in life, battle and death. Although the samurai were all but gone at the turn of the 20th century, Bushido remained a system of pride and valour in Japanese society.

The principles of Bushido emphasise honour, courage and skill in the martial arts. It is an ethical system rather than a religious belief system. The samurai warrior is immune from the fear of death and is motivated by his loyalty to his daimyo (warrior master), similar to the code of chivalry followed by the knights in feudal Europe.

If a samurai felt that he had lost his honour or was about to lose it, he could regain his standing by committing a rather painful ritual suicide called 'seppuku'. First, he would use his sword to disembowel himself, and when the pain was too great, his trusted second would quickly remove his head by sword.

Hiroki had been called to see Tokugawa Hidetada, who was the head of the Hidetada family of yakuza and lived in the Osaka prefecture. This was unusual as he received his orders from his father, Yoritomo. He would do anything Yoritomo asked of him; he owed him his life, and his loyalty was immeasurable.

They had travelled on the bullet train from Tokyo Station to Osaka, a large port city and commercial centre on the Japanese island of Honshu. The bullet train had covered the 520kms in just 2.5 hours.

They had left early this morning for their 11:00 am meeting. Now they had arrived at the headquarters of the Hidetada family of yakuza. It was a modern building of 15 levels, built in a style that retained elements of Japanese culture.

Hiroki walked beside Yoritomo, a symbolic gesture very few would experience as it demonstrated Hiroki's importance and station in the yakuza system. Then, finally, they neared the entrance to Tokugawa's office. Two imposing guards with swords stood on each side of the enormous doors.

The doors were constructed from centuries-old oak and stained red. They were decorated with scenes of battle, created from mother-of-pearl shells. These scenes were embedded in the oak and bordered by squares of gold beading.

The door handles were polished brass, and both doors were supported by three enormous brass hinges fixed to an equally impressive oak door frame. They were over three metres high, and each was 1.5 metres in width. It was an impressive entrance into the office of a very wealthy and influential yakuza boss.

Hiroki was wondering why they were meeting in person and knew this was an honour, very few experienced. He had met Tokugawa Hidetada once three years ago. It was after he graduated from his training and achieved samurai status. Tokugawa had welcomed him into the yakuza as his assassin and enforcer.

Feudal samurai were unpaid warriors; they received food and board only. In modern Japan, this had changed, and Hiroki was informed that he would be entitled to 5% of the tributes he collected. This was an incredible sum of money for such a young man; most warriors received 1% - 3%. Tokugawa considered him a mighty warrior worthy of the most challenging and rewarding assignments.

He was gifted with a beautifully crafted Katana sword forged by Yoshindo Yoshihara, considered the foremost present-day sword smith in popularity and skill. The blade and saya were of the finest quality and would have cost more than JPY13 million. It was the most expensive object Hiroki had ever held, and he felt tears of pride begin to well in his eyes. He quickly gained control of his emotions, bowed deeply and said, "Iroiro arigato gozaimashita" (Thank you for everything).

Hiroki's life had changed forever that day. Since then, he has done everything that was requested of him. He had killed more than 100 men and women; however, he had also spared hundreds more by convincing them that their tributes were insignificant compared to their lives and the lives of their families.

The guards bowed to them, turned and opened the two doors together so the men could enter the vast room. Sitting behind an enormous desk constructed from teak was Tokugawa Hidetada, dressed in a perfectly tailored grey western suit. He arose, smiled at them both and said, "Welcome, my most trusted and successful warriors. Please sit."

He gestured to a highly polished black wooden table surrounded by three silk cushions, each embroidered with a colourful exotic bird. They waited for Tokugawa to be seated, then sat cross-legged on the cushions.

Tokugawa rang a bell sitting on the table, and almost immediately, a door opened in the rich panelling of the wall and a beautiful girl dressed as a geisha walked towards them, her head bowed as a sign of respect. She carried a teak tray containing a tokkuri (sake flask) and three masu cups. Masu cups are small square wooden boxes made of Hinoki (cedarwood), which has a natural antibacterial property to keep food and drink fresh. The masu is used for special occasions and adds a clean woody aroma to the sake.

The girl placed a cup before each man and filled them with sake from the tokkuri. Then, she moved backwards away from the table, bowing to the men, her eyes cast downwards and exited the room through the same door she had entered. It immediately became undetectable, its presence hidden within the rich panelling of the wall.

Tokugawa raised his masu cup with both hands and said, "A toast to your health and the success of the Hidetada family."

"To the family," they responded, and all drank, savouring the flavour of the sake.

Tokugawa began, "We have trouble, gentleman. An unknown enemy threatens our family. Three of my businesses have been robbed in as many days. I have lost men; they have been freeing girls and customers have been killed. Also, word has gotten around to the other prostitutes in that prefecture, and some have stopped coming to work. Whoever these people are, they need to be stopped, and I want you to see that they are. I want their deaths to be an example and warning to all who dare to hurt my business. You will have access to whatever resources you require."

Hiroki and Yoritomo listened intently for the next fifteen minutes, listening to the detail and drinking their sake. Finally, when Tokugawa had finished talking, he stood. Hiroki and Yoritomo stood immediately and bowed deeply to him as a sign of great respect. Yoritomo said, "I will ensure security measures are in place to protect the other baishun yados in the prefecture that has been targeted. I will also ensure our interest in the people responsible is distributed swiftly with the incentive that any information leading to their capture will be well rewarded."

Tokugawa spoke, "My dear Yoritomo, you have protected our family for over 30 years, and I would like to have you in my employment for another 30 years. We cannot be seen as weak, or our competitors will try to devour us. I want you to take Hiroki to the

Shinjuku Processing Centre. I want you to ensure it is adequately secured to prevent these robbers from launching an attack."

"Rest assured, Master Tokugawa, I understand what is necessary, and it shall be done!"

<u>19</u>

Hirutu waited until they had all finished eating lunch and addressed Sakura. "Megumi has asked me if she could join the team in fieldwork. Until today, I have rejected her request. However, her technology knowledge will be invaluable for tonight's assignment when searching the accountant's office. Can you take her to the pistol range and teach her how to use a handgun properly, or at least well enough that she will not injure herself if she needs to fire it?"

"Of course, Grandfather, it will be my honour. Megumi, please follow me."

The pistol range was in the house's basement and was accessed by an elevator near her grandfather's study. Megumi and Sakura entered the elevator and selected the button for the basement. They exited the elevator and entered the firearm range. Sakura opened the firearms cabinet by keying the password. A heavy metal door measuring four metres wide, and three metres high quietly slid upwards to reveal a vast array of firearms.

She asked Megumi, "Have you ever seen a gun safe like this before?"

Megumi replied, "I selected this gun safe and had it installed for Hirutu as a birthday gift."

Sakura smiled at her. She was learning more about this exciting woman every hour of every day.

The cabinet was organised into different weapon types. On the right were the automatic weapons, an Uzi Submachine gun, AK47 and an FN Scar H. Below was an RPG (Rocket Propelled Grenade launcher). In the middle of the cabinet were military rifles. Descending from the top, the sniper rifles, an M82A1 chambered in 50 calibre rounds, capable of removing a man's leg at 1500 metres, a Barrett MRAD and a M24 SWS.

Below these were ten semi-automatic rifles chambering different ammunition depending on the purpose.

Finally, on the left side of the cabinet were the handguns and knives. Fifteen different types of pistols were available. At the top, the most powerful, a Desert Eagle 50 calibre (capable of penetrating 5mm steel armour from 25 metres), and descending in size to the smallest, a Glock 43 and the SIG P365.

Sakura selected the new SIG P365. Her grandfather had only recently purchased this weapon for her, a pre-release model. Sakura was petite, only 150 cm tall and 49kg; this firearm had a small grip that fitted her hand perfectly.

The gun had a polymer frame that was lightweight and chambered with 128-grain 9mm rounds. This firepower would be more than adequate for any up-close work. She had trained on a Glock 43, which was similar in size and was interested to see how this SIG P365 compared. She selected the Glock 43 for Megumi, a good training gun for her.

They walked to the range, and Sakura placed the Glock on the number 2 firing line bench. Then she walked to the firing line next to it number 1, hung a paper silhouette target on the bracket, and set the distance at 25 metres. Next, she pushed the button labelled 'forward', which took the target to the selected distance.

She handed Megumi eye protection and ear plugs and showed her how to use them by demonstrating on herself. Then she loaded the SIG P365 magazine with ten rounds. She looked admiringly at the magazine; it was tiny, similar to the Glock 43 magazine, but it held an extra four rounds. The Sig Sauer company had a game changer with this new double-stacked magazine; the weapon only weighed 14 grams more than the Glock 43 when loaded, including the four extra rounds.

She pushed the magazine into place, heard the click as it locked, worked the slide and chambered a round. Then, adopting her shooting stance, she fired three rounds in less than two seconds, the first two in the chest and the third in the head. This series of shots is recognised as a practical approach to eliminating a human target, indicating a professional hit. Next, she fired three more rounds, a similar pattern, then fired two rounds into the circle on the left shoulder and the final two rounds into the circle on the right shoulder. She removed the magazine and placed the pistol on the table. Then she pressed the button that returned the target.

She was happy with the result, two very tight patterns, one in the head and the other in the chest. All bullet holes were within a four-centimetre diameter, some of the holes overlapping. The shoulder shots were equally tight; all would have disabled someone aiming a gun at her. Her teacher would be pleased with this effort.

Sakura had trained every day for months to become an expert markswoman. This training meant her body could react autonomously without considering stance, breath, trigger pressure or her aim. She could shoot accurately and deadly in less time than the pause between heartbeats.

She held Megumi's elbow and walked back to firing line 2, hung the paper silhouette on the bracket, set the distance to 10 metres, and pressed the button that took the target to the desired distance. Then she removed her eye protection and ear plugs and signalled for Megumi to do the same.

"Megumi, I want you to forget everything you have seen in Western movies or gangster movies regarding shootouts. It is difficult to shoot a pistol accurately due to the short barrel length. It takes two hands, the right hand placed firmly around the pistol grip and the left hand supporting the underside of the pistol grip. Never hold the gun with one hand twisted 90 degrees like in modern gangster movies; this might look cool on the big screen, but it is ridiculous. Firstly, it provides little to no support to keep the gun pointing steadily at the target, and secondly, a spent casing, when ejected, is hot, and you don't want it flying into your eye or down your top. Your legs need to be positioned like this or this."

Sakura showed her two stances: a slightly side-on stance and a forward-facing one. "To aim the gun, you align the top of the front sight with the v-mount rear sight when pointed at your target. You can shoot with both eyes open. If you prefer with your left eye closed, that's a personal preference. I like both eyes open.

Your firing finger remains on the trigger guard until you are ready to fire. When firing, place a little pressure on the trigger, align your sights, pause your breath and squeeze gently on the trigger. If you jerk the trigger, the barrel will move, and you will miss. The distance you will miss is significant. For example, from ten metres, if the barrel is at a five-degree variation to the target, the bullet will be ninety centimetres off target." Megumi had a surprised look on her face. "Yes, you would miss by almost a metre, so you can understand why set-up is essential.

"Now, safety gear on and load the magazine with five rounds." Megumi put on her eye and hearing protection, loaded the magazine, slammed it into the grip as she had seen Sakura do, and cycled a round into the chamber. The first five rounds missed the target completely, but Megumi started to settle down and get the hang of it. After the fifty rounds in the ammunition box were extinguished, and the target returned, they saw she had put two rounds in the head and one in the heart.

"Not bad," said Sakura, handing her another ammunition box.

<u>20</u>

Takibi opened his eyes and then closed them tight. The sun was streaming through the uncovered window. It was like needles in his eyes. He slowly opened them again, allowing them to adjust to the light, but it didn't help his brain. His head was throbbing, a blacksmith hammering on an iron anvil type of throbbing.

His bladder was at capacity, and he needed to pee badly. His stomach was riding a roller coaster, and he was concerned he would empty his stomach on the way to his bathroom. He slowly sat up in the bed. The room was spinning; his stomach rumbled and threatened to release its contents. Then, finally, everything settled down a bit.

On unsteady legs, he made it to the bathroom and urinated. He started to feel faint, the effort of standing and peeing overloading his fragile system. Too late, he realised he was going to vomit; a stream of toxic, foul-smelling alcohol and stomach acid struck the toilet cistern, then the seat before he eventually managed to aim it at the bowl as he sank to his knees.

After what seemed an eternity, his stomach stopped heaving. He had dry-retched for the past two minutes. Exhausted, he laid his forehead on the cold porcelain.

Oh, it felt good. The toilet was filthy. Takibi wasn't a big clean freak; he never cleaned! The toilet was covered in weeks of dried urine and pubic hairs, but it didn't matter. He lay like that until he was woken by his phone.

Standing cautiously, he flushed the disgusting liquid in the bowl, made it to the bathroom sink, ran the water, and washed his face. Towelling his face dry, he started to feel better. They had drunk too much last night. They had robbed a second baishun yado. It had gone similarly to their first baishun yado. The layout was exactly as described in her instructions.

All these baishun yados seemed to follow a similar model. Two or three girls and two guards to collect the money and ensure their goods aren't damaged. She asked that they rob the baishun yado at 6:00 pm. It was the same approach as last time. They left two phones, collected JPY1 million each, and they kept the Berettas. Only law enforcement officers are allowed handguns in Japan, so these pistols were worth a considerable amount on the black market. They anticipated they could sell the four Berettas for almost JPY6 million.

They had made more income in the past two days than in the previous four months. They finished the job by 7:00 pm and decided to celebrate at 'Kirin City', a famous Tokyo bar with multiple boutique beers.

Unfortunately, the bar closed at midnight. Their celebratory mood had intensified from the alcohol surging through their body. Legal liquor licence hours expire at midnight, so they walked to an illegal underground bar run by Yakuza who sold whiskey at an obscene price. They had drunk till 5:00 am. Somehow, Takibi had made it home; he couldn't remember how. He also started to feel concerned with the conversations they had while there. In the early morning, two attractive girls joined them and requested an expensive Champagne.

His head started to hurt again, and his heart beat faster as his memory returned. They had bragged about their two jobs and the money they had earned. They hadn't mentioned the woman who had provided the information; he knew that for sure. She had threatened them with death if they revealed their source.

Regardless, Takibi was starting to feel very uncomfortable. He hoped Daku had arrived home safe, and then he remembered the missed call. He walked into his living room, finding his phone on the floor near his jeans and shirt that had been discarded on his way into his bedroom. He selected recent calls and saw that Daku was the last caller. He redialled.

"Hello?"

"I feel like shit. What the fuck did we get up to last night?"

"Crazy night, eh! Fuck me; I haven't checked how much I spent yet, but I suspect it was close to JPY500,000. I'm hungry; let's meet at the bar at noon for lunch." Takibi's stomach did flip-flops at the mention of food.

"Get fucked! I'm going back to bed. I will meet you tomorrow at noon." He hung up, looked at his watch. 11:10 am. Should he shower or have a coffee? He decided bed was the best option and climbed back in, pulled the sheet over his head and was snoring within five minutes.

21

Tatsuo was the first to enter the Ying and Yang Accountant business. It was 4:55 pm. He removed his hat and bowed towards the accountant, who had stood up from his desk when the little bell attached to the door rang. Tatsuo stood upright, looking humble, his hat in his left hand, and said, "Excuse me for my interruption to your day. I have an important matter which requires your attention." As he spoke, he moved slowly towards the accountant until he was within reach and quickly shot out his hand and struck the man's throat with his thumb and forefinger closing behind his trachea and pulling it towards him.

This strike is known as the 'Tiger Claw'; it is designed to stun not injure, and it did that. The man's eyes opened wide with disbelief, his hands went to his throat, and Tatsuo reached under his armpits and lifted him off his feet, roughly depositing him into the visitor's chair. Well, that's what he thought it was, as it was on the opposite side of the table from where the accountant had been sitting.

The bell rang on the door, and Sakura and Takeo entered the office. First, they walked through the premises to ensure there wasn't anyone there. Then Sakura asked the accountant, "Where is your security system?"

"There is no security system; I do not need one." However, Sakura wasn't convinced, so she and Takeo had a more thorough look around the premises whilst Tatsuo kept guard over the accountant.

"Looks clear," said Sakura. She walked to the front door and turned the Open/Closed sign in the window to 'Closed', signalling Kai and Megumi that entering was safe.

22

As they walked from the car towards the accountant's office, Kai and Megumi held hands. They wanted to give the appearance of a romantic couple having a pleasant stroll in the afternoon before dinner.

They had seen the team enter the premises and were waiting for the signal to join once the Saviours had secured the office and there was no threat to their wellbeing.

As they approached the accountant's office, Kai could see the Open/Closed sign still displayed Open. He did not want to walk past, so he pretended to kiss Megumi. He stopped, placed his right hand on her lower back, turned her towards him and looked deeply into her eyes. She was wearing a pale blue eye shadow which accentuated her green eyes.

She had green eyes! He hadn't noticed this before. Perhaps he had never really looked at her. But, in that instance, he realised that she was quite beautiful.

She had pulled her hair back and tied it into a ponytail, exposing her shapely face, which still held a youthful appearance despite her 33 years. Well, that wasn't that old; he was 32. She was looking up at him, a look of confusion on her face. Oh well, here goes, he thought; I hope she doesn't slap me. He bent his head towards her and gently placed his lips to hers.

Megumi was wondering why Kai had turned her towards him; he was looking down at her as though he was going to kiss her.

He was going to kiss her!

His mouth kept moving towards hers.

She stood still, her body stiff, and his lips touched hers.

A rush of endorphins flooded her body, her heartbeat accelerated, and her face flushed red. She reached her arm behind his back and pulled him towards her, pushing her hips against him. With her other hand, she held the back of his head and pulled his mouth harder against her lips.

It had been so long since she kissed a man, so long since she felt this fire that had started in her groin. She could feel her body tingling. What was happening to her? She never remembered ever feeling like this, and then, just as quickly as he had kissed her, he released her, gently pulling away.

Breathing heavily, he whispered, "They have changed the sign; we can go in now." Her legs felt rubbery; she had almost collapsed when he released his embrace and ended the kiss.

"Ok," she whispered, her voice raspy, her breath racing. He walked to the door, opened it and with his hand on the small of her back, he guided her inside.

Inside the office, Megumi saw the accountant sitting in a chair, the three saviours standing over him in an intimidating fashion. Sakura walked to his desk and picked up his mobile phone. When she pressed the home button to open it, she was asked for the PIN. No face or fingerprint recognition for the accountant; he wanted the certainty of a discreet sequence of digits to open his phone. "The code, please?" asked Sakura.

"Who are you people, and why are you here?"

Sakura ignored his question and asked, "What is your name?"

"Katashi."

"Well, Katashi, we know you are laundering money for the yakuza. We are looking for a girl, and we think you might know where she is being held. The people you work for are holding her. Now the PIN, please?"

Katashi remained silent, completely disregarding her. That was a mistake.

"Tatsuo, can you please hold his hand on the chair handle for me?" Tatsuo held his hand, and Sakura removed her kaiken(dagger), placing the blade hard against the skin just above the second joint of the left hand's ring finger. The skin separated from the sharpness of the blade and started to bleed.

"Last chance, phone PIN, please?"

More silence from Katashi, so Sakura sliced his finger off and handed it to Megumi.

"Can you bag that, please?"

He had a look of astonishment on his face, and then he screamed. Tatsuo pressed his big hand against his mouth to stifle the man's screams. Sakura placed the kaiken against the skin of the little finger just below the second joint. "PIN, please."

"Ok! Stop, please! It's '143289'."

Sakura keyed in the number, opened the phone and handed it to Megumi to reprogram the PIN to their usual 111111' code.

Megumi placed the phone into her bag and removed a small hard drive which she inserted into a USB port on the back of the PC. Then, she booted the PC, holding down the F2 key, forcing it to load the BIOS menu. She altered the PC's settings so it would restart using her USB drive as the boot drive. Once it restarted, Megumi typed in a copy command, and, just like that, all the contents of his PC began to copy to her hard drive.

Sakura asked for the combination of the safe which the accountant gave willingly, wishing to retain his remaining fingers. The safe contained bundles of US currency and gold bars.

"Takeo, can you remove these please, we will take them with us."

Tatsuo had bandaged the accountant's severed finger to minimise blood loss and secured his arms behind his back with cable ties. Kai joined him as walked Katashi towards their car. Tatsuo sat in the back with him, and Kai drove them away.

Megumi disconnected her USB drive thirty minutes later and said, "All done; we can go now." The three left the premises, Megumi returned to her office, and Takeo and Sakura went to her grandfather's house. It was 6:00 pm. Sakura was hungry. She was looking forward to dinner with her grandparents.

23

Kai was soaking in the onsen on the Takahata Club rooftop. It was a cloudless night; the stars were sparkling a brilliant blue, transitioning to white. Music was playing softly from hidden speakers. He knew the song, 'Japanese Garden'. It was a relaxing composition combining cello and piano.

The onsen's water was hot, 70 Celsius, which helped to soothe his pain from today's fighting. His abdominals ached, and his left thigh sported an ugly black bruise from Takeo's foot. The muscles in his back, legs and arms ached from overuse.

He knew his injuries would heal over the next couple of days, and he was feeling euphoric despite the pain. Today, he had become a Saviour! He had fought against two of them, each testing his ability. Finally, however, they had worked as a team to secure the accountant and extracted valuable information tonight, enabling them to continue their search for the abducted girl.

He was part of an elite team of four people, working for the leader of the Hirutu family. This was a fantastic honour for a man who had started life from humble beginnings. His parents had been murdered when he was nine; he had been adopted by a woman whose husband was a member of the Hotato yakuza.

He had worked hard to be the best he could be, and the yakuza had become his family. Today, he had been welcomed into Hirutu's home, a magnificent house unlike any he had ever seen. He was now connected to Hirutu's granddaughter and three of his most trusted friends.

He remembered the emotion he felt when kissing Megumi. It had been a long time since he had kissed a woman.

Today had been overwhelming.

He would sleep well tonight.

24

Megumi was lying in her bed, reflecting on the day. Her life had changed significantly over the past few days, so much so that there were times when she wondered if she was asleep and if this was just a dream. She was working with a fantastic team of people for a horrible reason, yet it excited her so much more than her regular day job.

Watching the fighting today awakened emotions in her that she hadn't felt since she was a schoolgirl. She had trained three days a week in a dojo from age eight until she fell in love at sixteen. She had enjoyed learning martial arts and had been good, attaining the black belt level. However, she had forgotten the thrill of utilising the skills learnt against an opponent. She was never at the standard she witnessed today. She could be, however!

Sakura was superb; she wanted to be strong, brave, and deadly like her! She would talk to Hirutu in the morning; she wanted to commence her training immediately. Hirutu had suggested she would train with Tatsuo. She would ask him if Kai could teach her.

Watching Kai today awakened a deeply hidden emotion, her ability to love. Megumi was 33 years of age, and she hadn't been with a man since she was sixteen. She had lived seventeen loveless years. The thought made her sad; that's far too long, half her life. Years ago, she had locked away her ability to love, deep within the inaccessible recesses of her mind. She had done this to avoid ever being hurt again. Today, Kai had freed those emotions.

She liked to sleep naked under her nightie. As she started to fall asleep, her hand moved seductively towards her womanhood. She could feel wetness on her thigh. She held the vision of Kai's shirtless body, glistening with perspiration, as she drifted into sleep.

The words 'far too long' echoed through her mind.

25

Sakura sat cross-legged at her tea table, sipping hot chamomile tea and reflecting on the day. Earlier, she had completed 45 minutes of meditation in preparation for sleep. Tea drinking was her before-bed ritual and usually resulted in a meaningful sleep.

Her body felt good, considering what it had endured today. Her tongue was beginning to heal, the painful bite no longer noticeable. Kai was a skilful warrior; he would prove to be a valuable member of their team.

She was concerned for Honoka Kondo. Tomorrow would be ten days since her abduction. What was happening to her? Would they find her in time to enable her to live an everyday life again? Could they save Honoka in time?

Sakura knew the impact of sexual assault and violence on a young mind. A sadness overcame her, emotions she hadn't felt for weeks, a sense of hopelessness.

Eventually, she fell asleep.

***

The nightmares returned, plunging her back in time. It was ten years ago. She was an innocent girl, unable to defend herself against the attackers who invaded their home, raped her and murdered her mother.

She had found peacefulness after revenging her mother and killing the five assailants. That curtain of tranquillity had now been torn away.

The stress and trauma from searching for Honoka had awakened her internal demons, resurfacing in her sleep like a festering abscess. She tried to fight them, but it was like fighting in water. Her arms were weak and restricted, she tried to run, but they were catching her, her legs were tiring, and she screamed.

Her screaming woke her. She hoped the others hadn't heard it. Her heart was racing; a thin film of perspiration engulfed her entire body. The window was open, and a light breeze blew the curtains, allowing the moonlight to dance in and out of the room. She was wearing a pale blue night dress cut low at the chest, she ran her finger along her raised flesh—the scars from her ordeal. The moonbeam danced upon her chest, revealing one of her ribbons, the tattoo ink providing an everlasting memento of a life she had taken to avenge herself. The familiarity of the tattoo and its symbolism eased her distress a little, these five ribbons reminding her those demons were gone. However, the past three days had confirmed that the world is full of evil men.

She got out of bed and walked towards the window. The cool breeze felt pleasant against her body. She looked out at the full moon. It was illuminating her grandfather's beautiful garden. She declared to the moon that she would purge the world of as many evil men as her strength, body, and breath would allow.

Then she fell into a restless sleep.
The nightmares made her body twitch, her face a tormented mask.

26

Hirutu closed the email. It had been a warning from the Chief of Police that the Hidetada family had deployed a great warrior to search for the people attacking their business. He is Hiroki, a ruthless killer, the Hidetada family's enforcer. He has supposedly killed hundreds of people. His father is the second-in-charge of the Hidetada organisation structure.

This was not a good development; he had assumed they would have more time before the dogs were unleashed upon them. However, he could not let the Hidetada family know it was him attacking them as that would present a great danger for his family.

He felt his anger rise and quickly brought it back under control; he needed to be calm to think clearly. He had spent his life creating a great organisation that was becoming more legitimate every day. A business creating wealth through innovation as opposed to the Hidetada business, which profited from drugs, prostitution and the destruction of lives.

He poured himself a glass of whiskey; he enjoyed a wee drop before bed. He sat in his comfortable office chair. He had told Megumi she could change his study as much as necessary, but he would still require a place for him to sit with access to his fine whiskeys and ice. As always, Megumi had come through and relocated these items into a spare guest room, only 10 metres from his bedroom.

He lit a cigar and pondered about this new development. The fine Cuban cigar was a pleasure he only allowed himself occasionally, necessary to assist him in resolving complex problems. Finally, he finished his drink, extinguished the cigar and walked to his bedroom.

Mirako was already asleep; he could hear her snoring softly. They had been married for 38 years, and he still loved her greatly. He would protect her and all his family.

He was starting to doubt his decision and his promise to find this girl. He had thought it would be something they could do quickly and discreetly, and of course, that hadn't been the case. They still didn't know where Honoka was being held captive, and the steps necessary to locate her were becoming bolder. He could also see the strain and stress it created for the Saviours, particularly Sakura.

As he fell asleep, a plan began forming in his mind.

Day 10 since the abduction

<u>27</u>

Kai was debriefing the Saviour team at the morning 'war room' briefing. He provided the detail he had obtained from the accountant once they had secured him in the iron chair at the Takahata interview room. It had only taken the lighting of the butane torch and the lick of its flame against his right eyelid for him to tell them everything. The accountant had provided them with the name and contact number of the man that controlled all the processing centres. He also provided the name and location of the processing centre he suspected held Honoka.

When asked how they had disposed of the body, Kai smiled and said the fish and prawns in Tokyo Bay would be very fat and tasty this season.

Megumi said, "To buy us some time, I will send a message from the dead accountant's phone to the boss in charge of all human trafficking operations. I will pretend his mother is ill and he must travel to Nagasaki to be by her side in the hospital, returning in three days. Hopefully, that will avoid any suspicion of him being absent for a few days.

"My team is working on analysing the computer information I extracted from the accountant's office. Preliminary results are promising, we have names and bank accounts, the analyses should be completed within 24 hours. I will present it back to the team when it's available."

Megumi displayed a satellite photo of the compound on the central display; the Saviours stood on either side, assessing the security systems and layout.

"This is the location where we believe they could be holding Honoka. It is the Shinjuku processing centre."

Hirutu spoke, "Megumi, we need to obtain intelligence on the compound layout and security systems. I have the Spotless van we used for surveillance for last month's project. Take Kai with you tonight under the cover of darkness to see what you can find out. Then, you can provide your briefing in the 'war room' update tomorrow morning so we can plan our attack on the compound."

<u>28</u>

Hiroki was driving the hire car, and Yoritomo was providing directions. Yoritomo had explained to him that a large proportion of the Hidetada revenue came from prostitution, which required a continuous stream of women from within Japan and other countries. They used compounds (processing centres) to contain and train them in their new duties. Today was the first of five processing centres they would visit to ensure the security systems were adequate for this new threat to their business.

They had been driving for 20 minutes when Hiroki turned left and saw the imposing structure at the end of the street. Although Yoritomo had referred to the building as a compound, this looked more like a prison or garrison, not a reputable business. It was surrounded by a 2.5-metre-high brick wall 50 metres wide and stretching rearwards a similar distance. An elevated brick column at each corner supported high-luminosity lights and security cameras.

They stopped at the gate; an intercom system near the driver's door squawked, "Please state your business?"

"Tokugawa Hidetada has directed the honourable Yoritomo to assess your building's security systems."

"Please drive through; we have been expecting you."

The whir of an electric motor could be heard as the heavy metal gates, each 3 metres wide and 2.5 metres tall, slowly opened inwards. Once opened, he could see the doors were 15cm thick. He thought these would be impenetrable to a vehicle or rocket launcher attack. He could also see that the wall was constructed from four brick courses. *This is a fortress; what are they protecting here?* His curiosity had been piqued.

He drove inside the compound, and a wire mesh fence stopped their progress four metres inside the external wall. This second barrier was three metres high and topped with a roll of barbed wire. It ran parallel to the outer wall, creating an area between the compound and the outside world. This construct, known as the 'deadman zone', is used in prisons to prevent escapes. Two men opened the gate, allowing their car to enter the compound. The dwelling wasn't as big as Hiroki had thought. A large area of land had been utilised for boundary security, and a further ten metres of cleared land surrounded the two-story dwelling. The building was constructed from stone blocks, and the roof was lined with terra cotta tiles and black varnished beams. It was a 17th-century hip roof with a central gable the four sides sloping down to large overhangs on the second floor. The first floor was constructed similarly using terracotta tiles and varnished wood; large overhangs created a wide verandah encircling the dwelling featuring traditional decorative and ornamental beams. The porch was three metres wide, and the ceiling height 3.5 metres. It was a grand building, probably an old Buddhist monastery.

A guard directed them to a gravel area with painted markings for parking. Hiroki parked the vehicle, and they stepped out into the sunshine. It was early, 7:00 am, and the sun was starting to heat up. The grounds were barren, with no grass and covered in stone pebbles. As the day heated up, he expected it would become sweltering inside the walls of this compound.

A guard bowed to them. They returned a slightly less formal bow as a sign of respect and denoting their status in the Hidetada family yakuza.

"Please follow me, honourable gentlemen," he led them towards the stairs and the impressive verandah. As they walked closer, Hiroki saw the exquisite details of the carvings on the thick wooden columns supporting the building. They were coated with rich lacquers of black, red and yellow.

The entrance was accessed through two oak doors, each with a dragon carving; their mouths open, the heads facing each other. They were painted in a rich lacquer, obviously by a master artist, the colours vibrant, red, yellow and orange, with highlights of black shading. It was magnificent.

A man came through the door smiling, his two front teeth slightly too large for his mouth, making the smile seem more grimacing than friendly.

"Good morning, gentleman; welcome to my humble business. I am Toyotomi Hideyoshi," then he did a deep bow. Hiroki and Yoritomo bowed in response, and then they shook hands.

Hiroki immediately disliked this man; his handshake was weak, and his stature was not that of an honourable man. He was in his late forties, and his stomach hung over his trousers. He wore an expensive grey suit, which achieved nothing towards impressing Hiroki. On the contrary, it looked out of place on this man. His eyes were too close together, and his brow protruded from his receding hairline. Hiroki thought this was probably the most unpleasant and ugly man I have ever met. He struggled to keep his face friendly and not betray his genuine emotions.

"Please come inside; I have arranged for tea to be served in the garden."

They followed Toyotomi into the building. The roof in the foyer was made from pressed tin and featured the most exquisite painting Hiroki had ever seen. Two brightly coloured pheasants sitting on a branch, obviously mates, their long tails wrapped around each other. A forest scene was painted behind them.

While appreciating the majestic building, he noticed a sweet sickly smell. It was a familiar smell; he knew he had smelt it before but couldn't remember where. As they walked along the corridor that led towards the rear of the building, they passed several rooms secured by solid doors. He thought he could hear crying behind them. It was faint, but he was becoming more confident that girls were crying. As they were led deeper into the centre of the building, the sweet sickly smell grew more noticeable. It was making him feel nauseous. What is that smell, he wondered.

They exited the building into a small garden with tables and chairs nestled within a pergola, the only area he had seen so far that wasn't prison-like. Toyotomi poured them tea. Hiroki asked if the head of his security team could join them; he wanted to ask him questions about the compound's defences and weaknesses.

"Of course," said Toyotomi, who stood and left to retrieve the man.

Yoritomo said, "Hiroki, are you ok? You appear uncomfortable."

"I don't like this commander; he has an aura of death and misery. I have never met a more dishonourable or ugly man."

"Hiroki, you need to ignore those thoughts. We must ensure this compound is well protected and Hidetada's prostitution business is preserved."

"I understand, but I tell you, Father, this place makes me feel, hmm, what's the correct word? Dirty. It makes me feel dirty like I need to shower, and what is that sweet sickly smell?"

The commander and his head of security arrived before Yoritomo could respond, and the two stood to greet them. He bowed towards them, "Welcome, it is my great honour to have you visit. My name is Yaomo." The men shook hands, and Hiroki studied the man; he was in his 30s, had an athletic build, and his handshake was firm but not disrespectful. His face was pockmarked from uncontrolled acne in his youth, and his eyes were cold. His lips were pale and thin. Yaomo means demon in Japanese. Hiroki thought the name fitting.

The four men sat, and the commander began.

"The compound had ten comfort rooms; six were used to house the girls while they were prepared for their new roles. The remaining four rooms were used to isolate problematic girls or for customers to sample a particular girl before buying. The facility could process 24 girls each week. When Hiroki asked what "process" meant, he was shocked by the response.

Toyotomi explained that he specialised in Thai and Korean girls who were usually tricked into travelling to Japan under the pretence that they had been accepted for a job in hospitality or as a maid for a wealthy businessman. He had over 100 operatives that sought out the vulnerable girls and arranged transport; they would be paid JPY100,000 for this service.

The Japanese girls were forcibly obtained. He had four teams of specialists that sought opportunities for abducting young girls. They had special vans fitted with blacked-out windows, restraints and soundproofing. A driver and two other men would kidnap then secure the girl in the truck for transit.

"The girls are distressed when they arrive, so we house them in a room with other girls who have been here for three to seven days to help them adjust. There is an element of training required, which I undertake personally to determine suitability for a private customer or whether they will be sold to one of our baishun yados. It's amazing how quickly a young girl can become completely submissive and accept her predicament. The troublesome ones we isolate and make available to the guards. Each girl is kept here for one week whilst we seek a suitable buyer. Eventually, they are sold for a minimum of JPY5 million."

Hiroki asked, "What is that sweet smell?"
Toyotomi responded, "It's a baby formula; this is what the girls eat. Baby formula has many advantages, it's cheap, nutritious and easy to make. The rooms have no cooking facilities, just a sink and plastic drink bottles. When hungry, the girls add the formula to a bottle, then warm water and shake until their meal is prepared."

They had finished the tea, and Hiroki stood, "I would like to oversee the security systems now if I may please?" He had been struggling to contain his emotions in the presence of this disgusting man. He wanted to run a sword through him; better to move away.
Yaomo rose and said, "First, I will show you the perimeter security." Then, they walked off, leaving Toyotomi and Yoritomo talking.

***

Hiroki had completed his assessment of the security system. The cameras were well-located and provided adequate notification. However, he didn't want to rely on them only, so he pulled out his cell phone and selected a number from his contacts. When the caller answered, he provided the address and requested he be there within the hour.

"Please advise your men on the front gate to allow Mr Yorimo Tando access to the compound under my authority."

"Certainly, sir."

"Can you please show me where the security monitoring station is?"

Hiroki was pleasantly surprised with the monitoring station; four large monitors could either loop through a predetermined camera pattern or be dedicated to a camera.

"Please explain the guard shifts."

"We have three shifts, each a duration of eight hours. The guards are to arrive one hour before their shift starts. We have two dedicated rooms, one for them to rest and another to sit while they wait. Between 6:00 am and 6:00 pm, we have two extra guards for the front gate. Base staffing is six people, one guard on the front door, two guards patrolling the inner courtyard, two guards on the rear door and a head of security in the security room.

All guards are issued with the Howa Type 89 military assault rifle chambered in 5.56mm high-velocity rounds and professional mobile radio (PMR) that utilises the Digital Mobile Radio (DMR) standard."

"I want you to change to four shifts of six hours, and I want the men to be alert. After their shift, they can rest in the guard room for three hours to ensure we have a stronger workforce if required. The next shift will arrive three hours before their shift, and they will relieve the previous guards, allowing them to go home until their next shift. Can you source these additional men, or would you like me to do that?"

"Sir, we use our Hidetada family security firm; they are ex-military. Therefore, I should be able to obtain the additional men."

"Plan for the additional shifts to start from 6:00 am tomorrow. Is that suitable for you?"

"Yes."

"I will be onsite tomorrow from 6:00 pm to 12:00 am to ensure the operations are working well, and Yoritomo will take over from 12:00 am to 6:00 am. Please let your other heads of security know of these changes. We fear this compound will likely be attacked within the week."

A guard entered the security room, "Excuse me, sir, Mr Yorimo Tando has arrived and is waiting in the compound."

***

Hiroki shook hands and said, "Thank you, Yorimo, for coming on such short notice. I want to install a microwave motion detector perimeter between the external and internal walls. Moreover, I'd like a system that cannot be deactivated remotely."
Yorimo nodded and then started to pace the distance between the eastern and western walls. Then he paced out the space between the northern and southern borders.

"I can install twelve detectors, and each will project a 360 degrees beam, overlapping, ensuring all areas are covered. They will be solar-powered, enabling them to be operational during an electrical failure. I assume you will want the alarm system to be directed back to the security station. This will require a physical ethernet cable for each device. I can terminate them in a junction box in the inner courtyard and run a single cable into the security room. I can get the guys here this afternoon to install the sensors and start the cabling. We will be able to finish most of it tomorrow. Integrating it into your security system will require access to the room and loading of new software. Once it is tested, we will bury and secure all the cabling, protecting it from external tampering. I should be able to complete all work within the next three days. Is that OK?"

"Yes, Yorimo, that will be adequate. Thank you."

Hiroki walked back into the garden pergola. His father was still talking to the commander. He politely excused himself and said to the commander, "I have finished planning the security improvements. I will return tomorrow at 6:00 pm to ensure the new motion sensor devices are active and the additional guard protocols are in place."

***

Hiroki was happy to be back in the air-conditioned comfort of their car. He sat in the driver's seat and began the short journey home. Yoritomo was the first to speak.

"I can sense you are uncomfortable with this assignment, my son. Does the fate of the young women bother you so much? Surely you must have realised before this visit where a substantial proportion of our funding was obtained?"

"Father, I have based my life and personal value on being an honourable man. I am struggling to convince myself that it is honourable to protect this disgusting man so that he can continue to traffic these women."

"Sometimes, my son, in business and war, it is necessary to do things that we would not willingly do. However, this is still honourable if done with respect."

For the first time in twenty years, Yoritomo was concerned that his adopted son may falter from the path he should follow.

***

Hiroki looked at the clock on the living room wall. 11:00 am. He decided to do a training session that always made him feel good.

First, he would shower. He needed to get the sweet smell of milk formula off his body.

<u>29</u>

The Saviour team were finishing lunch on the balcony. It was a rare occasion to have them all share a meal, and it had provided a valuable moment for them to forget the danger they were facing and enjoy each other's company.

The men said their goodbyes, rose and left the table. Hirutu, Megumi and Sakura remained seated. It was a beautiful day, the seasons transitioning from winter to spring. The sky was a sapphire blue, cloudless, the birds singing in the garden. Under different circumstances, Sakura would feel happy. However, today, she felt sad, anxious and ineffective. She needed to find Honoka soon. She felt their progress was too slow and worried for the young girl's daily well-being.

She stood and rested her elbows on the balcony railing, admiring the exquisite gardens. Two white vans entered the garden and parked at the rear of the house next to a similar third van. The signage on the side of the vans advertised Spotless Cleaning and included an image of a smiling Japanese maid holding a towel to her nose, a look of bliss on her face. Underneath was their motto, 'We take your linen dirty and return it smelling like new'.

Hirutu said, "Good, your transport has arrived."

The vans were parked, and the drivers started to replace the van registration plates. "There are hundreds of these vans in the city at all hours of the day, so they shouldn't raise any suspicions when we use them tomorrow night. We will alter the numbers on the van sides to avoid detection and fit different registration plates."

Hirutu pointed at another van, "That van is full of surveillance equipment. Kai and Megumi will use it to undertake tonight's reconnaissance. The other two we will use tomorrow when we assault the compound and rescue the women.

"Sit, Sakura, let me tell you of when I was in the cleaning business. Ten years ago, I had 55% of all the hotels in Tokyo using my cleaning service. I knew two other competitors well, and the three of us dominated the business. Any new entrants were persuaded to seek an alternative line of business. The three of us would decide when to increase our prices, and we would raise them in the same week. I used the firm to launder illegally gained money, and life was perfect until Spotless, a giant American cleaning company, decided they wanted to expand into Tokyo. They planned to enter the market by purchasing an incumbent and suggested a deal with me. I invited them to my office and had Megumi join me as she was the listed CFO for the company. They explained how they wanted to buy my entire business and were prepared to pay five times the profit from the previous year. Megumi took me aside and explained how she had understated the profit to minimise the tax commitment and that we should ask for five times last year's revenue. After 60 minutes of negotiations, the Spotless team phoned their CEO and then agreed to pay JPY13.4 billion.

"I had been considering exiting the cleaning business anyway, as the revenue generated by the technology business made this line of business irrelevant. The only issue was that I needed a business to wash the illegal money. Megumi explained that she had been working on another business strategy for a while. Megumi, please explain to Sakura what you did."

Megumi appeared slightly embarrassed, then regained her composure and said, "I established an IPO for the porn streaming business. First, we needed a business listed on the Japanese stock market. I spent JPY1 billion buying office space and established an accounting team with another JPY1 billion, with the remaining JPY11.4 billion. I bought 20% of our customer base from our porn streaming business. That provided 10 million accounts and the infrastructure we leased from our parent company. I developed the prospectus and established the executive team, Hirutu being the CEO and me being the CFO.

The initial float was 100 million shares, each valued at JPY200. CEO sign-on bonus was 40 million shares, and CFO sign-on bonus was 20 million, leaving 40 million shares for the IPO. In the weeks leading up to the IPO, I ensured all the major mutual funds and investors had a prospectus. On the day of the float, the 40 million shares were bought in ten minutes, creating a buying and selling frenzy over the day. The shares closed at JPY455. The company was now valued at JPY455 million. Paper profit for that day Hirutu JPY182 million, and I made JPY90 million. In addition to this, we had capital of JPY8 billion, more than enough to run the company effectively for the next five years."

Hirutu said, "It also gave us a new company to launder funds. It was so successful that we did a similar activity five years later. We were becoming a legitimate technology business."

Sakura looked at Megumi with new respect, she was not only intelligent and beautiful, but she was also a very wealthy woman. No wonder her grandfather treated her like family.

<u>30</u>

Hiroki stood, his masculine body gleaming with perspiration from two hours of intensive training in the sun. He drank icy cold water from his thermos flask.

He took a deep breath as he stretched his arms to the sky, pressing the four corners of each foot into the recently cut grass. Breathing out, he folded his body, his hands reaching down and touching the ground at his feet. Then, inhaling again, he slowly became upright. This simple yoga routine rapidly slowed his heart rate to his average resting rate of 42 beats per minute.

He collected the towel he had draped earlier over a garden statue and dried the remaining sweat from his body. Then, he walked from the garden and sat in the shade on his rear veranda to finish his water.

His phone rang; he looked at the caller id and answered, "Yes, Father, how can I help?"

"We have identified and located the two criminals interfering in our business. I need you to silence them publicly. We want to send a message that the Hidetada family does not allow this to happen. I have sent you photos of the men; most afternoons, they drink at the 'Red Lion Den'.

"They have robbed three of our businesses, killed two customers and four employees. They have also freed our merchandise, so please make it painful! Hiroki, I need you to do this today!"

"Yes, Father, I will prepare now and leave shortly."

Hiroki showered. After drying himself, he walked into his bedroom to dress. First, he selected loose-fitting slacks and a white long-sleeve T-Shirt. These garments allowed him to move unrestricted. Then, opening his weapons drawer, he chose his favourite 'chest harness' used to secure his swords to the front of his body.

The bedroom's eastern wall displayed his swords. There were ten, each crafted by Yoshindo Yoshihara, Japan's most skilled sword maker. The swords were arranged by size, with the longer Katana swords at the top and the smaller blades at the bottom. He selected two identical tantō swords; their shorter length allowed them to be concealed under clothing. Next, he secured the tantō sayas to the harness, configured in a cross across his chest. This layout permitted Hiroki to draw the swords using a cross-armed action. He had trained for years using this configuration and knew he could remove them swiftly and strike before his enemy knew what he was doing. Finally, he finalised his outfit with a plain white silk robe with long loose sleeves, it finished just below his knees. Hiroki studied his image in the full-length mirror; he could see the faint outline of his weapons but doubted anyone else would notice. He was ready, the simple action of wearing his swords increasing his pulse rate by 25%. His body was preparing for battle.

***

Hiroki sat at the farthest table from the door, a teapot and cup in front of him. To the other patrons in the bar, it would look like he was drinking Oyuwari instead of green tea. He recognised the men when he arrived. They looked very ordinary to him, unfit and unwell judging by the pallor of their faces. They were larger than the average Japanese man, yet their eyes lacked intelligence. He wondered how these men could have planned the robberies so thoroughly. They looked as though they would struggle to prepare a grocery list.

He sat calmly, regulating his body's sympathetic nerve system, lowering his heartbeat, and reducing the adrenalin being released into his bloodstream. He wanted to be at his peak when he confronted the men. The waitress came to his table. "Can I get you another pot of tea?"

"Yes, please. I will also buy a pot of Oyuwari for those men over there. Then, when you deliver it to them, please tell them it was from me."

The men turned to look at Hiroki when the pot of Oyuwari arrived at their table, holding their cups up high in a gesture of thanks. Yes, thought Hiroki, they are foolish. He smiled back at them and raised his cup of tea in response. How could they be so ignorant to think there would be no consequences for their actions?

Hiroki decided it was time to talk to these idiots. So he walked over to their table, bowing respectfully, and said, "Please forgive my rudeness for interrupting your afternoon drinks. Would you mind if I sit here? I have a proposition for you?"

At first, the men just stared at him; their faces set in a grimace designed to intimidate. It did nothing to Hiroki; he just sat down without their permission. "I understand you do freelance work of the criminal kind?"

No response.

"A man owes me money; I need him to be encouraged to pay me. I have been told that this is the type of work you excel in?"

The men just sat frowning, not responding.

One of the men spoke, "How much is the pay?"

"JPY100,000."

"You sit at our table, and you insult us?"

"I'm sorry, I humbly apologise. If you are already in the employ of someone, I understand."

"No! We are self-employed this week. We have been working on jobs we have planned for a few weeks. These are far more profitable than what you are offering."

Hiroki stared into the eyes of the man who appeared to be in charge and said, "I find it difficult to comprehend that you two morons could plan the robberies of the Hidetada baishun yados without assistance.

However, if you tell me who provided the information, I will allow you to leave here unharmed today."

Takibi burst out laughing. How dare this young man insult him. He spoke softly and said, "You possess an unhealthy confidence in your ability. We deal with people like you all the time. Now you can piss off, but first, you can give us the JPY100,000, and we will allow you to leave here unharmed. The money. NOW!"

Suddenly a semi-automatic pistol was in his right hand, pointing at Hiroki.

Hiroki decided he was finished talking with these men. He knew he should probe further to determine if someone had hired them, but decided they were so stupid they probably wouldn't be able to identify them. Most of the other bar patrons had heard the exchange of words and were looking at them now. Hiroki sat calmly, unfazed by the man's weapon. He leant back casually in his seat and crossed his arms. The tantō swords appeared as if by magic, taking the men by surprise. Hiroki pinned the man's hand holding the gun to the table with the sword held in his right hand. Simultaneously, the sword in his left hand swept in a wide arc and buried itself in the other man's right ear. The blade entered the auditory canal, penetrated his brain and exited from his left ear with little resistance.

Just as swiftly, Hiroki withdrew the sword, and the man's body folded forward, his head resting on the table, blood running from his ears. If you didn't know better, you would think he had drunk too much and was sleeping.

Using the same sword with which he had just killed the man, he pressed it into the neck of the man he had pinned to the table with his other tantō. The blade penetrated his 'Adam's apple', and a thin line of blood flowed down his neck.

The Adam's apple, or laryngeal prominence, is the lump or protrusion formed by the angle of the thyroid cartilage surrounding the larynx at the front of the neck. A kick or strike to this area is extremely painful because a cluster of nerve nodes surrounds it. Hiroki maintained sufficient pressure on his sword to maximise the man's pain but not too hard to result in loss of consciousness or cardiac arrest.

The man was utterly immobilised, his right hand pinned to the table by the other sword, and his gun had fallen to the floor.

"Last chance! I know you and your companion have attacked three of our businesses. Now tell me who provided you with the information."

"Please don't hurt me any further. A woman asked us to rob the businesses and paid us to deliver the phones taken from the guards. She demanded the young girls be freed, and we could keep the baishun yado's money."

"What is her name?"

"She didn't provide her name; she was disguised, she wore a Ninja hood and face mask, only her eyes were visible. She is Eurasian and speaks fluently and with authority."

"Is she big, small, tall?"

"She was seated, so I don't know how tall she was. Her clothes fit loosely, but I thought she was petite, probably weighing less than 50 kilograms."

Hiroki thought enough! He pushed the sword through the man's throat. The man's eyes widened as he realised he was about to die. Hiroki stood, and with a twist of his hand, the man's head flew from his body. The movement was so swift that the body's trunk stayed upright, blood spurting 60 cm into the air from the severed carotid arteries, still intent on delivering their blood flow to the brain. Hiroki pulled the sword from the man's right hand and watched as he slowly fell to the side and landed on the floor, other patrons moving quickly to avoid the blood splatter. He wiped the blades of both swords clean using the shirt of the dead man supported by the table.

Hiroki returned his tantō Swords to their sayas, adjusted the neck of his robe and turned towards the door exiting the room. All the patrons were averting their eyes, their heads bowed. No one wanted to be involved in what had just occurred. Unfortunately, the police would be unable to find any willing witnesses.

Outside, he flagged down a taxi, provided the driver with an address four blocks from his home, and then called Yoritomo.

"Hello?"

"It is done."

"Good; any witnesses?"

"Yes, plenty. We have a problem; the robberies were planned to obtain information. Someone is investigating our business. I will talk with you later to provide further explanation. Goodbye."

Hiroki terminated the call and pocketed his phone. He sat silently in the taxi, reflecting on the conversation in the bar; someone was deliberately disrupting their business. Who are they, and what is their intent?

This was unheard of; everyone knew the power the Hidetada family wielded in this area of Tokyo. He wondered what they were searching for if money wasn't the motivation.

South Korea

<u>31</u>

Yumi clipped the catch into place on her newly purchased suitcase, smiled, and breathed a soft sigh. She was feeling very excited. She walked to her dresser, opened her fake Louis Vuitton handbag and removed her passport.

The passport was brand new; she had only received it a week ago. She looked at her photo; she didn't like it; they had told her not to smile, and her mixed-blood features were more apparent when she didn't smile. Her dad was Australian, and her mother was half Korean and half Japanese. Because of these different ethnicities, she was fluent in English, Korean and Japanese, which led to the opportunity on which she was about to disembark. She fanned through the blank pages; she liked the smell of the paper.

She had answered a Facebook advertisement eight weeks ago. A Japanese couple sought a nanny for their six-year-old daughter to teach her English. A couple of days after sending her details to the family, she received an email with a video. The video duration was five minutes and included footage of a happy and wealthy family, showcasing their home and the grounds. They had a large backyard, certainly by Korean standards, complete with a swing set and fishpond.

Yumi was awestruck and begged her parents to allow her to go. She had completed year ten and had just turned sixteen.

The family was offering her a weekly wage of JPY50,000, which was triple what she could earn in Korea, including food and lodging. She had watched the video ten times and had fallen in love with them. Eventually, her parents agreed. She responded to the couple, and a FaceTime session was organised.

On the morning of the FaceTime video, Yumi was so excited she thought she might vomit. She had decided to make the appointment in their living room and was wearing her best dress, sitting in her father's chair, the fireplace in the background. As agreed, at 10:00 am, the FaceTime video window opened with the little girl smiling and waving, "Hello Yumi, my name is Minika." They spoke for thirty minutes; the mother joined after ten minutes and explained that Yumi would work four hours, five days a week, teaching Minika English. The indenture would be for six months, after which they could extend for another six months if both parties agreed.

Yumi found it difficult to conceive that conversation was only seven weeks ago, and today she was being picked up at 3:00 pm to be taken to Japan. The furthest she had ever been from her home city of Daegu was when they went on a family holiday to Seoul, 300kms away. Daegu was the third largest town in South Korea, with a population of 2.5 million. Today, she would travel 1150km to Tokyo, Japan, a city with a population of 14 million.

At 2:30 pm she carried her suitcase and handbag downstairs, leaving them at the front door, then hugged and kissed her mother and father. She had never spent a night away from them. Now they would be separated for at least six months, her living in a foreign land.

She was beginning to feel anxious.

Had she made the correct decision?

It had been surreal until this moment.

Her mother reassured her, and at 3:00 pm, there was a knock on the door.

A man stood there, neatly dressed, and said, "I have come to collect Yumi." Yumi hugged and kissed her mother for the tenth time and, with tears in her eyes, said, "I will miss you, Mummy!" and pulled away. Her mother smiled bravely, yet Yumi could see the tears welling in her mother's eyes.

Finally, she turned, picked up her suitcase, her Louis Vuitton bag and walked out to the minivan, feeling very grown up.

The driver opened the door, and she stepped up and into the minivan. She placed her suitcase in a storage area which held other bags and walked towards the remaining spare seat. There were seven other girls in the van, all smiling. She said, "Hello." The other girls all responded, "Hello."

Everyone looked thrilled, all going on an adventure. Yumi thought they all looked to be my age; she wondered where they were all going. Then she struck up a conversation with the girl next to her. Her name was Ari (the name means beautiful in Korean), a very fitting name for her. She told Yumi she was going to Tokyo to become a model. She had sent her photo portfolio to a studio she had found on the internet, and they had agreed to take her on retainer for JPY100,000 a week for three months to determine her popularity. Wow, Yumi thought, that's a lot of money.

She studied Ari's features.

She was gorgeous; however, she was surprised she had been accepted into a modelling career as she was less than 150 cm tall. Most Korean/Japanese models were much taller, at least 165cm.

When they passed the turnoff to the International Airport, Yumi asked the driver where they were driving to. He said, "We have a two-hour drive to Busan; from there, you will go by ferry to Fukuoka, which will take three hours. You will be collected there by our sister company in Japan and driven to your various destinations. I'm afraid you are in for a rather long day." He smiled at them. Yumi liked him, he seemed nice, and she was very excited. All the girls were excited.

They arrived at the International Marina at 5:30 pm. Instead of being taken to the ferry terminal, they were taken to a luxurious vessel, the SS Meroon. They collected their luggage, and the captain met them at the gangplank. He welcomed them aboard and asked for their passports. Yumi said, "Shouldn't we always keep these with us?"

"I will have all the passports stamped by immigration and keep them safe in my custody for the duration of the voyage. After that, I will have them validated again when we enter Japan as proof of legal entry into the country. This is standard procedure; the captain's responsible for ensuring the validity of passengers travelling on private vessels entering international waters."

They were escorted downstairs into a lounging area, the saloon, the door closing behind them. The girls sat comfortably, some in conversation, others either on their phones, brushing their hair or applying make-up. Ari was sitting next to Yumi, telling her how excited she was and how she had dreamed of leaving Daegu and becoming an international model. Now it was going to happen.

The engines rumbled into life, and after the mooring ropes were disconnected, the boat started to back away from the wharf. Yumi saw the water boiling near the ship's rear as it slowly turned its bow towards Japan. The engine noise grew louder, and the boat started to hum and vibrate as the speed increased. It was exhilarating. It was the first time Yumi had been on a fast boat. Finally, the bow lifted, the vibrations settled into a melodious hum, and they sped towards their new life.

***

Yumi had lost mobile coverage twenty minutes earlier, and now she watched the land disappear through a window of the SS Meroon. All that was visible was the incredible blue of the water.

They had been travelling for an hour, and two girls had become seasick; they had vomited into the small toilet next to the bedroom suite. She could smell the vomit, which made her feel nauseous. She felt unsteady on her legs and hoped the journey would end soon.

The door opened, and a man came in with a food tray. It was laden with small bowls, one for each girl. They contained Kimchi and Jangajji (an assortment of pickled vegetables) and a 200ml bottle of water. Yumi took her bowl and wooden chopsticks, ate the food, drank the water, and started feeling a bit better.

After ten minutes, the door opened again, and a man they hadn't seen before came into the lounge carrying a small bag.

"I need you to hand me your phones now, please."

One of the girls, Yumi thought she had told her earlier that her name was Binna, asked, "Why are you taking our phones?"

The man smiled, then slapped her hard across her left cheek. The blow so ferocious that she flew back and hit her head on the wooden rail running around the saloon wall under the windows. She started to cry. She put her hand behind her head, brought it out, and showed the man the blood on it. She had split the back of her skull from the force of hitting the hardwood rail.

The man smiled again and said, "Give me your phone, you spoiled little bitch, or I will slap you again." Binna handed over her phone, and as the man walked around with the bag open, each girl placed their phone into the bag without further objections.

Yumi momentarily hesitated before dropping her phone in the bag; her phone was essential. She was becoming frightened, first her passport and now her phone. As Ari placed her phone into the bag, the man leered at her and said, "Well, aren't you a pretty little thing." Then he left.

The girls started chattering again, louder this time and with anxiety blanketing the conversation. Binna was sobbing; one girl held a handkerchief to her scalp to halt the bleeding. The atmosphere of the saloon had transformed from sheer delight and excitement just one hour ago to desperation, fear and uncertainty.

The saloon door opened again, and three men entered. The man who had taken the phones walked over to Ari and said, "You come with me." Ari stood awkwardly. He grabbed her hand, walked her to the bedroom suite, opened the door, pushed her inside, and said, "Get undressed."

Ari started to cry, "No, please, no. Someone help me."

Two men entered the room and closed the door; the third man stood outside watching them. He was tall for a Japanese man, hair styled in a traditional crew cut, his face heavily pock-marked from teenage acne. He looked to be about 25 years of age. He was guarding the door. The seven girls looked at him, all feeling helpless.

Then they heard Ari screaming.

***

Yumi watched the three men leave. They had taken turns guarding the room, and Ari's ordeal had lasted more than an hour. To Yumi, this was the worst hour of her life, the worst hour of her 16 years. She could not comprehend how horrible it must have been for Ari. She got up and walked into the bedroom. Ari was lying on the bed, her knees drawn up to her chest in the foetal position, sobbing. Yumi could see a thin stream of blood trickling from her anus down the back of her thigh. She opened a drawer on the side table and found a hand towel. She used it to wipe the blood from Ari's thigh and then held it against her anus to stop the bleeding. She could see dark red palm marks where she had been slapped hard. Yumi whispered, "Are you ok, Ari?"

"I want my mummy," sobbed Ari.

***

The engine noise started to quiet, and shortly afterwards, it stopped. Yumi could hear men talking outside, and then the door to the saloon opened, and one of the men who had raped Ari was standing there with a pistol pointed at the girls.

"Grab your stuff and come up now."

Once on deck, Yumi looked around. It was a new moon, so there was little light, the sky black except for the stars. They had arrived at a small wharf. A van was waiting; the exhaust fumes grey against the dark of night, its headlights illuminating the empty road ahead.

"Hurry up!" the man barked, pointing his gun towards the waiting van. The girls walked across the gangplank onto the wharf. Yumi was happy to have solid land under her again, although it still felt to be rolling a little.

She was holding Ari's hand; she had helped Ari get dressed earlier. Ari hadn't said anything since the men had raped her. She just sobbed, her eyes hollow and glassy. They walked to the minivan, put their luggage in the rear, and took seats. A Japanese man slid the door shut, locked it and handed a package to the captain. Yumi assumed it was money. The captain gave the man the girls' passports, but there was no sign of their phones. This made Yumi sad, she hadn't been without a phone for six years, and it was a very odd feeling.

The captain and the man with the gun went back to the boat. The Japanese man sat in the passenger's seat, and they headed off into the night. She saw a sign saying 'Fukura 10 kms', giving her an idea of where she was. They had arrived in Japan; they had crossed the Korean Strait.

Yumi didn't know where they were headed. She knew one thing, though, that she was not being taken to the house where Minika lived; there would be no tutoring. She tried to understand what these men had planned for her, then started crying. She was the last of the girls to start crying.

Day 11 since the abduction

<u>32</u>

Kai was driving the van, and Megumi sat in the passenger seat. The time was 1:00 am. They were on their way to undertake reconnaissance of the processing centre. Sitting so close to him was having an uncomfortable effect on her; there was something about this man that excited her.

He was handsome, with an athletic build, and he was trained to kill.

Was it that trait that excited her?

She wasn't sure.

She knew her heart had pumped faster when Hirutu asked Kai to accompany her today.

She glanced down at her iPhone. "Turn left at the next corner, and we should be able to park behind the supermarket."

Kai left the vehicle running, allowing the air conditioning to continue operating. The van's rear compartment was full of electronic equipment, which produced considerable heat. They exited the van and walked to the rear. Casually looking around, they confirmed there wasn't anyone nearby, and Kai opened the rear doors.

Inside the van sat a large metal case. Kai removed it and positioned it next to the van before opening it. Inside the case was a Delta Quad long-range surveillance unmanned aerial vehicle (UAV). It was fitted with both a thermal and infrared imaging camera. It was capable of manual or autonomous flight with a duration of 110 minutes. The flight control panel utilised a virtual private network secured by military encryption and had a range of fifty kilometres. Kai removed the components from the case and attached the wings to the main body. It was a beast, 2.5 metres wide when assembled.

Kai carried the UAV to an open area in the car park while Megumi inputted the coordinates into the flight control panel. She set it to hover 500 metres above the compound to avoid guard detection. She pressed the launch button, and the four propellors on the wings started spinning. It was loud, the sound like a large swarm of bees.

The UAV launched vertically at speed, and within twenty seconds, it was just a tiny dot in the sky. Once it reached its programmed altitude of 500 metres, it commenced its course towards the compound. Kai entered the back of the van carrying the UAV case and deposited it inside. Megumi stepped in and sat at the bank of equipment against the wall while Kai closed the door. Over the next hour, they obtained the necessary footage to plan tonight's mission.

***

They had arrived at Megumi's home 90 minutes earlier. During that time, they previewed and discussed the footage from the UAV. Megumi completed editing and uploading the relevant UAV footage to the Saviour server and then turned to Kai.

"Well, I think it's been a constructive night. We have the information required to brief the team in the morning.

"Would you like a drink?"

"Do you have bourbon?"

"Yes, Gentleman Jack. How do you like it?"

"On the rocks."

Megumi prepared her drink and Kai's bourbon.

"Cheers."

Kai touched his glass to Megumi's and took a long swig from the finely cut crystal glass.

The bourbon was smooth; he felt its silky burn as it travelled down his throat and began to warm his stomach.

He watched Megumi take a long sip of her drink, her eyes never leaving his face. He found her green eyes mesmerising, she was a beautiful woman, and he realised he was falling in love with her!

She moved closer and reached out, placing her right hand against his chest. He could feel the heat from her palm through his thin cotton shirt. Her hand moved lightly across his chest, first resting on his right pectoral muscle, which she gave a squeeze, then it made its way to the left side of his chest, and she squeezed again.

Kai's heartbeat accelerated at this simple action, stimulating the release of endorphins and dopamine. She paused, searching his eyes and face for signals, and emotion, deciding if she should continue. Her stare, touch, and apparent desire for him kicked his heart into overdrive, and he became aroused. He took the drink from her hand and placed both glasses on a nearby table.

Megumi was breathing heavily, her body alive with long-forgotten emotions, something she had not experienced for years. Kai placed his lips gently on hers. She returned the kiss and felt his hand on her stomach. Slowly it moved towards her breast, a gentle squeeze, and he unbuttoned her blouse. He lifted her bra, exposing her breasts. He held one breast as he began to suck gently on the erect nipple of the other.

Her pleasure senses ignited; she reached out and unbuttoned his shirt as his mouth moved to her other breast. Moving her hands across his hairless chest, she admired his apparent strength beneath his soft, smooth skin. She pushed him away, reached down to unbuckle his belt, then dropped his trousers and removed his underwear. His penis sprung upwards when freed from the clothing and stood proudly erect. She stared at its fullness and considered taking it in her mouth. Before she could act, he bent down, lifted her into his arms with ease and carried her into the bedroom, laying her gently on the bed.

She reached for the zipper on the right side of her skirt and lowered it. Kai gently but quickly removed the dress, and then her underwear and butterfly kissed the inside of her thighs, moving slowly towards her throbbing triangle. Megumi removed her blouse and bra, throwing them into a corner of the room as she breathed heavily, enjoying his attention.

Kai lowered his body gently upon her, and they kissed passionately. Megumi could feel the hardness of his erection against her stomach. The kiss and his naked body pressed against her ignited emotions as ancient as humankind. She was fully aroused. She wrapped her legs around his waist and, with a strength that surprised them both, twisted him onto his back, positioning her on top, her legs straddling him.

She reached back with her hand to guide him and heard a loud gasp in the room, then realised it had come from her. She slowly drew him into her, grinding her groin against his, exquisite surges of pleasure penetrating her body, her moans growing louder as she worked to extinguish the fire within her.

During this primordial act, she had only one thought.
It had been far too long.

33

Yumi had been dosing but woke when the car's engine shut down. They had been travelling for nine hours with just one break in a rest area to use the toilet. The man driving had walked them in groups of two from the car to the bathroom and back. The other man previously in the passenger seat had driven the remainder of the way.

She looked at her watch, it was 6:15 am, and the sky was beginning to lighten from black to an overcast grey. It was a dreary day that matched her mood. The car had stopped in front of a walled compound with large metal gates; it looked like a prison. The driver spoke into the gate intercom from the car window, announcing them. The gates began to open, and the minivan moved forward through a second wire gate and parked in front of what looked like a monastery. Yumi thought maybe it wouldn't be too bad, but deep down, she knew they were in serious trouble.

She was a captive, but for what purpose?

Despite only being 16, she knew there were a few obvious options.

But she didn't want to think about it.

The guard in the passenger seat opened the locked sliding door to the minivan.

"Get out." Yumi reached into the storage area to collect her suitcase when the man yelled, "Leave it, just get out. Now! Quickly!"

The girls were separated into two groups of four and led into the building. The car containing their luggage drove away without unloading it. Now they had stolen all her best clothes, shoes and cosmetics.

Yumi's group was taken to a locked room. The guard opened the door and signalled for them to enter; she watched the other four girls being led to another room.

The four Korean girls stood there, trying to process what was happening. The room was dimly lit by a single opaque window, filthy from decades of grime, metal bars protected the glass. The furnishings were sparse, with just four futons covering most of the floor. In the corner was a sink with running water and a metal bucket that, judging from its odour, was their toilet.

There was only one girl in the room. She was sleeping restlessly, perhaps having a nightmare. She was asleep on a futon, with no pillow or sheets, wearing a night dress. Yumi went over towards her and kneeled next to her. She could see bruises on the girl's face. Her right eyelid was swollen, and a yellow fluid leaked onto her cheek. Her arms were skinny and covered in needle track marks. She thought that was what they were although she had never seen anyone taking drugs. She gently touched the girl's shoulder, trying to wake her.

No response.

She shook her gently at first, then harder until she saw she was arousing.

Suddenly, her left eye opened, and a look of sheer terror immediately appeared on her face. Once her eyes had focused on Yumi's smiling face, she relaxed.

Then, just as suddenly as before, her face changed into an expression of panic. She jumped off the floor, rushed over to the bucket and vomited for three minutes. Finally, when she had emptied her stomach, she washed her face and hands in the sink and walked back to lie down on the futon.

Yumi asked, "Are you sick? Where are we?"

"You are in hell; the men here have made me sick!"

"My name is Yumi, this is Ari, this is Binna, and this is Chaewon. What is your name, and how long have you been here?"

"My name is Honoka Kondo. I was abducted walking home from school eleven days ago. I am just fifteen. What these men have done to me is horrible. First, they brought me here by road and raped me repeatably during the journey. Then, when I arrived, they drugged me with heroin every eight hours, and the sexual abuse continued until I became compliant. Heroin will make you compliant, and it eases the pain.

"After seven days, they sent me to a baishun yado where I was expected to have sex with twenty men daily, with hardly any food or sleep. The heroin injections continued. I am addicted to it. The evening of my second day at the baishun yado, they told me I had one more client before I could have my medicine. I was furious. The man was nasty to me; he wanted me to suck his cock. He held my head so I couldn't move as he thrust it in and out of my mouth. I wanted him to stop, so I bit down hard, my mouth filled with his blood; he screamed and pulled away.

I looked at him defiantly as I spat his cock towards the floor.

"The guards came and beat me. The next thing I know, I'm back here for remedial training and education. Well, that's what they said. I think that was two days ago. They haven't given me any heroin or food as punishment. I am experiencing heroin withdrawal; it is excruciating. Every muscle and joint in my body aches. I want to die or get heroin; there is no other choice."

She got up again and vomited into the bucket, then laid down on the futon and quickly went back to restless sleep. The four girls were silent; the blood drained from their faces. They knew now what their future held. Suddenly Ari burst into tears, and the other three girls began crying. They hugged each other and, as a group, fell to their knees, trying to comfort each other from a fate they were starting to understand.

***

Yumi woke when she heard the door being unlocked. She looked at her Apple Smartwatch; it was 8:30 am. She had slept for a couple of hours. The four girls had slept two to a futon, cuddled against each other as the room was cold, and there were no sheets or blankets. Cuddling provided some comfort, allowing the girls to fall asleep.

A fat ugly man entered the room first, followed by a woman carrying clothes and another man carrying a medical bag. The lead man, probably the boss since he was wearing an ill-fitting suit, said, "Get up! Now!" The four girls all stood. Honoka remained snoring on her futon. The man addressed them, "Welcome, girls, to my humble establishment. I hope your transport options were comfortable." The other man snickered when he heard this. "You have probably guessed by now that the job opportunities you thought were available here in Tokyo were a complete fabrication. Your new profession will be prostitution. I have your passports, and I will return them to you when you have earned JPY7 million, as this is the amount necessary to repay your new owner their original bondage payment. You should make sufficient money within three years if you service twenty men daily. That's not so long now, is it? You are all young and will still be young when you pay for your freedom.

"Now, please remove all your clothes and dress in the nightgowns being provided by the nurse. She will also examine you to determine if you are intact and suitable for your new occupation."

Binna was the first to be examined, and the nurse asked her how she had split the back of her head. Binna told her it had happened on the Korean boat trip, and the woman frowned. Next, she put a glove on her right hand and asked Binna to bend over. She forced her fingers inside her, and Binna cried, "You are hurting me!"

All the girls underwent a similar embarrassing examination, with Yumi noticing that the nurse never changed her glove.

The nurse said to the commander, "You will need to do something to stop that boat crew from damaging our goods, one girl requires stitches to the back of her head, and the other has severe vaginal and anal lacerations that will take six to eight days to heal with the correct treatment. I will take them both back to my medical practice so they can get the required care and medicines. I will return them when they can perform their new duties."

It was evident to Yumi that the commander was unhappy with this medical assessment. He begrudgingly accepted her advice and grumpily replied, "OK. What about the other girls and the state of their pussies?"

"All of them have normal functioning vaginas and should be able to work in the business. They all could pass as virgins except the girl raped on the voyage to Japan."

"Excellent, thank you. Repair the two girls and return them to me as soon as you deem fit. You can leave now."

The commander stood in front of Chaewon, "Do you speak Japanese?"

"Yes, a little."

"What's your name? How old are you, and what was your planned occupation in Tokyo?"

"I am Chaewon; I am 14 years old. I am an exchange student. I was to live with a Japanese family for three months to improve my Japanese skills."

"Well, little Chaewon, good news, you will share my bed tonight and have the advantage of learning your new skills from me, not the guards."

He turned to the guard, pointed at Honoka and said, "Wake her."

The guard roughly grabbed Honoka by the shoulders and dragged her onto her knees. Her head drooped forward, and he slapped her hard, the noise reverberating in the room. She was instantly alert and started crying, the tears running down her cheeks, already beginning to dampen the collar of her night dress.

"So, this is Honoka. The girl who bit off my customer's cock! My dear girl, if my customers lose their cocks, I will get no more business from them! If other men discover I have cock-eating girls in my baishun yados, I will lose more business. Do you understand? Cock-eating is a public relations disaster and must be handled quickly and efficiently.

"I have a Korean client willing to pay me twice the usual amount for a young Japanese girl. Do you know why he is willing to pay so much?"

Honoka shook her head slowly, first to the right side, then to the left. Yumi could see that Honoka was afraid of this man.

"In 1942, his grandfather was murdered by Japanese soldiers, and his grandmother was taken to be an ianfu, a comfort woman for the Japanese soldiers. She was nineteen years old. His father, who was four then, had his right hand cut off by a sword. The soldier holding the young boy's arm laughed at his colleague, encouraging him to see how cleanly he could cut. They left his father to die. Luckily, he was saved by a neighbour who had hidden and waited till the soldiers left. At the end of World War 2, evidence of the conditions and abuse the Japanese soldiers forced upon comfort women was reported.

His father's anger and hate for the Japanese was passed onto him. His mind was poisoned, by his father's stories, recollecting the terrible abuse his grandmother would have endured. He wants a young Japanese woman so he can exact his revenge on our race.

"I'm not an evil man, Honoka, but I need to protect my business. So, do you want to become a comfort woman for Korean men, enduring who knows what atrocities they will inflict on you? Or would you prefer to pay off your debt here in Japan and become a free woman in a few years?"

Honoka pleaded, "Please let me stay here; I will be good. I need my medicine; I am very sick." The commander undid the belt on his trousers, dropping them along with his underpants to the floor. He stood, his tiny penis just inches from Honoka's face. "I am a generous man. Show me that you can satisfy a man by swallowing his seed without eating his cock. Then, if you do a good job, you will be rewarded with a heroin fix."

Yumi and Chaewon watched in horror as Honoka was forced to provide fellatio. They had heard stories at school, but neither had seen it done before. Chaewon was wondering what she would need to do in his bed tonight.

When it was over, he said, "That was ok, but you must be able to do much better than that. Today, I will let my guards visit you as often as they desire, and if you satisfy them, you will receive a quarter of a fix. If you perform well, you will end the night with a beautiful high and a full belly.

"Jintu, please administer a quarter of a fix for this girl and take her to room number one. Secure her and leave a vial of heroin in the room so the guards can reward her. Every good blow job rewarded with a quarter fix should instil an improved reward response from her. Also, give each of these girls their first fix, just a half for this morning and another half at 5:00 pm after they have their dinner bottles."

The commander left the room, and the guard placed his bag next to the sink, filled a syringe with the substance from a vial and then applied a rubber band around Chaewon's little arm. He pressed the syringe into her arm and pulled the plunger back. Yumi could see blood enter the needle and discolour the liquid inside it. Then he pushed the plunger a third of the way and removed the needle. Chaewon gasped, her eyes went glassy, and she started falling. Yumi caught her and lowered her to the futon. She looked pale and lifeless.

Next, the man attempted to apply the tourniquet to Yumi's arm. She pulled away.

"Do that again, bitch, and I will stick the needle into your eyeball!"

"But you need to use a clean needle."

"Give me your arm, or it's going into your eyeball."

Yumi held out her arm, and he injected her; instantly, a metallic taste was in her mouth. She could feel the heroin racing through the arteries of her arm. Her heartbeat slowed, she felt calm, euphoric, and the room started closing in on her. Her peripheral vision became a slowly expanding dark ring until the room disappeared.

***

Yumi opened her eyes. She felt nauseous; she could smell vomit; she looked over to her left and saw Chaewon lying on her side; she had vomited on her futon. She studied her and saw her tiny chest slowly rising and falling. Good, thought Yumi; she knew that she was still alive; they both were.

She looked at her watch, and it was missing!

At first, she couldn't believe it, then she burst into tears, sobbing uncontrollably.

"No, no, no," she cried.

How is it possible for someone's life to change so quickly in less than 24 hours? She had transitioned from feeling elated from securing her dream job into desperate misery. They had stolen her best clothes, shoes, iPhone, passport, and now her watch. She wore a night dress that still held the scent of the perfume from the girl who wore it before her. Her only remaining possession was her innocence, but for how long she wondered, after that, I will have nothing, I will be nothing, just a vessel to serve men. She closed her eyes to stop her tears, but she couldn't, and her tears fell relentlessly.

Eventually, she did stop crying and opened her eyes. She noticed a smudge of blood on the edge of the futon. Looking closer, she could see it was a bloody fingerprint. Further examination revealed a thin strand of wire sewn into the edge to strengthen the futon. She followed it. It continued around the entire futon; someone had worked away at the point where it joined. They had been successful in breaking the join.

She thought, if I can remove this, I may be able to fabricate it into a weapon, but she wasn't sure how she would do that.

First, she had to get the wire out.

For the first time since she had been abducted, she felt a glimmer of hope. She worked tirelessly to push the metal through the futon, freeing it. She worked from both ends until she could pull it from the futon.

Yumi considered her skills and how she could use these skills to make a weapon.

She knew how to braid hair; maybe she could break it into lengths; it was less than 1mm in diameter. She selected a point 30 cm from the end and bent the wire back and forth. It only took a few bends before it broke. She smiled, thinking this might work.

It had taken her almost three hours to make her weapon, probably because the heroin was muddling her brain. First, she had plaited three wires together and fabricated nine of these. They were each 3mm thick and not particularly strong, but she had a powerful weapon once she braided the nine pieces into three thicker plaids and then braided them together. Then, she bent one end into a bulb to aid her grip.

It felt good; she had fashioned a strong blade, a total of twenty-seven pieces of the wire interlaced. She could use this to defend herself if she had an opportunity. She hid it under her futon and, exhausted, fell asleep.

34

Hiroki arrived at the compound at 4:00 pm, two hours earlier than he had advised. He wanted to confirm that the improved security preparations were complete and that the guards were alert. He was immediately provided access to the compound and was pleased to see the installation of the microwave detection units. Unfortunately, he could see that the main cable was snaking across the ground, it had yet to be buried.

The additional guards had been obtained; the shift durations had been reduced and overlapped. He spoke to each guard individually to ensure they understood that they were under threat and must maintain awareness and be always cautious. Regardless of how minor, they were to radio immediately if they saw anything unusual.

At 5:30 pm, he was met by Commander Toyotomi, and they shook hands. When he released his grip, Hiroki concentrated hard to avoid wiping his hand against his trousers. Toyotomi smiled and said, "Honourable sir, I want to thank you for improving the security of my compound and for personally overseeing this evening's shift. My men and I will be forever grateful".

Then he added, "As a sign of my appreciation, I would like to present you with a gift. Please follow me."

***

Yumi was woken roughly; a guard was shaking her. "Come on, you slut, wake up; we have a nice surprise for you." He dragged her to her feet, and together they left the room. She had no opportunity to grab her knife. She felt ill, the effects of the heroin wearing off and the thought of what she would now need to endure. The man led her to a room at the end of the corridor, opened the door and said, "Wait in there, shortly an important man will arrive. You will do whatever he desires if you know what is good for you. He is a killer."

When the guard had left, Yumi surveyed the room; a sizeable western-style bed with clean sheets dominated the room. There was a small dresser with a mirror, and a ceramic jug sat upon it. She opened the lid; it was filled with water, with six ice cubes on the surface to keep it chilled. She opened the drawer and gasped. Inside were sexual accessories, different-sized dildos and some items she had never seen before and wasn't sure of their use. The drawer also contained four sets of handcuffs with keys.

She examined the door, it was solid wood and thick, at least ten centimetres, the single window was secured by bars, and the walls were constructed of stone. She wondered how many girls had been in this room before her, and what atrocities had been committed.

She felt as though she had been transported from the modern 21st century into a time when barbarians ruled the world. She sat on the bed. It was either the bed or the floor, as the room lacked any other furniture. Despite trying to be brave, she couldn't hold back her tears. She rested her face in her hands and sobbed, uncontrollably, wishing she had never accepted that fake job. After fifteen minutes, she was able to gain her composure again. She felt sick, and she was tired, so she laid down and drifted asleep.

She awoke when she heard the key turn in the lock, and the door opened. She sat upright, and Toyotomi, the commander, entered the room, followed by a younger man.

"Hiroki, please accept my gift for your help securing our compound.

This Korean girl is new and untouched; please take your time and enjoy."

Displaying a grotesque leer, the commander turned and left. The other man just stood, a bewildered look on his face. A minute passed, and he didn't say or do anything, just surveyed the room. Occasionally his eyes would glimpse briefly at her then he would look away.

After another minute of silence, she thought she should start the conversation.

"My name is Yumi.

"I have been tricked into travelling to Japan, only to find I am being forced into prostitution.

"I am a virgin.

"These people are ruthless, drugging me and the other girls trapped here.

"Are you going to rape me?

"I will fight back if you try. I do not consent."

"My name is Hiroki. I am not here to rape you. Please tell me your story."

Day 12 since the abduction

35

Hiroki looked at his watch. 2:00 am. He had left the compound at midnight after his father had arrived to oversee the midnight to 6:00 am shift. He had laid awake since he had gone to bed, his mind mulling over the young Korean girl's story. Sleep was impossible.

They had spoken for thirty minutes. He had found Yumi to be intelligent and full of optimism. She had been at the compound for less than twelve hours and had seen and experienced things no young woman should endure. He also worried about the other girls, in particular, Chaewon. She was only fourteen years of age. A child, forced to spend the night with the Commander, a man he disliked before and now despised.

Hiroki had hurt and killed many people, yet he still considered himself honourable. His crimes, so to speak, had been executed on behalf of his daimyo under the samurai code of Bushido. But unfortunately, these men were treating these young girls as merchandise, showing no compassion or providing for their basic human needs.

He was not looking forward to returning and defending these men. It was his duty, though, and he would execute it to the best of his ability. He would do it for his father, whom he loved.

36

Yumi slowly opened her eyes, adjusting to the dim light. A shadow moved towards her. Her body felt heavy, the heroin she had received hours before still drugging her body. She searched under her mattress for the wire weapon she had fabricated earlier and grasped it in her right hand. The man moved towards her; he was one of the new guards. She heard the rustle of fabric as he pushed his trousers down and removed her panties. He lifted her legs over his shoulders, preparing to rape her. He moved closer, and she could see his face now. Her eyes had adjusted to the dark, her adrenalin fighting against the stupor of heroin.

She struck him swiftly and as hard as she could, aiming for his left eye. She was surprised how easily the roughly made tool penetrated his eye and plunged its full length into his brain. His back arched upwards for a moment then he collapsed upon her. A warm fluid flowed over her hand onto her chest. The exertion of killing the man had exhausted her, he was much heavier than her, and she couldn't move him off her. Quickly, her adrenalin resided, and the heroin effects overcame her lucidity, and she fell asleep, liquid oozing from the man's eye and pooling on her chest.

37

Megumi was watching the complex using the drone's thermal imaging camera. It was 3:00 am when the human body was at its lowest awareness. The Saviours hoped to use this to their advantage. She watched two guards patrolling the inside wall walking in opposite directions, which resulted in them passing each other on the southern and northern sides of the complex. This patrol pattern was effective as it kept each man alert and halved a guard's time to investigate a particular area. However, it made them vulnerable as they would be alone for most of the circuit.

A third guard was stationed at the front door, and two more guarded the back door. Inside, she saw two in the security surveillance room and four more in what they considered the guards' waiting room. Four occupied rooms, each containing four to six sleeping bodies. She was sure the girls were being kept hostage. The bedroom, they believed was the commander's, held two bodies, one a lot smaller, probably a young girl. She provided this information to the Saviours, who were in the agreed positions, - Sakura on the south wall, Tatsuo on the eastern border, and Takeo on the western wall.

Kai was sitting in the driver's seat of the first van, Dr Uni was in the driver's seat of the second van, and Megumi was sitting in the back of the truck, which contained all the sophisticated technology required for tonight.

Sakura said, "Megumi, please commence disabling their security systems. Advise when complete." Inside the van, Megumi activated the mobile data jammer. This would prevent any calls into or out of the complex and surrounding areas within a 200-metre radius. Next, she completed her hack of the complex's internet router, disabling the camera feed and replacing it with the five-minute loop she had recorded earlier. Inside the security room, it would appear everything was normal.

Megumi watched as the two guards passed each other on the southern side of the compound and then turned to patrol the different sides of the building. "You are good to go."

Sakura was the only person to move. She was nimbler than her older colleagues, and years of training had strengthened her lower body. She quickly scaled the external wall and, standing on the top, launched herself into the 'deadman zone', a four-meter-wide space between the outer wall and the interior wire wall. Anyone caught in this area was an easy target for the guards.

Megumi's team had rendered a 3D digital model of the complex to determine if any areas were free from detection by the motion cameras. They had done an excellent job ensuring the entire area was covered. However, Megumi believed there was one spot, just one meter by one metre, that was clear. Sakura had leapt into this area and immediately began to cut the interior wire fence, listening for the sound of an alarm.

After thirty seconds of silence, she mentally thanked Megumi for accurately predicting this location. Then, she entered the internal courtyard and stealthily closed the distance between her, and the two guards stationed at the rear entrance. If they had been attentive, they may have noticed her. Instead, however, they were smoking and talking under the light.

Sakura removed two throwing knives from her tunic and held one in each hand. She was equally skilled throwing with either hand having practised throwing at two targets simultaneously for a decade. She took a moment to calm herself, paused her breathing, and then threw the knives as one, each silent and deadly, striking the guards simultaneously.

One blade entered the guard on the right through his left ear, travelling along the internal auditory canal. It severed the vestibulocochlear nerve, which caused the left side of his face to spasm comically until the blade passed through the cerebral cortex, causing him to stiffen before he fell to the decking dead.

The other blade entered the guard on the left through the right eye socket, embedding itself deep into the temporal lobe; death was instant, and he collapsed like a rag doll to the decking. Sakura silently made her way to the rear door, checked it to find it was unlocked, smiled to herself and thought these people were amateurs.

Near the rear door was a recently installed ethernet cable for the motion detectors yet to be buried. This weakness in their system meant she could disable them, enabling the older and bigger Saviours to enter the 'deadman's zone' undetected. Sakura cut it with her wire cutters.

"I have disabled the motion sensor and am entering the complex," she advised the others.

Megumi watched the guards complete their patrol of the east and western boundaries and said, "Saviour two and three, you are good to go." Immediately, Takeo and Tatsuo scaled the external wall, ran to the internal wire wall, and commenced cutting. Each man was through the wire in forty seconds and made their way to the front of the building, their backs hard against the wall.

As the guards rounded the building commencing another patrol circuit, she said, "Initiating power failure." Megumi pressed the red button on the detonation transmitter, and a radio signal was sent to the charge Kai had placed on the transformer providing power to the complex. She heard a soft bang, and all the lights illuminating the complex went dark. The patrolling guards rounded the corner as the lights went out, they were temporarily confused. Tatsuo and Takeo were using their night vision goggles, the guards visible to them in the darkness. They killed them silently.

Sakura made her way past the security room towards the guard's room. She expected them to be resting or, hopefully, to be sleeping. She lowered her night vision goggles, and immediately the world turned green. Slowly, she pushed the ancient handle downwards and felt the catch slide upwards from its latch. She expected it to make a noise. However, it remained silent. She pushed the thick door open slowly. There were four sleeping guards, their snores reverberating throughout the room.

It's difficult to kill someone silently, despite what we see in the movies. Human bodies are resilient, and the will to live is robust in most people. Sakura was concerned about the risk of the death throes of a guard waking the others. She assessed her options and decided the Nieves Fernandez technique was her best chance of success in this situation. She had studied the Fernandez technique in the final five years of her training at the temple.

Nieves Fernandez was a filipino schoolteacher during World War II when the Japanese army invaded the Philippines. Women became vulnerable targets of sexual assault during the occupation, and the Imperial Japanese Army used many forcibly as comfort women. Worried that Japanese troops would come for her girl students, she became the Philippines' most famous female guerrilla commander. She once commanded an assault team of 110 men responsible for killing over 200 Japanese soldiers in a single night.

Fernandez was perhaps the world's most famous silent killer. Before she became the commander, she would hunt solo at night, shoeless and wearing a black dress. She used the filipino bolo knife, an easily accessible tool primarily used for trailblazing and agricultural purposes such as clearing vegetation. Her technique was to sneak up from behind her targets and stab behind and below the earlobe, severing the anterior carotid artery, which delivers blood to the brain, causing immediate unconsciousness. Next, the blade would be thrust to a depth of five centimetres and then twisted upwards at a ninety-degree angle, severing the exterior and interior jugular veins. If performed correctly, the blade twisting caused the victim to suck in air, preventing screaming.

Sakura had practised on straw-filled mannequins; she had never performed this manoeuvre on a living human. So first, she calmed herself, encouraging her muscles to replay the hundreds of hours she had practised. Then, removing her kaiken, she quickly dispatched each guard, delivering them to their new eternal resting place.

"Guards are dealt with, just security and commander rooms to be made safe," Sakura said over her radio.

Megumi responded, "Front door guard is enquiring about the property's power. He has been warned to remain in position and be ready for when the backup generator comes online."

Tatsuo threw his kaiken at the guard; it lodged in the man's throat, causing him to drop his rifle and reach for his throat. Tatsuo moved swiftly, slamming his left forearm against the man's forehead and dragging his kaiken viciously back and forth before removing it. The cut went so deep that the man's head fell backwards, opening a massive wound. The blood squirted out in a thick stream and just as quickly stopped as he dropped to the ground, lifeless. Tatsuo lifted his night goggles an instant before the lights came on again.

Megumi said, "Security is asking for the guards to report status immediately, the voice urgent, suspecting an issue."

Takeo made his way to the rear of the building and joined Sakura as she exited the guard's room. The front door opened, and Takeo entered and joined them. The Saviours all moved towards the room they believed was the security room.

<u>38</u>

Yoritomo was tired; he had taken over the watch from Hiroki at midnight. It had been many years since he had been awake after midnight, and he was starting to regret his decision to do the graveyard shift. He should have let the younger man do it. But instead, he watched the security cameras. The same video feeds had been repeating for the past three hours, the pictures lifeless except when the guards patrolled past them. He wondered if the people attacking their business would be bold enough to take on this fortified complex. If they did, they were very brave or foolish.

He had dressed in his favourite samurai outfit and was fully equipped with weapons. On his back, in their Sayas, were his Katana and tantō swords; his kaiken was secured in his belt. He had five throwing blades hidden in his right sleeve and another five in his left. He was wearing his leather fighting sneakers.

Suddenly there was an alarm. Yoritomo turned to the guard, "What alarm is that?"

The guard typed on his keyboard, and a message was displayed 'MOTION SENSOR DETECTION – OFFLINE'. "It's the newly installed motion sensor system. It has either failed or someone has disabled it."

The light went out, and all the monitors went blank; only the blue emergency light on the ceiling illuminated the room. Yoritomo was instantly alert, his renal glands dumping a spike of adrenalin into his system, increasing his heart rate and preparing his sympathetic nerve system for fight or flight. The man next to him muttered, "Shit!" Thirty seconds later, they heard the emergency power generator cough twice before settling into a steady 'thrum, thrum'. A moment later, the room came alive again. First, the lighting and monitors returned online, whilst the security systems rebooted.

He studied the four monitors intensely, searching for clues. Every thirty seconds, the monitors would cycle to a different camera view. The first cycle was focused outside the compound, it looked normal, and then the monitors flickered, focusing on the 'deadman's zone'. The cameras conducted a slow pan covering their respective areas.

"Stop the pan there," yelled Yoritomo. He could see breaches in the eastern and western internal wire walls. "Guards, report your status!" he yelled into the security mike. No one answered. The camera feeds then focused on the internal compound, and he could see the guards' bodies lying in the areas where they had been killed. He reached towards a stainless-steel console that housed the main controls for the security systems; he lifted a small cover protecting a red button stamped 'ALARM' and pressed it.

Nothing happened.

He pressed it again.

The door of the security room flew open.

<u>39</u>

Takeo kicked hard at the door; the heel of his foot slamming next to the lock. The jamb splintered, and the door flew open, revealing two people. One was the security guard; judging by his uniform, an older man was dressed as a samurai. All three Saviours threw their kaikens as one, Sakura targeting the security guard. The blade entered the man's mouth as he shouted a warning. It severed his spinal cord and lodged deeply in his throat, three centimetres of blade penetrating to the outside; he dropped to the floor. Tatsuo's and Takeo's blades had targeted the samurai, who, in one fluent move, drew his Katana sword and deflected both knives away from his body, each falling harmlessly to the floor.

The security room was small and unsuitable for combat; the samurai would have the advantage as only one saviour could enter and attack him at a time. So, without speaking, the Saviours drew their swords and backed away into the large room adjacent to the security room, each positioning themselves a few metres apart, waiting for the samurai to decide. Finally, he did, and with a calmness that concerned Sakura, he confidently stepped into the room, adopting the classic Jodan-no-kamae samurai stance in preparation for combat.

Each of the Saviours carried firearms, and they may have been able to dispatch this warrior to the gods with a bullet quickly. However, this man was obviously a warrior, and killing him with a gun would be dishonourable. The authentic Japanese warrior understands that honour comes from defeating your enemy with skill, and the satisfaction of drawing blood with a well-positioned sword strike can never be achieved with a firearm.

Time stopped as the four warriors studied each other. All were standing motionless, their swords raised in the Jodan-no-kamae stance. This is one of five classic sword stances and is executed with the left foot pointing forward and the right foot positioned behind and at ninety degrees to the body. The torso is slightly twisted to the right, which reduces the exposed strike area. The arms are raised above the head, the left hand is closest to the opponent, gripping the rear of the hilt. The sword points backwards and upwards at an angle of forty-five degrees. This stance enables the fighter to strike at their opponent with a powerful downward motion in any direction. The left hand controls the direction of the strike, and the right-hand drives the sword downwards with incredible force, easily able to slice a man in half.

Sakura stood between Takeo and Tatsuo, directly facing the samurai. She studied him. He was perhaps in his fifties, yet he held his balance like a much younger man. His face was calm, his eyes intelligent, cruel, emotionless. She suspected he was a Kensei, a master samurai swordsman. He had probably killed many opponents.

Her mind replayed a memory from her training at the Sohei Temple, a story told to her by Master Shi Yan Ming. "Sakura, there will be times when you face a larger, stronger, more skilled opponent. Do not fear this moment, as these experiences strengthen your spirit. Instead, be grateful for the privilege of fighting a more formidable opponent. Consider what your opponent will see, a young, diminutive woman. They will most likely underestimate your strength and skill. This will be your advantage and their downfall."

The man stepped forward quickly, covering the distance in a blink of an eye and struck his sword downwards in a frightening blow targeting Sakura's head. She responded instantly with a blocking stroke driven entirely by muscle memory from years of training. Their swords clanged together with force, the shock of the blow painfully running through her arms' nerves and muscles. Her grip almost failed her, and her grip was legendary. She had not had a weapon dislodged from her hands for a decade, yet this man's powerful strike had weakened her and forced her to drop to her left knee.

Luckily, she had Takeo and Tatsuo at her side. They quickly attacked the samurai, forcing him to deflect their strikes and move backwards into a temporary defensive position away from Sakura. The two men rained sword strikes at him simultaneously.

Sakura took a moment for her body to recover, watching as the three men fought. Their swords circled their bodies at speed, each blade a blur until it was deflected or stopped by another sword. Both Takeo and Tatsuo were master swordsmen, yet against this man, the two of them could not penetrate his defence.

Sakura decided to circle behind him to see if she could attack from the rear. She reached an attacking position, and now the three Saviours struck blows at him from three sides. Miraculously, he repelled each attack, skilfully deflecting their swords, his body spinning in controlled arcs of 180 degrees to ensure he could defend from in front and behind.

Sakura aimed at the samurai's shoulder, her muscles propelling her sword the fastest she had ever struck. He blocked it; however, she could see that her blow had startled him. She sensed that he might be weakening, the speed and ferocity of their attack unrelenting.

Tatsuo attacked with a strike to his head, which he blocked, opening a gap and enabling Takeo to lunge forward and drive his blade into the samurai's right thigh. The samurai plunged his sword, a full half of its length through Takeo's forearm, and immediately extracted it.

Blood fountained from the wound in Takeo's arm. He was out of the battle and staggered back towards the wall to attend to his injury, leaving his sword in the samurai's leg. The samurai reached down and slowly pulled the sword from his leg, his face expressionless as the Saviours watched with awe.

Who is this man? thought Sakura.

The injury would have stopped most men in their tracks, yet this man stood before them, blood running down his leg, staining his trousers.

He held Takeo's blade in his left hand and his sword in his right; he attacked, wielding the two swords.

Another blow stunned Sakura, and she was forced backwards, almost losing her balance and exposing her body; however, before he could finish her, Tatsuo struck, and his blade cut through the tunic on the samurai's right shoulder, revealing a gaping wound.

The samurai's attention had been distracted momentarily due to the immediate pain in his shoulder. Still, just as quickly, he ignored it and attacked Tatsuo, wielding both swords in figure eight.

Each blade struck after the other in a savage arc, targeting his head. Tatsuo was forced to duck, and the samurai plunged Takeo's sword into Tatsuo's right thigh, all the way to the hilt. Tatsuo screamed out in pain and stepped unsteadily backwards; the samurai raised his sword above his head, both hands gripping the hilt.

Before he could complete the killing blow, Sakura raced in and drove her blade into his left leg and quickly withdrew it. She didn't want to lose her weapon and be forced to fight this warrior with a smaller blade.

The samurai turned and faced Sakura. He adopted the classic Ko Gasumi stance. His injured left leg extended forward at forty-five degrees, his right leg behind and bent at a slight angle to support a fast-attacking blow. He held the sword above his injured right shoulder at eye height, the tip facing towards Sakura. They made eye contact. Sakura adopted an identical Ko Gasumi stance. The samurai nodded and slightly bowed towards Sakura, an unexpected sign of respect. She responded with a similarly polite bow and then leapt high towards him, her powerful legs propelling her towards him.

She plunged the sword towards his heart.

He defended, his sword forced to move in an arc across his body to protect him, which deflected Sakura's sword upward. She harnessed the upward motion and redirected it, leveraging its power to strike down at his neck, the tsurgi sword easily severing his head from his body. The arterial spray fountained from his neck, his knees bent, and he collapsed to the floor with dignity, a warrior even in death.

A single throwing blade was dislodged from his right sleeve as he fell. It spun two times on the floor, then stopped, the blade tip pointing at Sakura.

Sakura wiped the sweat from her brow. Her heart was pumping at peak speed, her chest rising and falling quickly as she sucked oxygen into her lungs.

Suddenly she felt exhausted, the adrenalin leaching from her body, and then she remembered her colleagues.

"Megumi, we have killed all the guards except the commander. However, I need assistance; Tatsuo and Takeo have been injured and cannot continue fighting. I need Kai to assist me and Dr Uni to bring his medical bag; we are in the rear end of the house."

Sakura returned to the security room and retrieved her kaiken from the guard's throat. This blade was priceless to her.

<u>40</u>

Yumi awoke. She was having difficulty breathing. The dead guard's weight was pressing on her chest. Using all her strength, she was able to roll him off her. Her heartbeat was racing now, the heroin was wearing off, and she was terrified. She had avoided being raped but wondered what would happen to her for killing a guard. She thought about what they did to Honoka for biting off a man's penis.

She wondered if her parents were worrying about her. Had they contacted the police? How would they find her? She knew it would take a miracle to find her, so she would need to escape!

She stood and washed the blood, brain and eyeball fluid off her hand, arm and chest. It was disgusting, and she felt bile rising in her stomach; however, she avoided vomiting. She checked the door; it was unlocked. Slowly she opened the door and stepped out into the hallway. She knew there were several guards but didn't know how many or where they would be stationed. She could hear noises, so she walked towards the sound. It increased with each step, and then she heard a grunt. Turning a corner, she saw four people fighting with swords. She didn't understand what was happening but could see it was no game. One of the men had already been injured. She watched the fight, and the petite woman killed the man. Two other men lay wounded. She wondered who these people were. She was afraid and ran back to her room and hid inside.

Maybe she would be rescued.

41

Kai heard Sakura's strained voice through his earpiece, and before she had finished the sentence, he had started the van and was driving towards the compound. He stopped the van fifteen metres from the main gate, walked around to the back of the van and opened the rear doors.

Inside the truck were ten backpacks and a smaller bag which held the gate-breaching charge. He grabbed the bag and ran towards the gate with its massive steel doors. There was a 30mm gap between the doors, and Kai could see the thick steel locking device, a rectangular slab of solid steel, 30 mm thick and 100 mm wide. He placed the charge bag on the ground, opened it and removed the orange stick of Semtex. He unwrapped the wax paper and rubbed the plastic explosive between the palms of his hand. In a few seconds, he had the desired shape he wanted, a 20mm thick sausage about 20cm long. He used the gap between the doors to wrap the explosive around the locking beam. Next, he removed a twenty-second detonation plug and pushed it into the sausage. When he was happy that it was all firmly in place, he pressed the small red button on the end of the detonator and ran back to the van. He opened the driver's door, dived inside and lay across the seats.

There was a loud BOOM! He sat up, started the vehicle and slowly drove towards the gate, waiting for the smoke to clear. Three metres from the entrance, the smoke had cleared sufficiently for him to see that the locking bar had been destroyed and the gates were standing slightly ajar. They were severely deformed from the blast. He used the van's front bumper to open them fully, then drove to the inner gate. He breached the locking device on the inner gate by using a hydraulic bolt cutter, which easily cut through the retaining bolt. He opened the gate. "Compound gates are open; you can drive in now." Then he parked the van in the inner compound, turned off the engine and stepped onto the gravel.

He could see the three dead men towards the front of the building. He raced towards the front door, opened it and stepped inside. "Sakura, I am inside. Where are you?"

"Walk down the main corridor towards the rear of the building. I am waiting at the door, with a bronze plaque marked 'Office'.

Kai hurried through the corridor, noticing the closed doors on either side and smelt the sweet, sickly smell that permeated the building. Then, finally, he rounded a corner and was relieved when he saw Sakura.

He embraced her, "Are you ok? Where are the others?"

"I'm ok. Takeo and Tatsuo are injured. They are sitting down in the rear entrance room."

They heard the other two vans sliding to a halt on the gravel. Shortly after, Megumi and Dr Uni ran through the front door and joined them. "Dr Uni, Takeo and Tatsuo are in there. Please see to their wounds." Dr Uni and Megumi raced off in the direction Sakura had pointed to tend to their colleagues.

<u>42</u>

Kai put his ear to the office door to listen. He couldn't hear anything, so he carefully opened it. The room was pitch dark. It was an interior room without windows. He put on his night vision goggles, as did Sakura, and they panned the room. There was a large wooden desk on the opposite side of the room, behind it a decorative bookcase. It took up most of the wall, stopping half a metre from a door which led to a connecting room. Against the wall to their left were two metal storage cabinets, each had two doors and stood three metres tall and two metres wide. To the room's right was a coffee table surrounded by four comfortable chairs.

Sakura looked at Kai, pointed towards the door, and together they moved towards it, neither making a sound. Sakura stood to the right of the door, Kai to the left. He was waiting, his hand on the door handle. Sakura held her kaiken at the ready. They had made considerable noise in the past five minutes, whoever was in that room would know the facility was under attack.

A thin line of light escaped under the tight-fitting door; someone was awake and waiting for them. They lifted their night vision goggle. These would prove useless in a lit room, a disadvantage as the brightness would temporarily blind them.

Sakura nodded, and Kai slowly turned the handle until the latch disengaged, and then he threw the door open, diving into the room to the right, executing a commando roll as he hit the floor. Bullets slammed into the wall, chasing him across the floor. Sakura leapt into the room and threw her kaiken at the man who focused on Kai. It penetrated his right shoulder; the gun fell from his grip as he screamed and reached across with his left hand to pull the knife free. Sakura drew her tsurgi sword from its Saya; it sang that eerie note from the finely made Japanese steel blade drawn across its bamboo sleeve.

Before the man could do anything else, Sakura had the tip of her sword resting against the triangle of skin just above his Adam's apple.

"Please place my kaiken on the bed and back up to the wall behind you."

The commander's bedroom was five metres by five metres, the headboard of a king-size bed against the wall opposite the entrance door. A young girl was sitting up in the bed. Her pyramid-shaped pubescent breasts, evidence that she was only a child.

Sakura felt her anger rise within her.

She knew what it felt like to be abused as a child.

She could barely contain her fury.

It would be so easy to push her blade into the man's throat ending him now.

Kai gently touched her shoulder and said, "I have him; you attend to the girl."

Sakura walked over to the bed and smiled at the little girl.

Then, she raised her hood so the girl could see her face.

"My name is Sakura. What is your name?"

"I am Chaewon."

"Are you ok? Did he hurt you?"

She started to cry.

Sakura saw bruising to the left side of her face, a blackened and partially closed eye and a small cut on her lip.

"He hurt me. He drugged me and did things to me."

"Kai, take him out into the office so we can interview him."

"Do you know where the other girls are?"

"Yes, they are in the rooms off the main corridor."

"Have you met this girl?" Sakura showed her the picture of Honoka.

"Yes, that is Honoka. They took her from our room yesterday morning. She is here somewhere, the guards are abusing her, and she is very sick."

At last, Sakura thought, we have found her.

Kai finished securing the commander into his office chair using cable ties.

Sakura dragged a chair towards the commander and sat opposite him.

She hadn't replaced her hood, since she spoke to Chaewon.

She wanted him to see her face, and she wanted him to know she was a woman.

"I am Sakura Bianchi."

She stared at him silently, watching him grow angry.

"I am Toyotomi, the commander of this facility and a respected member of the Hidetada yakuza family. You and your friends have just forfeited your lives by attacking this building. You are effectively attacking Tokugawa Hidetada. You are walking dead, as is your immediate family."

Sakura sat patiently, just staring at him.

"You are as stupid as these whores if you think you can get away with this."

Sakura was tired of this rude man. She would let him sweat a bit more before proceeding with the next part of her plan.

She stood and walked toward the storage cabinets. She opened the doors of one and her eyes went wide with astonishment. The cabinet had ten shelves, each separated by thirty centimetres and was filled with passports.

Sakura removed a stack of passports and shuffled through them. They were all Korean. She counted thirty passports in the pile. Each shelf was six stacks deep and twenty stacks wide; a quick calculation, 3,600 passports were on each shelf. All the shelves in this cabinet were full. It held 36,000 passports. She briefly checked the other shelves. Passports were from multiple countries: Russia, Britain, Thailand, the

USA, Australia, New Zealand, Finland, Israel, France, Hungary and Romania.

Sakura opened the second cabinet, which was half-full, and did another quick calculation. The cabinets held more than 50,000 passports, or more disturbingly, 50,000 girls had been trafficked through this one operation. Sakura walked back to the commander.

"Have all these girls been forced into prostitution?"

He said, "Oh, there have been many more. When the cabinets are full, I burn the passports in the cabinet which is holding the oldest. Usually, every six years as it's unlikely the girl will return to collect her passport after six years."

Sakura said, "Kai, can you check the kitchen and find some garbage bags or something in which we can transport all these passports, please? We are taking them as evidence."

Sakura focused back on Toyotomi.

"I'm looking for Honoka Kondo; where is she?"

"Oh, the cock eater!

A nasty piece that one, and not much good on the suck either; I have sampled that personally. My guards have been offering her a chance to practise all day and night, and I have many guards. She is in room number one."

Sakura walked down the corridor, found the door with the numeral one and entered. The room was hot and smelled of semen, sweat and fear. The room was sparse; there was a table on her right, a doctor's bag sat on it, and there was a vial with a small amount of a brownish liquid. On the bed was a naked man. He had a rubber band tightened around his bicep, and a syringe needle was sticking out from his forearm. He wasn't breathing.

Next to him was Honoka. She was naked and manacled to the headboard by both arms. She was looking up at the roof, her eyes lifeless. Sakura didn't need Dr Uni to check. She knew Honoka was dead. She felt a sharp pain in her stomach, an ache like a giant hole had formed within her. She began to weep.

She was too late.

Composing herself, she closed the door and went back to the commander.

Megumi had pushed the commander and his chair away from the desk and typed on his keyboard. She looked up when Sakura entered the room. She didn't need to ask; she knew by Sakura's death mask that Honoka was dead. She hadn't seen that look on Sakura's face before, which frightened her. She looked at the commander and saw that his expression had also changed.

"Glad you are back. He is the most disgusting man I have ever met. He has zero respect for women, you have no idea about our discussion, but I am into his computer now."

Sakura looked at the man's injured shoulder, and the blood flowed freely from it, much more than when they had restrained him. It looked as though the wound had been opened wider. Well, Megumi, you are full of surprises, thought Sakura.

Sakura stood in front of Toyotomi, her face red, obviously furious.

"Who is your controller? Who is the man that controls the prostitution business for Hidetada?"

"Ha, ha, you stupid slut, why would I tell you this information?"

His disrespect for Sakura ignited her fury. She struck him in the nose with the heel of her right palm. She had targeted a spot ten centimetres behind the impact point to ensure she hit him with maximum force. The human body will subconsciously protect itself. Even when intentionally striking at a target, the brain will reduce the energy used just before contact. Professional fighters aim at an imaginary point behind the strike area to avoid this subliminal response. The man's nose collapsed from the force of Sakura's blow and made a squishing sound which delighted both her and Megumi.

Years ago, a fellow student had told Sakura that it was possible to kill a man by forcing the bridge of his nose into his brain. She had been doubtful and asked a Sohei warrior monk. She still remembered the look of disappointment on his face. He said, "Sakura, over the past eight years, you have learnt about the human body, its vulnerable areas, how to induce pain without killing, how to maim. You know that the human nose is constructed from cartilage, and the bones of the skull protect the brain. It is impossible to drive cartilage through bone regardless of how hard it is struck. To kill by this method is an urban myth. However, a powerful blow to the nose is excruciatingly painful, making it difficult for an opponent to breathe. This strike will end the fight in most men."

Toyotomi screamed in pain. Sakura burst into laughter when she saw the damage. His nose had flattened against his face like an egg, transformed from a three-dimensional point to a flattened circle. The nostrils were positioned in the middle of the egg, just below his eyes, two black holes in his face. They gave him the appearance of a pig.

Megumi said, "Oink, oink", and they laughed hysterically.

Sakura opened the dressing gown he was wearing to reveal his peanut-sized penis. "No wonder you select the smallest and youngest girls. You could never satisfy a woman with that tiny thing. I think I will add it to my collection."

She drew out her kaiken and pushed the blade against his fat belly, slicing downwards towards his penis.

"Please stop! I will tell you everything you want."

Sakura decided he would retain his pathetic manhood but couldn't resist pushing the tip of her kaiken into the head of his penis, smiling as a drop of blood emerged.

"Stop! Please stop!"

It only took five minutes, and Sakura knew the name of the leading operative, his office address, his home address and the security protocols protecting him. He was a direct report to Tokugawa Hidetada. If they could get to this man, they would have details of all the processing centres. While interviewing the commander, Megumi had been investigating the computer system.

"Megumi, have you found any information that will be useful?"

"Yes, I have downloaded a complete system copy to my hard drive, which my team can investigate back at the office. I have been looking through the security controls. Shit!"

"What is it?"

"I have just found another server that uses a VPN tunnel and a landline. It looks like it stays dormant for five minutes, then activates and forwards security footage to a cloud storage centre. It is cleverly hidden, unable to be detected remotely."

"Yes, you stupid bitches, there are hidden internal cameras, and since you entered the building, video of you has been sent to a remote system. Smile, I have a camera up there"; he glanced up at the bookcase above him.

"The Hidetada yakuza family have video and audio of all of you. Now you are finished.

"Women are put on earth for two reasons - to serve men and have children. Just the thought of your filthy bodies, lust, and infidelity disgusts me. I would keep you all on chains like dogs to serve...."

A red flower appeared on the commander's forehead, accompanied by a gunshot. Sakura turned to see Megumi holding the Glock 19, a small plume of carbide smoke drifting upwards from the end of the barrel. Sakura held her hands out, palms up, and shrugged her shoulders in a gesture representing, what the fuck?

Megumi responded, "I don't like that man."

43

Sakura turned towards Chaewon.

"Chaewon, can you show me your locked room?" Sakura and Megumi followed Chaewon down the hallway until she stopped. Sakura entered first. One girl occupied it and what looked to be a dead guard. Chaewon ran past her and hugged the other girl.

"Are you ok, Yumi?"
"I am! Are you ok, Chaewon?"
"Yes."
Sakura asked, "What happened to him?" and pointed to the dead guard.
"He was trying to rape me, so I killed him with this," replied Yumi, holding out her wire knife. Sakura admired the prison-styled shank the girl had made and smiled at her.
"I am Sakura; this is Megumi. Nice to make your acquaintance. We need to free all the girls and get out of here quickly. Check the other rooms and assemble the girls out the front of the building in the car park."

Sakura walked back to check on Tatsuo and Takeo. Dr Uni had bandaged Takeo's arm and placed it in a sling. He looked to be ok. Tatsuo was pale, sweat on his brow, his head tilting downwards. He did not look well. Dr Uni had cut the leg out of his trousers, bandaged the wound and used his belt as a tourniquet. He had inserted a cannula into his arm, and Kai held a saline bag to replenish his fluids.

Dr Uni said, "He needs to undergo emergency surgery, the femoral artery has been severed, and he will bleed out without immediate surgery. So, we need to get him into the van and to the hospital. He is a big man; I don't know if I am strong enough."

Sakura said, "I am! Kai and I will be able to do it." Sakura took the shoulders, Kai the legs, and Dr Uni carried the intravenous saline drip.

"I have sedated him; he shouldn't feel too much pain."

When they lifted Tatsuo, he gave a weak grunt, drifting in and out of consciousness. The three of them carried him to the van containing the technology equipment. It took all of Sakura's strength to walk the distance to the van. When he was finally settled, Dr Uni secured the saline drip to the inside wall of the truck using a bandage and checked that it flowed correctly. Sakura and Kai returned to collect Takeo and Honoka; all three would be taken to the hospital.

In total, twenty-two girls had been freed and loaded into the two empty Spotless vans, twelve in one van and ten girls in the other, along with the bags of passports retrieved from the commander's office. Yumi was assigned the lead in the truck with the passports, and another girl, Saisunee, a Thai national who spoke fluent Japanese, was made the lead of the second van. The girls were told to record the names, nationalities and dates of birth of all the girls in their vans. They were also told to explain that they were being taken somewhere safe with proper beds and food.

Sakura sped out of the compound and headed for the hospital. She was driving the technology van with Dr Uni attending to the injured men in the rear. Shortly after, Megumi moved the van containing twelve girls 200 metres from the compound and waited for Kai to follow.

***

Kai was the last to leave the compound. He had removed ten backpacks of C4 explosives from the van and placed them throughout the building. He had also emptied twenty litres of diesel throughout the building to act as an accelerant. He drove out of the compound and parked behind the van Megumi was driving. He armed the detonation device and then pressed the trigger. A bright flash, followed by a thunderous roar, and the van lurched side to side. He saw a massive fireball a hundred metres wide rolling upwards into the night sky.

He smiled. It was done.

"Let's see what Mr Tokugawa Hidetada thinks of that."

44

Kiticha opened his eyes, instantly alert, seeking the sound that had disturbed his sleep. He was a light sleeper, and this genetic trait had contributed to him being alive into his fifties. The sound was coming from his home office. It was an alarm. He sat up and swung his legs over the side of the bed. He glanced at the clock. 4:10 am. He took a deep breath, stood and walked into his office.

The room had nine monitors on the wall, three rows of three. From here, he could monitor all his baishun yados and, more importantly, the five processing and distribution centres. All the monitors displayed images except monitor #5 (Shinjuku Processing Centre); it was blank except for a red bell icon, with the words 'FIRE ALARM' flashing every 2 seconds. He reset the alarm, sat down and started to go back through the video feeds to see if he could determine if this was a real emergency or a computer glitch. He found the last video image; it was a flash of flame and then nothing. The alarm must have been triggered before the building communications were destroyed.

He logged into a CCTV camera of a nearby business. He had hacked their system years ago. He took control of the camera and panned it towards his compound. Flames rose hundreds of metres into the sky, destroying their business. He returned to the compound's security footage and scrolled backwards. First, he watched the assassination of Toyotomi and then the battle between the three invaders and Yoritomo.

He picked up his phone, scrolled through his contacts and called Hiroki, who answered on the second ring. "Kiticha, for what do I owe this early morning call?"

"The compound has been destroyed. I'm sorry to inform you that your father has been killed. Please come to my home immediately. I will message my address."

Hiroki looked at his watch. 4:18 am. His phone made the tone for an incoming message. He copied the address into Google Maps, informing him that the time to the location was 42 mins. He knew he could do it in under 20 minutes this time of day. He dressed quickly, jeans, a long-sleeved shirt and his Italian leather motorcycle jacket. He walked into his customised garage.

He had sacrificed the third bedroom to build a garage to store his prized possession, a Ducati Panigale V4 R. The motorbike had been equipped with the Moto GP race tuner and engine kit. It pumped a tyre-shredding 240 horsepower at the rear wheel. He put on his gloves and helmet, straddled the powerful machine, turned the ignition key, pressed the starter, and the powerful motorcycle roared to life.

He felt his heartbeat accelerate with the anticipation of the ride. He opened the garage using the remote, and as the roller door started to open, he kicked the side stand up, selected first gear and rolled slowly from his garage. Clear of the garage, he pressed the button on the remote to close the door, then twisted the throttle and released the clutch. The beast roared as it accelerated instantly, sliding onto the road surface and fishtailing down the road as Hiroki shifted through the gears.

***

He parked the bike in the garage of Kiticha's residence and killed the engine. The ticking of the engine cooling replaced the deep note of the twin exhaust. Kiticha was waiting by the lift for him.

"I'm sorry about your father; he was an honourable man. Come, and I will show you the footage."

Hiroki rewound and played the footage again; it was the fifth time he had watched his father's death. Finally, he spoke, "I will find this

Sakura Bianchi and revenge my father. Does Tokugawa Hidetada know of this destruction yet?"

"Not yet; I will call him at 7:00 am. I expect he will be outraged. You and your father have failed to protect his business interests. Perhaps if you can find this woman quickly and determine who is behind these attacks, you will find his favour again."

Hiroki understood the veiled threat. But he wasn't concerned; the loss of his father weighed heavy on his heart. It was personal now, and he would hunt this woman to the end of the earth to avenge his father.

He rang his chief of security. The phone rang five times before it was answered by a voice just waking from sleep.

"Hargi speaking."

"Hargi, it's Hiroki. I need you to conduct an immediate search for Sakura Bianchi. I want to know everything about her, where she lives, and her affiliates. I am sending you video footage of her. She is a petite woman: weight under 50kgs, aged in her early twenties. She has killed my father and destroyed one of our businesses. This has the highest priority. Drop everything else. Search the hospitals in Tokyo for two men with sword wounds, one in the arm, the other in the leg. Call me as soon as you have information."

<u>45</u>

Megumi and Kai parked the vans outside the empty apartment building. Megumi had named it 'The Terraces' because of the grand balconies hanging off the front of each apartment. Megumi and Hirutu had built a significant property portfolio over the past ten years. Tokyo had been in a recession for decades, and banks were more than happy to clear their balance sheets of old debts by reducing the sale prices and providing cheap funding. So Megumi was using the revenue of the streaming business to pay the mortgages and claiming the interest payments as a tax reduction.

The Terraces had been completed two months previously, but she had recommended that Hirutu leave it vacant so they could claim the loss of income to reduce this year's tax liability.

The apartment building was ten floors and held forty apartments, a mixture of two and three bedrooms. They had allowed the girls to choose who would flat together. It took thirty minutes to accommodate the girls across eight apartments. Yesterday, the flats had been stocked with essential food products: rice, eggs, fruit juice, coffee, tea, fruit, vegetables, fish, chicken, miso soup, udon soup and noodles.

Two armed guards were stationed at the front desk, and the doors had been locked to ensure the girls remained safe. They would need to stay here for a few days to recover from heroin withdrawal and the trauma of their ordeal. Dr Uni would return once Takeo and Tatsuo had been treated in the hospital to assist the girls with their recovery.

46

Sakura was sitting in a chair in room 4012 in the intensive care unit. The hospital staff had only allowed one visitor, so she was alone except for Takeo and Tatsuo, who were both asleep. It was 9:30 am, and she was feeling exhausted. Her friends had both undergone surgery for their injuries early this morning and had not yet woken. A doctor had visited an hour ago and explained to her that the surgery was successful, and he expected both men to fully recover over the next two to three weeks.

She had dozed, but sleep was difficult. She was feeling extreme sadness, her heart heavy. They had been too late to save Honoka. How would she explain her failure to Honoka's parents? Two men she loved had been seriously wounded during the raid on the compound, and her cover had been exposed. This would mean great danger for her grandparents and herself when the Hidetada family found her. They would find her; money can focus people; it was just a matter of time. She felt helpless, and the sadness was having a debilitating effect on her. The only time she had felt like this was ten years ago when she awoke from a coma to discover her mother had been murdered.

Her phone rang, and she saw it was her grandfather calling her.
"Hello, Grandfather."
"Good morning, Sakura. I am outside; I have come to relieve you. Megumi is waiting to drive you back home so you can rest. I will sit in vigil with my most trusted men."

"Ok, I am exhausted and depressed. I have failed the Kondo family."

"Sakura, whilst you were indeed unsuccessful in saving Honoka, you have rescued twenty-two other girls who would have faced years of forced prostitution. There will be many families relieved to have their loved ones returned."

"Yes, I keep telling myself that, but my pain remains. I am on my way. See you soon."

47

Hiroki sat in the hospital waiting room with Botan, his number one assassin and enforcer. They had been waiting for twenty minutes. His Chief of Security, Hargi, had notified him earlier that a hospital nurse had reported that a slightly built woman was in the ICU with the injured men. Her description matched Sakura, and the men's injuries matched those he had viewed on the video.

He was waiting for Sakura to leave so they could capture her outside. He had his best female assassin, Kira, waiting outside for her. Botan would go to ICU and deal with the injured men who had attacked their facility. He would ensure their deaths would act as a warning to all who threatened the Hidetada family.

The elevator doors opened, and a slightly built woman stepped out. Her eyes were red and puffy from crying. He wondered how this woman had beaten his father in combat. He would not have believed it if he hadn't watched the security footage. She walked past him, paying no attention to them, consumed by her thoughts and emotions. The automatic doors opened, and she exited the building.

Hiroki dialled a number on his phone. Kira answered. He said, "Kira, you are on. She has just walked out of the hospital." He turned to Botan. "Go and kill them. Make it obvious it is payback. I want their eyes and tongues. We must send a strong message to the other families that attacks on our business will not go unpunished."

"It will be done," replied Botan.

***

Sakura hugged her grandfather, who stood just outside the hospital door. He had disguised himself as a frail old man in his 80s.

"The doctor said they will be ok. They were still sleeping when I left."

"Go home, darling, have some rest; you look terrible. The car is over there; Megumi is waiting for you." Hirutu pointed towards the rear of the car park. Their quick embrace ended, and she walked towards where she had been directed.

A woman struggled with a suitcase and a baby in a car seat capsule, her left arm in a cast and sling, making it difficult to carry the bag and the baby simultaneously.

"Can I help you with that suitcase?" asked Sakura.

"That would be wonderful, thank you. My car is over here."

Sakura followed the woman to the far side of the car park, away from where Megumi was waiting in the car. The woman opened the car trunk.

"Can you put the suitcase in here, please?" As Sakura laid the case in the car's rear trunk, a strong arm crossed her chest, and a hand covered her mouth. The woman removed a syringe from the baby's capsule and injected her in the neck. Sakura could see that the baby was a doll. Then the realisation struck her as she started to lose consciousness: they had found her. She wondered how they had achieved it so quickly.

The sliding door of a black van parked next to the car opened, and Hiroki placed Sakura inside. He turned to Kira. "Good work. Now wait for Botan to complete his task and leave before the police arrive."

****

Hirutu walked towards the elevator. There was a man already standing there waiting for the elevator to arrive. The doors opened, and three people got out; then Hirutu motioned for the man to enter before him. He watched him select floor four, the level containing ICU and his men. Hirutu studied the man whilst the elevator ascended. He was powerfully built, with broad shoulders for a Japanese. A scar ran from below his right eye across his nose and finished on his chin. It was deep and had not healed well. Hirutu suspected it was an old sword injury. He decided to start a conversation to determine why this man was there. He had a bad feeling.

Hirutu said, "I'm visiting my wife. She is dying from cancer, and I suspect she will pass away today or tomorrow. We've been married for fifty-five years. Whom are you visiting?"

"I am visiting my mother. She is also unwell."

There was no further discussion. This man was not the talking type. Finally, the elevator arrived at their floor, and the man exited first and walked to the nurse station. "Who are you here to see, please?"

"Room 4012."

The nurse checked the computer and said, "OK, you are cleared to go."

Hirutu's heart skipped a beat when he heard the man ask for the room which held his sleeping men.

The nurse asked him, "Who are you here to see?"

"Room 4010, please." The nurse checked her computer as Hirutu watched the man walk down the corridor.

"Ok, you can go."

Hirutu could see the man had reached room 4012 and was opening the door. Hirutu quickened his step and entered a moment after the mysterious man, whom he suspected was an assassin.

The man held a short dagger in his right hand, a simple weapon, easy to conceal, as he didn't expect any resistance. Hirutu twisted the cane handle he had been using as his old age prop and drew the sword from its saya. The man turned, facing him,

"Old man, if you want to live, leave now." Hirutu removed the old man mask he was wearing.

"So, Hirutu Hotato, you are behind these killings. Whatever has possessed you to take on the Hidetada family, have you become senile in your old age?"

Hirutu did not respond; he moved swiftly and thrust his blade directly into the man's chest, penetrating his heart and ending his life. Then, just as quickly, he withdrew his sword, and the assassin fell dead to the floor at his feet.

He locked the door, then rang the Chief of Police. Naturally, this situation would need to be handled delicately to protect the Hotato family's name.

48

Sakura slowly regained consciousness. She was nauseous from the drug they had given her. She realised she was restrained, her arms behind her back and her ankles tied to the chair she was sitting upon. She gazed around the room. It was a library judging by the shelves of books. The chair she was seated upon was clearly out of place and must have been positioned there to restrain her. Looking down, she could see the floor was covered in a richly coloured, thick-piled carpet. A transparent plastic sheet had been laid over the carpet.

Are they protecting it?

From what?

She could see her ankles were held to the chair by black cable ties, and she suspected cable ties had also been used to secure her wrists behind her. She tested the movement in her wrists. It felt like a single cable tie had been used to hold her wrists together, the back of the right wrist tight against the underside of the left.

The door opened, and a large man entered the room. He wore a dark grey suit, a white shirt and a pale blue tie. He had broad shoulders, and the suit had been tailored to fit.

"Where am I?"

The man remained quiet, walked towards her and checked her restraints. Then, he placed his hand under her chin and lifted it gently to look into her eyes. His eyes were dark brown and emotionless, and his facial features were Japanese. He gave a 'hmppf' sound, then turned and left the room.

A short time later, he returned accompanied by two other Japanese men, the three of them standing an arm's length in front of her.

It was intimidating, yet Sakura remained defiant.

"Where am I?" Sakura repeated.

"You are my guest, Sakura Bianchi," replied the smaller man.

"My boss, Tokugawa Hidetada, is very interested in meeting you. Your interference in our business has been very frustrating and costly. We will need to make an example of you and all your family. The Bianchi bloodline will end for what you have done." He slapped Sakura's left cheek to punctuate the point. He wasn't a strong man, and the strike's sting only lasted a few moments, although she knew her cheek was already reddening. He could see he hadn't hurt her and raised his hand to strike her again. The other man grasped his wrist in a fluid motion, quickly preventing his strike.

Sakura recognised the agility and strength of a warrior in that action. She expected he was highly skilled; he was lean yet displayed a powerful chest and strong shoulders. He was young, perhaps a similar age to her.

"Careful, Kiticha, we do not want to damage her beautiful face, or we may be in trouble with Hidetada. I suspect he will want that pleasure for himself."

"I want to interrogate her! I want the names of her accomplices. Hidetada will want to know as well," yelled the smaller man at the warrior; his face had grown red with his anger.

"She has destroyed one of our compounds, we have lost men and merchandise, and it will take months to rebuild or locate alternative premises, impacting our revenue stream."

Sakura assessed her situation, and it was grim. She suspected the bigger man was security working for the smaller man, as his demeanour was subservience towards him. The other man, the warrior, was obviously in a position of authority.

"Who are you?" Sakura asked of the warrior.

"I am Hiroki, Miss Bianchi. Not only have you embarrassed me by penetrating and destroying our compound, but you also killed my father. Both actions are unforgivable."

"A small price for you to pay for human trafficking," replied Sakura.

"Hidetada would disagree with you. However, I will introduce you to him later today once the transport is arranged."

"Kiticha, I will be back in a couple of hours. Can I trust you to ensure Sakura Bianchi is in a fit state for her introduction to Hidetada?"

Hiroki stared at Kiticha. At first, he met Hiroki's stare, then respectfully bowed his head and said, "I will."

49

Hirutu was experiencing panic, an emotion unfamiliar to him. Generally, his life was relatively ordered. However, the past few days' events had been frantic, requiring significant planning and organising: the attack on the compound, the accommodation and logistics for the freed girls.

His most valued men and personal friends were injured and lucky not to be murdered in the hospital. They had been relocated back to his house, putting further pressure on Dr Uni and resulting in the acquisition of two nurses, one helping the girls with their heroin withdrawal and the other caring for Tatsuo and Takeo. Megumi had just called and asked him to meet her in the 'war room'.

***

Megumi was standing at the transparent monitor, displaying a Tokyo map. A pink dot was flashing.

"What is it, Megumi?"

Sakura never met me at the hospital. I waited thirty minutes and tried to ring her cell phone, which went directly to voice mail. So I came back here to search for her. Unfortunately, her cell phone has been disabled, so I am using the Saviour tracking device sewed into her outfit."

"You have put tracking devices on the Saviours?"

"Yes. A small C2322 battery powers them. They send a location signal to the Global Positioning System every thirty minutes. Their location is recorded on the Saviour Server. Sakura is here." Megumi pointed to the flashing pink dot.

"It is the location of the man who oversees Hidetada's human trafficking operations. The commandant provided us with his details, and this is the address he provided. I can go there with Kai and see if we can free her."

Hirutu shook his head; his mind was racing. He was trying to focus on the multiple risks.

He couldn't lose Megumi or Kai.

He was struggling to process everything.

His mind felt like a cage of startled parrots, flying erratically to avoid a disturbance but trapped within the boundaries of their cell, unable to escape.

It was overwhelming.

"I will arrange for three men to accompany you and Kai. You will need to plan the mission with Kai. I have important calls to make. Contact me when you have a plan."

<u>50</u>

Sakura lifted her head when the door closed behind the two men.

They had beaten her until she feigned unconsciousness. She had endured perhaps an hour of punishment after Hiroki had left. The larger man was skilled and knew the areas of the body to inflict maximum pain: targeting her liver, spleen, kidneys, ovaries and solar plexus. She had cried and begged him to stop; the other man laughed at her distress and demanded she tells them who had ordered the attack.

The smaller man was weak, and his blows were primarily intended to degrade and humiliate her by attacking her breasts and groin. The strikes to her groin and bladder were painful, and she had urinated, soiling her clothes. She knew her breasts would be badly bruised, but the damage was superficial, and she would recover quickly.

She had remained silent, withholding the information they sought.

She had survived the first interrogation. The men had tired and taken a break, and she knew they would return. She would be ready for them next time. She closed her eyes, let her head dip slightly, and focused on breathing.

The Sohei monks had taught her how to control the parasympathetic nervous system, and now that training would prove invaluable.

She entered a deep meditative state, imagining a flame being held to her wrists. After a moment, she could feel her body respond, perspiration surfacing under the cable tie providing lubrication. Next, she pictured the Median Nerve in her left hand, which supports the muscles used to bend the thumb, index and middle fingers. She needed to override two of its primary responsibilities: 1 to ignore the pain and 2 to allow the thumb and fingers to be extended past their predefined limits to avoid injury. Once she was ready, she dislocated her thumb, index and middle fingers. Immediately the cable tie loosened, and she slid her wrist from the restraint.

Once free, she used her right hand to force the thumb and fingers back into their proper positions. She shook her arms before her to assist the blood flow. Her shoulders ached from being held in that uncomfortable position, and her left hand throbbed as her immune system sent its first responders' inflammatory cells and cytokines to repair the trauma she had caused. She tried to free her feet but couldn't slide the cable tie from the chair as it was fixed above a leg support rail; she would need to cut them away. She knew the guard had a knife; he had threatened to cut her during the interrogation. She relaxed but stayed alert as she waited.

Perhaps half an hour had passed when she saw the door being opened. She returned her arms to where she had been restrained, and the guard entered. Her head was resting on her chest, pretending to be unconscious. Then, she heard him walk towards her and stand before her. He held her chin tightly in his hand and lifted her head to stare into her eyes. She could see he was angry.

"You are embarrassing me in front of my boss! Your time is short; soon, you will be relocated to Osaka and held within our largest compound. There you will meet Hidetada and his henchmen. They are very skilled at extracting information. They will keep you there until they have what they want."

Sakura struck his chin with the palm of her right hand, the blow forcing his head upwards and backwards at an angle exceeding the human body's design specifications. As a result, the rear of his skull smashed into the C3 vertebrae, causing it to fracture and sever the spinal cord. He fell to the floor, paralysed but still able to breathe. He would remain alive, albeit in a quadriplegic state.

Sakura could bend over and reach the knife, removing it from the sheath he wore on his belt and using it to free her legs. She stood on unsteady legs, enjoying the sensation of blood returning to lower extremities. She turned the guard over so he could look into her eyes.

"How does it feel to be helpless, unable to protect yourself?"

She smiled at the man, her eyes cold and unforgiving.

"This is my gift to you." Then she drew the knife across his throat, cutting deeply through the jugular and carotid arteries. He would be dead within the minute.

Sakura stood. Now to find the boss, she would enjoy ending his life. She located him in his office. He was viewing the security video. She silently approached him from behind, wrapped her left forearm around his neck, secured her grip with her right arm and squeezed hard. He struggled and tried to gouge her eyes with his hands, but Sakura's positioning behind the chair prevented any effective defence against her choke hold. She felt his hyoid bone fracture, its displacement further disrupting his windpipe.

As his life force slowly left his body, she whispered, "Didn't your mother ever teach you not to strike a woman?"

Sakura checked the remainder of the apartment, but there wasn't anyone else present. She was considering how she would make her escape when she heard the door open; it was the warrior, Hiroki, returning. She held the knife she had taken from the guard in her right hand in a defensive position. Her left hand was still throbbing and tender from the dislocation earlier and would not be very effective in a fight against this man.

51

Yumi was feeling pleased as she pressed 'Finish'. She had completed the task Megumi had assigned to her six hours ago. During that time, she had drunk four cups of tea and eaten some fish and miso soup provided by a housemaid. She was in the home of Sakura's grandfather.

She never imagined that a home could be so splendid. It was like living in a castle. She had been brought here after the girls had been housed in the apartment. Megumi and Kai had explained that she was to organise all the passports by nationality. Of course, there had been many passports, but it was a relatively easy activity as they had been bagged mainly by nationality, and she only needed to view the covers to organise them. There were twenty piles of nationalities, three piles dominated by numbers: South Korea, Thailand, Philippines.

Once they were organised, she could locate the freed girls' passports. They also asked that she find thirty recent passports issued in the past twelve months for Australian, British, American and Israeli nationals. This had taken over three hours, and now she had scanned the detail pages showing names, ages, addresses, etc., for each passport into four files that had been saved onto the Saviour server.

Hirutu entered the room, a maid behind him. "How is it going, Yumi?"

"I have finished; the four files are saved where Megumi told me."

"Excellent. You look tired, and it's been a long night for you. Would you like a bed to rest?"

"That would be wonderful, thank you."
The maid took her hand, "Follow me."

The bedroom was spacious; a blue chaise lounge chair was positioned near the window with a delicate side table and a book sitting on it. The bed was four-poster and massive. There was a writing desk and a phone. The maid said, "You can call your parents and tell them you are safe." Yumi lifted the phone receiver as the maid left the room and dialled 010-82, then her home number; on the third ring, her mother answered, her breathing laboured as though she had been running to reach the phone.

"Hi, Mum, it's Yumi. I have arrived." Then the tears streamed down her face. It was hard for her to believe it had only been two days since she had left Korea. It felt much longer.

***

Hirutu sat down at his computer and logged onto his email account. He sent four emails, each with an attachment containing the scans of thirty passports with which they could verify the email's intent. The emails were addressed to contacts he had acquired over the years, in the USA, the CIA; in Australia, the SAS; in the United Kingdom, the Royal Marines and in Israel, the Mossad. He needed assistance and a military force to destroy the other processing centres and bring the downfall of Hidetada's human trafficking operation. However, he knew he couldn't trust the Japanese army or Japanese police as the Yakuza's reach was too deep.

He would wait sixty minutes and then start the phone calls to discuss the emails with his contacts. He expected that by then, they would have confirmed that the names he had provided from the passports were women listed as missing.

52

Hiroki sensed something was wrong; decades of training enhanced his sensory abilities. The apartment was too quiet, and he could smell the metallic odour of blood. Cautiously he moved through the apartment, checking the library first. Sakura was gone, and the security guard was lifeless on the floor. He approached Kiticha's office when he sensed a displacement in the air, slightly behind him and to the left.

He reacted immediately, stepping aside, dipping his body forward and away from the threat. The flash of the blade moved swiftly through the space that had just a moment before contained his body.

The girl was fast, but he was faster. A right cross caught her on the chin, and her legs buckled under her; a left to her solar plexus completed the combination. Sakura fell backwards, dropping the blade, falling heavily onto her rear and sucking in air. He removed a cable tie from his pocket and secured her wrists behind her back. He pulled it tight against her skin and knew it would be uncomfortable. They had a short forty-minute helicopter flight north, and he did not want her misbehaving in the helicopter.

"Miss Bianchi, if you continue to misbehave, I will sedate you again. We have a short flight to Osaka, where Mr Hidetada eagerly awaits to meet you. He is very interested in which family or organisation deliberately disrupts his prostitution business. He wants to end this inconvenience, so life can continue as it has for decades."

Sakura glared at him!

Hiroki wondered what this woman had endured, such a beautiful and innocent face unable to hide the hate emanating through her eyes.

He could sense that she was furious and strong-willed, and he knew extracting the necessary information from her would be difficult.

"I'm assuming that Kiticha could not obtain any meaningful information from you. Unfortunately, it will not be easy to escape where I am taking you. It is Hidetada's oldest and most secure facility. It has a garrison of twenty men and rooms specifically designed for interrogation of unresponsive captives. I am afraid that if you continue to resist, your health will deteriorate quickly. It is not an honourable place, and the interrogators have little interest in our Bushido code or respect for a warrior. Perhaps you can tell me who oversees this operation? If you cooperate, I can promise that your future will be short and less painful.".

"You, of all people, should know that I will never betray my daimyo."

Hiroki lifted her by the wrist restraint; she gasped in pain as the cable tie cut into her and led her from the room into the elevator. They rode it to the top of the building, took the stairs up to the rooftop and opened the door. The sound of the twin Bell 230 turbine engines was deafening as he led her into the helicopter and strapped her into the rear seat. Her seating position would be awkward and uncomfortable with her wrists secured behind her. However, he knew this was just the beginning of her discomfort.

Sakura tried to maintain a brave face despite being terrified; she knew her predicament was dire. Her grandfather would discover she had been taken but would not know where to find her. At best, he would need to engage Hidetada in a diplomatic resolution for her release. She knew that would be unlikely. She had failed Honoka, and now she had failed her grandfather. The blade speed and engine noise increased, and she felt the helicopter lighten and lift off the rooftop.

53

Sakura was dragged from the helicopter, which had landed on the road leading to the compound. The gate opened, and she was frogged-marched through the gates, across a twenty-metre 'deadman zone' and then through another security gate. Another twenty-metre walk took her to the front step. This building looked as though it was an old hotel. It was constructed from sandstone blocks and had three wings, one on each side of the door and one pressing out to the rear. It stood impressively over three levels.

She was taken inside and into a large formal room in the east wing. A big man sat at a ten-seat dining table. He rose and said, "So this is the bitch causing me so much trouble." He walked towards her and stood very close, a position designed to intimidate her, but Sakura was unfazed. So, this is the famous Tokugawa Hidetada, she thought.

Glaring down at her, he said, "I want you to meet Yaomo. He is my best interrogator; he has never failed me. We can do this the easy way or the hard way; either you tell me what I want to know, and then I will end your life quickly, or you will suffer terribly, and I will still get the information I want. So, what is it to be?"

"I don't know who is responsible. I receive a message on my phone telling me what to do."

"Bullshit! Sakura. Strip her; I want to see what she looks like naked." Two guards stripped her roughly; she almost fell when they removed her underwear, her wrists were still restrained behind her back, and they had to cut her Saviour tunic from her.

Sakura stood boldly, unashamed of her nakedness. The men leered at her. She stared into each man's eyes. When she got to Hiroki, she saw he was looking away. It appeared that he was uncomfortable with what was happening. Hidetada grabbed her right breast roughly and squeezed hard. She screamed; it was very tender and bruised from the treatment she had received earlier. Hidetada laughed, enjoying her discomfort, her scream pleasing him; he was a pig of a man. He forced two thick fingers into her vagina. She screamed again. Another smile appeared on his hideous face. "I look forward to sampling this tight pussy once you tell us what we want to know." Then he released her from his torment and turned to Hiroki. "Can you stay a few days to assist Yaomo with the interrogation?"

"Of course, Mr Hidetada."

Day 13 since the abduction

<u>54</u>

Megumi was showing Hirutu, Kai and Tatsuo the location of the other four compounds, including Google Street View and satellite images. These complexes were much bigger and better secured than the compound they had taken. Megumi couldn't help but wonder how many young girls had been detained at these places; their lives changed forever as they were forced into prostitution.

Last night, she and Kai, along with three of Hirutu's men, had entered the premises of Kiticha, the man responsible for managing Hidetada's human trafficking operations. She had downloaded all the information contained within the servers. She had quickly scanned some of the data during the copy process and realised it held a wealth of information: banking accounts for washing money and, more importantly, the addresses and details on the other compounds; she now knew there were four more processing facilities.

She knew that Sakura had been moved to the Osaka processing centre and the two dead bodies in the apartment evidence that she had left there alive.

Overnight her team extracted the primary information from all the sites, and she was now sharing it. She was pleased to see that Takeo was well enough now to join them, and they expected Tatsuo would be able to get out of bed tomorrow.

Megumi had the room's full attention. "Yesterday afternoon, Sakura was taken to this facility. It's Hidetada's pride and joy and incredibly well-defended. I was able to access the resource records for guards and timetables. Twenty armed guards on patrol twenty-four hours a day, a backup detail of ten more men. It will require an army or elite forces to extract Sakura from this premise."

Hirutu said, "Megumi, please obtain as much intel as possible about all four sites. If successful, I have enacted a plan that will enable us to take control of these four facilities. I will be able to tell you more tomorrow."

55

Sakura was lying on the bed naked, shivering. She had no idea of the time; the cell was windowless but brightly lit, like a stadium. It also had music, just one song, 'The Real Slim Shady' by Eminem, playing very loud all night. She had been unable to sleep. Combined with the ordeal of the past twelve days, she was exhausted.

She started to doubt her ability to survive the next few days. She didn't know what to expect today, yet she knew it would be unpleasant. All night, she thought about what they might do to her, her imagination probably more frightening than reality. The lack of sleep and fear of the unknown depleted her energy and resolve. She had tried to meditate, this usually helped settle her mind, yet it was impossible under the bright lights and blazing music.

The door opened, and her interrogator entered with two guards armed with Tasers, the warrior Hiroki was also with them. She knew she had no choice but to comply in her weakened state.

***

Sakura awoke. Startled, she sat up. She was in the cell, the lighting was dimmed, and the music had stopped. Her heart raced as her memory recalled the morning's session. They had used waterboarding on her. It was a practice discussed at the Sohei Temple, but the monks had made a pact never to use this form of torture. She never thought she would be so terrified in her wildest dreams. They had secured her to a board that could pivot. They had positioned her head downwards, her feet above her, covered her face with a cloth, and poured water over it. Some water would soak through the fabric, but the real kicker was that the water restricted the air that could be sucked through the cloth, making it feel like you were drowning. She couldn't scream, she couldn't move, they continued until she was almost unconscious and mad with fright. Then, after a brief respite, they would repeat it. She had no idea how long she had endured it. Eventually, she could no longer tolerate the punishment and passed out.

She stood up on shaky legs.
She was hungry; they hadn't provided any food.

***

Several hours later, they came for her again, and the waterboarding continued. She didn't pass out this time. Instead, she was able to gain some control over her body's response to drowning. She thought that she could completely shut down the drowning response with practice, making the ordeal somewhat bearable. They had returned her to the room, which was once again brightly lit with the Real Slim Shady blasting from the speakers. No dinner again, the second night a repeat of the first. However, she could get some sleep; her body was exhausted.

Two men entered the room perhaps six hours after she had returned from the waterboarding.

Day 14 since the abduction

56

Megumi presented the intelligence they had obtained to the three men and women in the 'war room'. Each country Hirutu had contacted was appalled that so many of their citizens had been trapped in this human trafficking ring and had agreed to help.

Kai, Tatsuo, Takeo, Hirutu and Hiroki sat on the couch and watched the interaction. Hirutu had admired Megumi's intellect and drive for many years. However, seeing her confidently presenting the security controls to these military folk today was another dimension of her abilities. His heart swelled, knowing he had provided the resources to enable this fantastic woman to grow.

He was worried for Sakura. He knew how ruthless Hidetada was, and he knew it was only a matter of time before she would have no option but to disclose his involvement. Yesterday, Sakura's tracking device left the compound and was dumped in Osaka's largest waste disposal processing centre. He was sure it had been Sakura's uniform in the rubbish, and she was still alive. Any other outcome was unbearable for him to consider.

He watched as Megumi convinced these international soldiers to help rescue Sakura and destroy Hidetada's human trafficking business forever. Finally, Megumi's presentation was completed, and the soldiers assessed the information and agreed on which compounds each unit would take together. Further conversations revolved around the resources required and how they could access the country with weapons and men.

The Australian SAS took the largest and most heavily secured compound containing Sakura. It was agreed that a simultaneous strike on all four compounds was the best approach, and a plan was established for each specific location. Troops and munitions would be finalised today and flown to Japan tomorrow. If everything arrived as planned, a decision would be made at 7:00 pm tomorrow to commence the raids at 03:00 am the next day.

Hirutu was encouraged that they had a plan to rescue Sakura, yet saddened knowing that she would need to endure another fifty hours as a captive. He tried not to think about the treatment she would receive at the hands of Hidetada's barbarians, something a grandfather should never have to experience.

The soldiers looked tough; all hardened veterans, the men square-jawed, alpha males. The woman was Israeli Mossad. Hirutu found her exotic features quite beautiful, yet knew she was as deadly as these other soldiers. Nevertheless, he thought that Sakura would like her.

<u>57</u>

Sakura awoke when the door opened. It was the same detail as yesterday: the interrogator, two guards and Hiroki.

"Please remove these men from the room and advise their commanding officer of their indiscretion so that he can warn the remainder of his guard," demanded Hiroki.

It was obvious what had transpired here: two men, thinking they could take advantage of a defenceless young girl, now lay dead. Hiroki recalled the number of people he knew that Sakura had killed or wounded; it was starting to reach legendary status. This woman warrior was extraordinary, and he felt sorry that he was a participant in this process to determine whom she was protecting.

The water boarding continued, she dealt with the psychological torture as best she could; the sensation of drowning was tough to overcome. She could tell the interrogator was becoming frustrated. She heard him and Hiroki arguing about enough is enough.

That's when the torture method changed to electricity.

Hiroki watched for ten minutes, then excused himself. He walked from the room, a man in torment, pained from watching this warrior woman brutalised. He was a Samurai who lived by the code of bushido. What was occurring here was barbaric. He decided to go home and ponder his future. He was astounded that his world had changed so quickly. He took the bullet train home. It gave him time to think, but his thoughts were erratic, like bats awakened by a threat in their nesting cave, flying in panic towards the entrance.

58

Hiroki sat under his rear veranda, overlooking his beautifully designed Japanese garden. He had made tea and sat cross-legged, waiting for it to finish brewing. He was looking forward to enjoying a moment of reflection and relaxation. These past three days were, without question, the most emotionally distressing of his lifetime.

His father was dead, and his friend and best assassin, Botan, also dead.

Hidetada was holding him accountable for protecting the remaining processing centres and he was no closer to discovering who was attacking their business. He disliked the human trafficking business, and he hated the processing centre commanders, yet he was tasked with their protection.

He disliked Hidetada! It was as though his father's death had opened his eyes, and the lens with which he now viewed the world was grossly inconsistent with his bushido code.

The woman, Sakura, was having an unusual effect on him, promoting emotions he had never experienced. She was the enemy, and he needed to interrogate her, yet he became more attracted to her every time they met.

She was a wonderful woman. He didn't care that she wasn't pure Japanese; he was mesmerised by her exotic Eurasian features. She was a mighty warrior, and although diminutive in stature, she had beaten his father in battle. He had watched the video many times and was surprised by the skill and strength she had displayed.

She had also escaped her bonds and killed Kiticha and his second-in-command. She had unleashed devastating destruction on Hidetada's operations, and Hidetada was furious. They had held her for three days, and she had provided no information. Tomorrow he was to take her to Hidetada, which could not end well for Sakura. He wasn't sure what the man would do, yet he knew it would result in her death.

He was saddened that such a dishonourable man would kill such a mighty warrior.

It just felt wrong!

Until recently, he had always felt pride in serving his father and the Hidetada family. Now he was doubting if he had been honourable or rather a disillusioned instrument to create pain and suffering for an evil regime.

There was a knock at the door.

He stood and walked to his front door, held his eye against the peephole, and then smiling, opened the door.

"What a pleasant surprise. How long has it been since we have seen each other?"

"Five years," replied Kai.

"Please come in. Join me for tea in the garden. It should be brewed now."

The two men sat cross-legged on cushions, facing each other across the ceremonial tea table. A butterfly alighted on the teapot, flexed its wings then flew away. The Samurai believe butterflies are reincarnated Samurai; it symbolises immortality, eternal life, and indestructibility. A reward for their service to their daimyo during their lifetime. This was a good sign.

Hiroki poured the tea. When he had finished, he laid his forearm on the table, displaying the two faded Japanese characters on his wrist. Kai did the same, displaying identical characters on his wrist but in a different order. Both men had received these tattoos when they were young, Kai was nine, and Hiroki was a baby. Their parents had tattooed them, hoping they would find each other someday.

"My brother, I am looking for a warrior woman. I am hoping you can help me find her. She means a lot to me. Her name is Sakura Bianchi."

Hiroki smiled, "I know where she is."

The Story of Hiroki and Kai

Twenty-three years earlier

The baishun yado wars had been raging for five months, and many owners and prostitutes had been sacrificed. Saoriko was the owner of her family, baishun yado, passed down from her grandmother to her mother and now to her. She considered her business a family heirloom and was determined not to let Tokugawa Hidetada take it from them.

During the past weeks, they had witnessed attacks on other baishun yados, and the violence was accelerating as Hidetada's men grew braver, refining their techniques. She knew it was only a matter of time before they would be attacked, and she had prepared as best they could. They had weapons, and she had hired two Ronin as protection; however, the cost was starting to deplete their cash reserves.

The girls were scared and frequently failed to show up for work; four girls who lived on the premises had snuck out early one morning and had not returned. They were frightened by the rumours of Hidetada's men murdering the prostitutes in the baishun yados they attacked. The number of customers serviced had halved as stories emerged of customers murdered during the attacks.

Hidetada was running a fear campaign, reducing the baishun yados owner's income and impacting their ability to buy protection. Unfortunately, the strategy had been effective, and many owners eventually surrendered their businesses.

Saoriko was determined that would not happen to them. She was concerned for her two beautiful boys. Today, the tattooist came, and Kai had his name and Hiroki's name tattooed on his wrist. Just two symbols: Kai first, then under it, Hiroki. He had cried, Saoriko had cried, but it was necessary. She held Kai's wrist and rubbed the liniment softly onto the red and raised skin. She kissed him, and he bravely stopped whimpering. He sniffed, and she wiped clean the two lines of snot that had run from his nostrils.

"Kai, we are in danger. I need to move you to a safer place. I have secretly agreed with a woman whose husband is a member of the Hotato family to support you and embrace you as one of their children. Your brother will stay with us, he is just a baby, and the tattoo on your wrist will remind you of him. If we are killed tonight, then in the future when you are older you are to find your brother and reunite yourselves. The tattoos you share will act as evidence of your family bond, helping him to believe. Any reunion must be kept secret because if the Hidetada family discovers your identity, they will kill you."

They embraced, and then her husband entered the room and said, "Come on, son, I need to take you to a safer place." Kai did not want to leave his mother, he started to cry again.

"No, I want to stay!"

"Be brave, my son; this is for the best. I know that you will be a mighty warrior and seek your revenge one day."

***

Saoriko had closed the baishun yado at 10:00 pm and sent the girls away. Only Ronin, her husband and Hiroki, who had finally fallen asleep, remained. She had held her baby for hours as he cried from the pain of the tattoo. She had continued to apply liniment to provide some relief, the black ink of the Japanese characters wickedly raised against his delicate skin, which was a hideous red and hot to the touch. She looked down at him in his cot, sleeping restlessly. She was concerned for him; surely Hidetada's men would not kill a baby?

She had heard rumours that tonight they would be attacked; Hidetada had tired of her resistance to hand over her business and was sending his most ruthless man, Yoritomo Ito, to oversee the operation. She hoped the Ronin she had hired could defend against this man. She decided to go and see what precautions they had taken. When she entered the room they had occupied for three weeks, she saw they were no longer there, nor was their equipment.

They had fled; it was just her husband now and her. They would be no match against these men; she had no choice but to surrender her business.

A tear rolled down her cheek; they would lose everything, but at least they would have their lives.

There was a loud noise, and she heard the front door splinter, then a scream from her husband. She ran downstairs; six men were standing there. She recognised Yoritomo; he was cleaning his sword on her husband's tunic. Her husband lay dead in a pool of blood, his severed head three metres from his body. Saoriko screamed, "You can have the baishun yado; please let me get my baby, and we will leave."

Yoritomo raced up the steps towards her and plunged his sword into her stomach, the tip exiting her body a full fifty centimetres.

"It's too late for you; the opportunity to live has passed."

He savagely drew the sword upwards, opening her abdomen; a length of her intestine fell out and dangled towards the floor; he knew this was incredibly painful.

He watched her eyes, waited till her life left her body, then let her fall to the floor.

***

Yoritomo told the menoto (wet nurse), "You will nurse him until he is three years of age and then bring him to me. I will expect him to be toilet trained and tutored. I will be his father and teach him to be a warrior. If anything happens to him if you do not keep him in the peak of health, you will die and all your family with you, do you understand?"

"Yes, Yoritomo, I will look after him better than if he was my son."

***

As promised, the menoto delivered Hiroki to Yoritomo when he was three, and an influential father/son bond was established over the years. Hiroki was fifteen when a young girl bumped into him while he was shopping at the market. Later that night, he found the note she had slipped into his pocket. It was written with a quill pen and ink, the Japanese symbols precise and crisp on the rice paper.

It simply said:

Destroy this note once read.
I have vital information to share with you.
Meet me Friday in Shinjuku Central Park.
I will be sitting on the bench near the statue of Kusunoki
Masashige.
I will be wearing a blue hat and reading a book.
Tell no one.
Kai

Hiroki looked at the tattoo on his wrist; it had started to fade. The tattoo was old, older than his earliest memories. He only understood the significance today, just two symbols: his name and the symbol for Kai underneath it.

They had met, and Kai had explained that they were brothers; the encounter was brief as they did not wish to be discovered. They met the next time after Hiroki purchased his home, and they enjoyed tea. Kai had told him the fate of their parents and that Yoritomo had killed them. Hiroki had become angry with his brother; he did not want to believe him.

He could not believe him. How could the only father he had known be the man that had made him an orphan?

***

This was their third meeting, and now Hiroki did believe Kai. They spoke for an hour, Kai revealing that Sakura was the granddaughter of

Hirutu Hotato. He impressed upon him that the Hotato family was honourable and planned to kill Hidetada and destroy the human trafficking business.

Together, the two brothers developed a plan.

Day 15 since the abduction

<u>59</u>

Kai collected Hiroki, and they caught the 5:30 am bullet train to Osaka, arriving at 7:00 am.

Hiroki terminated the call on his cell phone and smiled. He had convinced Hidetada that they had broken Sakura and that she would reveal the man and organisation behind the attacks, but only to Hidetada.

Hidetada had sounded pleased with the outcome and had agreed for him to deliver her at 11:00 am to his office. Hiroki confirmed she would be restrained, and another of his highly skilled warriors would assist him.

<u>60</u>

Sakura had laid awake for hours. Sleeping was impossible because of the lights, Slim Shady blasting in the background and her electric shock torture injuries. Not only was her body badly hurt and weakened after days of torture, but she was also afraid she was losing her mind.

Her mind was full of negative thoughts, darker, more menacing than ever. She had weeds growing inside her mind where once flowers bloomed. In just a few days, the absence of sunlight and the inability to track time, along with torture and starvation, had significantly altered her physical and mental health.

The door opened, and despite her usual resolve, she burst into tears. She knew they would break her today; she could not endure anymore. She would betray her grandfather; they had succeeded. The waterboarding was debilitating, and the electric shocks were unsustainable. She could not survive another day. She would tell them what they wanted to know. She would plead for mercy and ask for a quick death. She knew she would never be leaving this place.

Hiroki walked through the door; another man was following him; he was carrying a suitcase. He walked towards her and placed the case on the floor near the bed.

"Hello, Sakura. I have been looking everywhere for you."

She looked up through teary eyes, "Kai? Is that you?"

She stood, he hugged her, and for the first time in days, Sakura felt her strength returning.

She felt safe but confused.

How was he here?

Both men saw the bruising of her upper torso, breasts, groin and thighs. There were only a few places on her body where her pale skin was unblemished. They could see electrical burns on her nipples. One nipple was a translucent bubble full of fluid. The blister on the other nipple had ruptured, lymphatic fluid weeping from it, flowing along the curve of her breast and down her body.

Sakura remembered her nakedness and used her arm to cover her breasts and her hand to cover her groin. She was embarrassed and bowed her head.

Kai quickly said, "I have some clothes for you," and opened the suitcase. He took out fresh underwear, and a fresh Saviour outfit. He also handed her a shoulder holster and her SIG P365 pistol. Sakura took hold of the gun, released the magazine and smiled when she saw it was loaded. She slammed it back into the handle, cycled the slide, and a round slid into the breach. She set the safety and slipped it back into the holster. Kai noticed that all her fingernails were missing on her right hand. The soft skin, usually protected by the nails, was red and inflamed from the trauma inflicted upon them once the nail had been removed.

She hugged Kai, "Thank you," forgetting her nakedness.

Kai silently thanked Megumi for providing him with the clothing, something only a woman would consider under the circumstances. Then, as Sakura dressed, the two men averted their eyes, focussing on the suitcase. Kai removed the other items he had brought: a chicken sandwich sealed in a zip-lock bag and a small thermos of miso soup.

While Sakura ate and drank the miso, Kai explained that Hiroki was his brother and that they had been separated from each other twenty-three years ago when they had been orphaned. Then, they presented their plan and that Sakura had to dress in a prison inmate's transport outfit, consisting of an orange jumpsuit with a belly chain, handcuffs and leg restraints.

***

They arrived at Hidetada's apartment and office just before 11:00 am. Two men guarded the car park elevator. A call on the intercom confirmed they were expected, and they rode the elevator to Hidetada's floor. Hiroki thought it was only six days ago that he first walked down this corridor towards these magnificent doors and the two giant guards. Finally, the doors were opened, and they escorted Sakura into Hidetada's office; he was seated at his desk.

"Bring the bitch over here," he barked at them.

Sakura studied him, this man who had caused so much misery to innocent girls. She could not mask her hate and contempt for him.

"I hope you enjoyed my hospitality in 'Osaka Processing Centre'; now tell me who is behind these attacks."

Sakura remained silent, glaring at him, her mouth turned up into a grimace. She could see his face beginning to redden; Hidetada was a man used to getting his way. He slammed his fist on his desk and stood up, looking down at Sakura, then he walked around the desk to stand in front of her, just inches apart.

Sakura thought, why do these men always try to intimidate her by standing so close? Don't they realise that this places them in the danger zone?

That's when she struck. Kai had unlocked the handcuffs before entering the building. She quickly shook them loose and, reaching out with her right hand, grabbed his groin, her fingers wrapping tightly around his scrotum. Once she located a testicle, she positioned it between her thumb and first finger and squeezed. He screamed, and she felt his testicle pop like a grape; years of carrying ten-litre jugs with just her fingers had given her incredible grip strength. Finally, she released him, and he fell to his knees, clutching at his groin.

Kai yelled, "Sakura, behind you!" As Sakura turned, she reached inside her tunic and removed the pistol. She saw a hidden door opening amongst the beautiful wall panelling and a guard entering. He was carrying a gun and was raising it to target her, but he was no match for her speed. In less than a heartbeat, Sakura had flicked off the safety, adopted the shooting stance and fired two rounds into his heart and a third round into his forehead. He fell to the floor, never firing his weapon. A second guard stumbled over the fallen man, his face covered in blood from the leading guard's head wound. She moved quickly towards the opening to see a third man exiting, whom she dispatched in hitman style, two rounds to the heart, one to the forehead, then she put three rounds into the head of the second guard as he struggled to rise.

Kai and Hiroki had positioned themselves in front of the main entrance door. The guards rushed into the room, alerted by the gunshots. They didn't get far; Kai and Hiroki dispatched them quickly. Sakura quickly checked the hidden room; it was full of security monitors but no guards. Hidetada was groaning on the floor. Hiroki grabbed him roughly and slammed him into a chair.

"Hiroki, your father will turn in his grave knowing you have betrayed me."

"It is you who have betrayed me. You had my parents killed."

Kai spoke into his radio, "All clear, you can come up."

The front doors of the limousine opened. Megumi emerged from the driver's side; Hirutu stepped out of the passenger side, wearing his old man disguise with the cane. Together they walked towards the elevator to Hidetada's apartment. The guards watched suspiciously as the couple approached, appearing harmless and non-threatening. That was a mistake. When they were within striking distance, Hirutu used his sword cane, running the blade through the hearts of both men before they could react.

***

Hirutu enjoyed the confused look on Hidetada's face when he entered the room; he didn't recognise him in his elderly man disguise. So, he removed his old man mask, revealing himself.

"Hirutu Hotato, you are responsible for this? Why?"

"I could no longer tolerate your human trafficking; it is an offence against humanity. So today, we will destroy your business, free the girls you have enslaved and do everything we can to free those distributed around the country."

Hidetada boldly yelled, "I will have your ancestry name removed from history. I will ensure everyone is killed, including all your employees except those I select to work for me. Who is this Sakura Bianchi? What relation is she to you?"

"She is my granddaughter and will change the Yakuza structures within Japan and perhaps the world. She is a great warrior."

"Looks just like merchandise to me, a vessel for my seed," boasted Hidetada.

Sakura laughed, "I think I have significantly impacted your ability to rape any more girls, you vile man."

He rose angrily from the chair, "I have dealt with stronger women and broken them to serve my will. You, too, will serve me, you little slut."

Sakura pivoted on her left foot, directing a roundhouse kick to Hidetada's kidney. The flawlessly performed blow transferred a brutal force wave through his body fat and ruptured his kidney. Once again, the big man screamed in agony and bent over, trying to release the terrible pain in his lower back and groin. She kneed him hard on the jaw, forcing him upwards again, and then she struck him with a three-finger punch, crushing his larynx, restricting his oesophagus and inflicting a flight response from him. He stumbled backwards, his face white with fear, his eyes wide in alarm.

Sakura spoke softly, "You have destroyed so many lives, not just the girls you kidnapped and tortured but their parents and siblings. I aim to remove you from this earth, along with all those who served you. But, unlike you, my threat is real and will be executed over the next twenty-four hours."

He could not respond; his voice box had been destroyed, his coughing continuous, a thin film of blood spraying from his mouth and splattering onto the carpet.

Sakura took a moment to savour this moment, content in her knowledge of the pain and fear she had instilled into this evil man. She knew the three injuries would generate waves of pain and were life-changing; however, they were not life-threatening.

While she was his captive, Sakura had considered how she would end this man's life if she got the chance. She knew many ways to kill a man. She slowly walked towards him; his confidence had evaporated, and he was backing away from her, his arms outstretched in a pathetic attempt at defence. Her eyes were black and cold, the eyes of a killer showing no empathy. Whilst his eyes were wide and white, betraying his terror. Eventually, his movement was stopped as his back struck the wall, "plsjsygg."

He had grunted something incomprehensible, perhaps a final plea for mercy; it didn't matter. Sakura would show no leniency; she hated him and everything he represented. She struck him with a short punch, the impact point just above his solar plexus and below his sternum. The punch is known as 'Dim Mak' or 'Death Touch' and used a secret technique only taught to a few students because of its deadly effect. The punch force increases after contact with the body, its momentum continues deep into the body. The lethal blow sent pressure waves of energy through his chest cavity, tearing the muscles of his heart and rupturing the aortic heart valve.

His face turned an ashen grey as he went into a type of cardiac arrest, 'Commotio Cordis', a condition caused by the sudden arrhythmia disruption to his heart. He reached for his chest, his mouth agape, pain etched on his face and fell to the ground.

He wouldn't die immediately; some people could writhe around in pain for ten minutes or more; it depended on the individual. The 'Sohei Master' who taught her this technique explained that the injury results in intense pain for the victim.

He deserved this death, and she hoped he would endure the pain for minutes.

Megumi entered the room. She had witnessed the final blow and the death of Hidetada. She held up a disk drive, "I have copied it all. I know everything, his offshore bank accounts, his cryptocurrency wallet, we have access to over 100 billion Yen."

<u>61</u>

Hirutu was listening to each of the commanders describe their battle readiness. It was 4:00 pm, and the troops required for the assault on Hidetada's four compounds had all successfully been deployed to Japan. The team agreed they would simultaneously attack the four compounds at 3:00 am. The Saviour team would make emergency calls to the local police and hospitals at 3:30 am, which should enable the soldiers sufficient time to kill all the guards, free the captive girls and destroy the buildings. After that, the soldiers would go to the respective airfields where private flights had been arranged to return them to their countries.

If it all went well, the ambulances would transport the girls to the hospital for treatment, and the police would ensure the areas were made safe for the public. Finally, the team wished the soldiers good luck as they departed to collect their men and fly to the four regions across Japan for their missions.

At 5:00 pm, Yumi said goodbye to Hirutu and Megumi, crying as she thanked them for saving her from her captives. Yumi had found her passport amongst the Korean pile of passports, and Hirutu had reserved a seat on Korean Air, departing Narita at 8:00 pm and arriving in Daegu at 10:30 pm. Yumi was excited, knowing she would soon be reunited with her parents and safe in her room.

Day 16 since the abduction

62

Hirutu, Megumi, Hiroki and the four Saviours, were watching the news reports in the 'war room'. Takeo and Tatsuo had argued that they were well enough to leave their beds, and they all wanted to see the impact on Hidetada's business. The 5:00 am Nippon News covered the four locations of the burning buildings and had footage of many distressed and disoriented girls being loaded into ambulances. They flicked through a few channels, and all channels broadcast similar footage. The Minister of Police was asked if this was a terrorist attack.

Within a few hours, the news story became clearer (with some subtle phone calls from Megumi). Evidence emerged that the assets were owned by a businessman called Tokugawa Hidetada. By 6:00 am, interviews from the hospitals started being broadcast. The girls interviewed were more recently captured and are less dependent on heroin. They told their stories of how they had been kidnapped or tricked by promises of employment and had instead become captives of human trafficking destined for prostitution.

When three plastic bags of Japanese passports were delivered to the Nippon News Network, the nation was outraged as people began to understand the scale of the human trafficking operation. Later, photos of piles of international passports were leaked to the world press, and the story became international news.

Journalists visited several embassies: Korea, The Philippines and Thailand. The interviews were short; the embassy representatives only said they had anonymously received many passports, and early checks on a sample of the passports had revealed the owners were listed as missing persons. Investigations had commenced on the whereabouts of the owners of all the passports. The Korean embassy confirmed that two girls had walked into the embassy yesterday afternoon, claiming to have been kept captive in a clinic, whilst they recovered from injuries sustained in their abduction. Sakura smiled; she suspected these would be the two girls that had been transported with Yumi and Chaewon. She was happy they would finally be safe.

Megumi had provided the locations of all the baishun yados to three news networks and the Minister of Police, who had no option but to instigate raids and shut down these businesses across Japan. This was to become the largest police operation on prostitution for twenty-three years. As a result, 800 women were freed, and 350 Yakuza were taken into custody.

Megumi had transferred all the cryptocurrency to Hotato's crypto wallet. Next, she emptied Hidetada's overseas bank accounts, moving the money evenly between Hirutu's and hers. Finally, she transferred five significant commercial buildings into the Hotato family property trust by hacking the Japanese Real Property Registration System and changing the ownership details. Hidetada was dead, so no one would ever know.

It was almost a perfect outcome, except the other Hidetada businesses were still operational. Megumi called Hirutu, Sakura and Hiroki over to the couch and motioned for them to be seated. "It has come to my attention that there is a global bounty on Sakura and Hiroki. Each of you is valued at US$5 million. The bounty is for your capture or proof of death." She passed her phone to Hirutu, who read the message, then passed it to Sakura and Hiroki. The three of them looked at Megumi with concerned expressions. "It has been issued globally, meaning every assassin, hitman, and organised crime group will be looking for you. Japan is not safe. You must travel somewhere overseas to hide until people stop looking for you."

Kai had explained to Sakura about Hiroki's history, how the brothers had been re-united, and that Hiroki had been tricked into obeying his adopted father, the man responsible for him being an orphan. Sakura had argued with her grandfather and Kai for days: she did not want Hiroki as a travel companion. It was difficult for Sakura to forgive Hiroki for delivering her to her torturers. While he hadn't participated in the punishment, he had stood by and watched as she was beaten, waterboarded, sexually assaulted and electrocuted.

As each day passed, it became more urgent that she leave the country. Her grandfather had impressed upon her that many men and women were searching for her, the bounty incentive tempting the most dangerous assassins and murderers in Japan.

Eventually, she agreed to have Hiroki accompany her to stop the arguments. That night, before she fell asleep, she considered Hiroki's fate. She would have her revenge. Unfortunately, while he would be her travel companion, that relationship would be short-lived.

One week later

<u>63</u>

Sakura was in her room. She opened the specially designed luggage case she would take with her. Her grandfather had his technicians prepare the case so she could transport her swords and other weapons through airports. Each corner of the bag had ornamental brass bracing, impervious to X-rays. Sakura unzipped and removed the lining, revealing compartments in each corner. She used three to store her ammunition and the other for her kaiken.

She packed enough clothes for a week, including her Ninja Yoroi, a special outfit that consisted of a black jacket, black trousers, light leather slippers and a hooded cowl that enabled her to hide all her face except her eyes. She flicked through the five passports. Each had a photo of her and a different name, three were Japanese, and the others were American Passports. How her grandfather and Megumi had been able to achieve this, she was uncertain and hadn't asked. There were matching Visa Cards with bank accounts attached. Megumi selected five different banks and opened each account with US$5 million. Hiroki also had five passports using the same surnames; they would travel as brother and sister.

Sakura walked to her wardrobe to collect her tsurgi and tantō. These swords had been gifted to her by Shi Yan Ming, a great warrior monk and leader of the Sohei Temple when she graduated. She was the youngest female ever to reach the Sohei Warrior status, and she had achieved this status in ten years, a remarkable feat when most students took a minimum of fifteen years.

The tsurgi sword is a two-edged sword used in the 10th century by Samurai and Sohei warriors. Very few exist, and this was Sakura's prized possession. It was an incredible honour for her to be gifted this priceless weapon. Due to the age of the sword, more than 1000 years, the original binding of the hilt had deteriorated. Her grandfather had the bindings rewound by Tokyo's greatest Masamune (sword maker). The handle of the alder wood was wrapped in the traditional battle wrap style known as Katate Maki. To achieve this, the handle was first covered with stingray skin, a coarse texture that helps keep the silk wrap in place and prevent slipping. The contrast of the fine black silk over the whiteness of the stingray skin resulted in a beautiful design that was practical for its purpose.

As Sakura removed the tsurgi from the saya, the sword sang a soft "TING". She studied the sword, admiring the new bindings and the shine of the ancient blade; it was beautiful. When viewed from the tip, the blade was a diamond shape, with each side a sharp cutting edge. The sword showed wear from its use over the centuries, primarily chips and scratches. Sakura poured some oil on a linen cloth and wiped the blade. She then took her grindstone and ran it along each edge several times to ensure the blade was as sharp as the day it was made. Finally, she wiped off the excess oil and returned it to its saya.

Next, she removed the tantō from its saya and repeated the process, ensuring it was sharp for this mission. The tantō was also gifted to her on her graduation day and complimented the tsurgi. One of the tantō's purposes was to enable a Samurai to commit Seppuku. She returned to the luggage case and pressed the hidden buttons that allowed the carrying handle to be entirely removed. Once removed, a cavity was revealed, one on each side, that was specially made for these swords. They could be secured behind the handle, protected in a metal tube lined with rubber and manufactured specifically for each sword. She was ready!

64

Yumi was flicking through Facebook posts on her new iPhone 14; Megumi had given it as a farewell gift. She was bored, and the social media posts were childish and time-wasting. Since she had returned home, she had caught up with her school friends, but she had found the conversations meaningless; the girls were immature, more interested in their hair and nails than building strong personal relationships.

She had phoned three of the girls who travelled to Japan with her. She thought their shared captive experience would build a strong bond, but she couldn't connect emotionally with them. Instead, they had settled into the life they had led before they left for Japan.

Yumi had told her parents about the kidnapping but had withheld some of what happened: the rapes, the drugs, and that she had killed a man. Before returning home, she had decided it was best that they didn't know.

She had been considering her future this past week and had decided on her fate. She wanted to be like Sakura and Megumi: a warrior helping people in distress, punishing evil men. She had realised that she could never live in Daegu, working in a hair or nail salon. She wanted to do something meaningful to be trained in martial arts. She desired to be strong and deadly.

She opened Contacts on the iPhone and made the call.

"Hello, Yumi. Are you enjoying being back home?"

"Megumi, I need to talk to you about my future."

<u>65</u>

Sakura admired the tray the air hostess had placed on the flight table. She was on her grandfather's private jet; they had been in the air for an hour. The silver tray held a small bottle of Evian sparkling mineral water, a crystal glass and a dish with a salmon and avocado sushi roll, which had been cut into four equal portions, each piece lying flat, positioned to create a shape that resembled a flower, a dollop of wasabi at the centre where the four pieces touched. Black wooden chopsticks and a small bowl of soya sauce completed the arrangement. She filled the glass with water, selected a piece of sushi, dipped it in the sauce and savoured the mixture of tastes.

It was delicious.

She looked over at Hiroki, sitting across the aisle from her. He had a similar tray which included a tokkuri (ceramic flask) of sake which he was pouring into a choko (sake cup).

Sakura watched Hiroki eat his sushi. He was a handsome man, only a year older than her. She considered their similarities; both had been orphaned at a young age and were warriors, assassins, and killers. They were unusual travel companions; Sakura had killed his adopted father. Hiroki was now a ronin, having betrayed his daimyo and allowed Sakura to kill him. They would both be hunted by the yakuza until they were found.

Hiroki turned to face her. He held his sake cup in a salute and said, "To our new lives!" He sipped from the cup and smiled at her. Sakura held her glass of water up, "To our new lives," and smiled back at him. He had no idea she would kill him when the opportunity arose.

Then she laid back in the seat and closed her eyes. Her heart was racing, she felt her cheeks reddening, and she was confused. Was it the thought of killing him or his smile which had caused this effect upon her body? Finally, she settled into a meditative state, attempting to slow her heartbeat.

United States of America

<u>66</u>

Sakura and Hiroki were eating dinner in a local diner in a small town in Washington State. Last week, they had arrived in Vancouver from Japan. They had spent the week sightseeing, masquerading as tourists, travelling on fake passports as brother and sister.

Today, they had travelled across the border into America. They needed to remain on the move and avoid leaving a digital footprint which would enable them to be located. Hiroki appeared troubled. Finally, he looked up from his meal and at Sakura. She saw his eyes were moist, and then a tear rolled down his cheek.

"Sakura, I am so sorry you suffered because of me. Each night, in my nightmares, I relive the scenes of your punishment, reliving your screams and your requests for mercy.

"I am ashamed, I knew it was wrong, yet my loyalty to Hidetada prevented me from intervening. I know now that my loyalty was misplaced; my heart is heavy with that burden. I will never forgive myself, so I have decided to end my life as retribution. I will commit to seppuku. I ask that you be my kaishakunin (appointed to behead me) and end my life once the pain is too great. I wish to die with some honour."

Sakura remained silent, staring at Hiroki, a minute passed as she considered his request. She thought seppuku would be an appropriate ending to his life. As his kaishakunin, she could prolong his pain, ensuring he suffered. It was perfect.

"Hiroki, I am honoured and agree. We will travel to Colorado, where a Shinto Shrine is in the Shambhala mountains. We will conduct the ceremony there in the Japanese gardens."

It would take them a month or longer to make the journey. Sakura would make him wait, she wanted him to suffer, in the knowledge he would die by his own hand.

***

They travelled east through Idaho, stopping at various towns for three days, then onto Great Falls in Montana. The beauty of the wilderness overcame Sakura, and they stayed for a week, spending their time on day trips through the forest. A waitress suggested they visit Whitefish, telling them it was situated by a large lake, so there is abundant wildlife. They left the next day, found accommodation and paid for a week. Sakura had purchased hiking boots and a small daypack. She was ready to tackle more challenging terrain exploring the area. On the first day, they trekked to Whitefish Lake's popular picnic and swimming area. It was a lovely spring day, and whilst it was too cold to swim, she enjoyed the area's serenity. They had it all to themselves, and it felt like they were the only two people in the world. There was no evidence of humanity for as far as she could see.

The following day, they left early in the dark. Sakura was keen to hike to a mountain peak that overlooked the lake. It was a ten-mile hike to their destination and ten miles return; it would be a long day. She had planned for ten hours, taking warm clothes and a torch in case they had to return in the dark. They arrived at the track head just as the sky was starting to grow light. They finished their coffee, leaving the Styrofoam cups in the car and set off at 6:30 am. The sun was beginning to rise in the east. The trail was less used than previous hikes they had recently completed and had overgrown during the winter months.

She needed to urinate a couple of hours into the walk. Then, looking for a suitable area, she spotted a grassy clearing through the trees. It was 20 metres walk from the track, through the woods, to reach it.

"Hiroki, I need to relieve myself; I am going there. Can you wait here for me, please?" She walked through the undergrowth to the clearing and looked with awe. It must have been logged decades ago, and now it was a manicured grassy plain hundreds of metres in diameter. It appeared to be a favourite place for grazing animals, deer, and maybe even moose. It was empty now, though; she couldn't see any animals, which felt wrong. A shiver spread through her body. That's when she spotted the cute bear cubs; she had heard tales of grizzly bears roaming but had assumed it was the locals just joking with her.

67

Artio watched her babies drinking from her teats, their meal was finished too quickly, and her milk was exhausted. After their morning feed, she washed them, savouring their scent on her tongue, embedding their uniqueness into her memory. They had been born two moons ago and were big enough now to venture outside. She had decided today they would leave the den, which had been her home for five moons; the first three, she slept, then her birthing pain aroused her, and her beautiful cubs were born. This was her second litter and knowing what to expect had made it easier.

She could see her skin sagging, the fat she had accumulated before her big sleep had been depleted, and today's feed was inadequate for the growing cubs she needed to hunt to restore her milk. The cubs had drifted into a restless sleep, their bellies half full. She nudged them with her nose, then stood and shook her body, starting at her tail and ending at her head. She was hungry, ravenous, and looking forward to a hunt. There was a clearing nearby she decided to start there; she walked to the cave entrance, the sun had climbed above the ridge, and she could feel its warmth. She took a deep breath, the smells of spring enticing her to move quickly; she bounded down the hill, the cubs clumsily chasing her.

They reached the clearing; she found a safe place for her cubs to play and told them to stay whilst she hunted. She walked towards the other side of the clearing, an area populated with rabbits, and they would have their litters out playing in the sun. She glanced back at her babies, who were playing, rolling on the ground. The boy was on top of his sister, already more muscular and larger than her. She hadn't named them yet. She would do that after their third moon; by then, they would have a good chance of surviving.

She got low on her haunches and walked stealthily through the clearing; she could smell the rabbits; there were many. As she got closer, she saw a young family eating the grass. She was upwind so that they couldn't smell her. She moved closer, waiting for the right moment, and then launched herself at the young rabbits. She captured two, one in each of her massive front paws, her claws easily penetrating their soft bodies, impaling them. She quickly removed their heads with her powerful jaws and dropped them to the ground. The meal was small, just two bites in each rabbit, but it felt good to have warm food in her belly. She reached down, grabbed one of the severed heads, and delicately removed as much of the tongue as possible with her claws. Tongues were a delicacy. She enjoyed the texture, which was very different to the fur-covered meat.

She made her way over to a beehive in a tree's hollow, honey was her favourite treat. Standing upright, with a reach of three metres, she could easily extract large amounts of honey with her paws, which she greedily sucked upon. Suddenly her meal was interrupted by a faint scent, the wind had briefly changed direction, and her keen instincts immediately recognised the danger. Once, a long time ago, she had stalked a two-legged animal. As she made her attack, it raised a long stick; there was a loud noise and pain in her front leg. She terminated the hunt and ran off, bleeding and feeling weak. She had spent seven days lying by a creek, letting the wound heal. She remembered that pain and had ensured she always gave these two-legged animals a wide berth.

She scanned the clearing, first checking on her babies. That's when she saw the threat between her and her cubs. Her motherly instinct overcame her fear of these two-legged animals, and with a ferocious roar, she bounded forward. The two-legged animal turned at the sound of the roar, screamed, and then ran towards a large pine tree. Artio increased her speed; the noise of her 250kgs crashing along the ground sent the birds to flight. She was gaining on it; the scent of its urine was strong on the ground, reminding her of her hunger, driving her to run faster, despite her already tiring.

She heard another yell, turned and saw a second animal had entered the clearing. It was running in the opposite direction, carrying her girl baby. She turned so fast that large sods of grass flew into the air, and roaring, she chased after this second animal.

Shortly into the chase, it dropped her baby; she stopped briefly to check it was unharmed, then continued her pursuit. They would feast today on these animals. Finally, it reached a tree and unfortunately, climbed quickly out of her reach, just as she crashed into the pine tree without slowing. There was a large crack, and the tree swayed, but the animal had wrapped its arms around the trunk and was determined to remain there. She backed up and ran at the tree again. She could not dislodge the animal. She turned to see the other animal pointing something at her from her perch in the tree. Remembering the pain from last time; she decided to end the chase. Disappointed she would not get to eat these animals; she turned and ran towards her girl cub. Licks and low growls soothed the infant, and together, they walked back to the boy baby.

<u>68</u>

Sakura watched as the grizzly bear chased Hiroki; he had saved her life. She knew the bear would have reached her before she could climb the tree. She removed her iPhone from her pocket and videoed the bear chasing Hiroki. She would send this to the Saviour team; they would never have believed it otherwise.

When the bear broke away and walked off with its cubs, Sakura realised she had soiled herself. Her trousers were wet; she must have emptied her bladder when she started running. She wasn't sure how long to wait to ensure she was safe from the bear. They had been travelling for two hours and were probably six miles into their journey. Her heartbeat was starting to slow; she realised she had been terrified, an emotion she had rarely experienced. Hiroki had climbed down and was walking towards her. She also decided to climb down, embarrassed that she had wet herself.

"Are you ok? That was an adrenalin rush!"
"I'm Ok, but I have had enough of the wilderness for a few months; let us move on to more populated areas. Let's start heading towards Colorado."

Six weeks after leaving Japan

<u>69</u>

Hiroki awoke at dawn. It had been a restless night, his last in this life. Since he had agreed to seppuku, he had not slept well. Knowing he was to take his own life and die in a foreign land did not promote peaceful sleep. On the contrary, every day he spent with Sakura reminded him of what he had done.

As if dying wasn't enough to endure, he had fallen hopelessly in love with her. Sakura had physically healed from her injuries, yet he could see her hate for him in her eyes and her body's stiffness when he stood too close. She had seemed eager to be his kaishakunin, almost happy at the prospect of finishing his life, and he didn't blame her.

Her grandfather had spoken to him about Sakura's history as a young girl, and now he had made her suffer more indignities. His conscience haunted him each night, punishing him for subjecting such a beautiful and mighty warrior to further atrocities.

The weeks had passed quickly, and they had travelled through Washington state to Montana, then Idaho, Wyoming and eventually Colorado. Today, they would travel to the Japanese Shinto Shrine in the mountains to end his life. He looked out the window, the birds began to chirp, and the sun's rays felt warm upon his shirtless body. He smiled; it was a good day to die.

70

Sakura was struggling with her morning meditation, her mind restless, thinking about what she would do today. She had agreed to use her swords in today's seppuku ceremony as it had been too dangerous for Hiroki to return home and retrieve his swords after they had killed Hidetada.

At first, she was elated by the knowledge that he would die by her hand and her beloved weapons. However, over the past six weeks, she had begun to grow fond of him. Perhaps it was the shared danger, knowing they were being hunted, or the isolation of only having each other's company to share. He was a handsome man, and when she looked into his eyes, she could see his pain, his guilt.

Could she forgive him? She understood that he had been bound by his bushido code and loyalty to Hidetada. She wasn't certain if her discomfort was because she would end his life today or because she would be travelling alone in the USA with murderers chasing her.

***

They parked the car and walked through the spectacular red archway denoting the pathway to the shrine. They made their way towards a large cherry blossom tree. Sakura had carried the swords wrapped in a blanket. The blanket had now been laid under the cherry blossom tree, and the swords were positioned for the ceremony. Hiroki wore a silk robe, shirtless underneath and knelt upon the blanket. Sakura selected her tsurgi sword and adopted a stance behind and to the left, enabling her to perform the Kiritsuke, the final cut to remove Hiroki's head.

Hiroki lowered his head and whispered the seppuku prayer; these ageless words had been spoken for centuries, assisting the samurai to complete the ceremony with honour and transition them into the next life. Then, with both hands on the hilt of Sakura's tantō sword, he positioned the sharp point against his stomach just above his belly button.

"Sakura, are you ready?"

"Stop, Hiroki! I forgive you! I release you from your pledge."

Hiroki lowered the blade and looked at Sakura. Her face was flushed, her hands still raised, holding the sword. She looked amazing, powerful, and beautiful. He stood and bent down to kiss her. He stopped when he felt the tip of her sword press against his groin.

"You have saved my life twice in the past two months. One would not have been necessary if you hadn't handed me over to Hidetada. So today, I will let you live.

A life for a life. It does not mean that I forgive you."

"I love you, Sakura. I want to spend my life with you."

Nine Months after leaving Japan

Epilogue

Sakura focussed her gaze out the limousine window. The church stood majestically amongst the red outcrops of the Sedona desert, the clear blue winter sky framing it in contrast to the reds of the surrounding landscape. There were 150 steps from the car park to the church; she had counted them last week when finalising the wedding arrangements.

Her grandfather squeezed her hand, and she turned to face him. He was smiling and looked regal in his perfectly tailored dark grey suit. Kai opened the limousine door. He had positioned a red carpet cut in a semi-circle shape at the door. Sakura swung her legs out and placed her feet on the carpet whilst remaining seated in the car. She settled her dress around her feet, hiding the four-inch stilettos she was wearing. Kai moved back, "Smile," pointed his iPhone towards her and proceeded to take photos. He had volunteered to be the wedding photographer, and Sakura had reluctantly agreed, but she trusted Kai with her life. Literally!

Her grandfather walked around the car to her. She stood and Kai took more photos with them standing together on the red carpet, the shining white limousine in the background.

"We better get going. They are waiting for us," said Kai.

Sakura looked up at the church; it looked beautiful in this dry, harsh landscape. She hoped the steep climb wouldn't ruin her makeup. Kai lifted the train of her wedding dress, and Sakura grabbed the sides. She was determined to keep her dress well above the fine orange dust as she climbed the stairs. The three started the journey upwards, the church bells chiming happily, welcoming them to this sacred place.

Upon reaching the church doors, her grandfather opened them and beckoned her into the vestibule. He closed the doors behind her, trapping the red dust outside. Kai let go of the wedding dress train and re-arranged it so Sakura could enter the main section of the church.

Hirutu smiled at her, "Are you ready?"

"Yes," whispered Sakura.

He opened the door to reveal a smiling Yumi.

"Hello, Sakura, you look beautiful! Hiroki is a fortunate man."

An organ began playing the bridal chorus, the words 'Here comes the bride' instinctually playing out in her mind. Yumi was carrying a basket full of rose petals, scattering the delicate petals as she walked towards the front of the church. They fluttered to the floor, pinks and reds, decorating the path for Sakura.

Hirutu squeezed Sakura's hand and whispered, "Wait." He allowed Yumi to walk a few metres ahead of them before saying, "Ok, let's go."

Sakura started her walk to the bridal party, her heart pounding in her chest, a mix of emotions. Seeing Yumi again made her happy in the knowledge that she had been able to rescue her before any harm had befallen her. On the other hand, however, she felt sad knowing she had been too late to help Honoka Kondo.

As she neared the bridal party, she looked at everyone. They were all smiling, happy for her and Hiroki.

Hiroki, the man who had captured then rescued her, and finally stolen her heart. She never knew she could love so deeply for someone. Even now, looking at his handsome face made her heart beat faster, awakening butterflies in her stomach. Over the past four months, she had fallen deeply in love, and now they were to be wed. It felt surreal.

To his right stood the groomsmen, Tatsuo, Takeo and Kai. The left side of the bridal party consisted of her grandmother Mirako, Megumi and Yumi. All her family and closest friends were here to celebrate this day with them.

The priest asked, "Who gives this woman to marry this man?"

"I do," said Hirutu, then he released Sakura's hand and stood behind her as the bridal party turned to face the priest. The church pews stood empty. The priest was the only other person present. It had been crucial that the wedding be kept secret and that the gathering of this family is hidden from the Yakuza, who were still searching for Sakura and Hiroki.

The priest was an attractive middle-aged woman with long blonde hair named Kirsten Boyse. She was the first ordained female priest in Arizona. Sakura enjoyed the symbolism of being married by a woman priest, another century-old barrier breached by the tenacity of the modern woman. The ceremony began.

***

Sakura and Hiroki had been travelling as brother and sister, so they had always had separate rooms or beds. Now they were married and using the same names, travelling as husband and wife.

Tonight, was the first time they would share a bed: the bridal suite bed, and it was enormous.

Her grandfather had booked the entire Red Agate Resort for the wedding. It was a beautiful resort in a spectacular location not far from the church she had been married in today. They enjoyed an incredible wedding reception and delicious meal.

Earlier in the day, when they had entered the bridal suite and then the bedroom, Hiroki had held her, kissed her and said, "I love you so much, Sakura. Would you like me to sleep on the couch tonight?"

She had looked up into his eyes, which were sparkling with anticipation. "I want you to sleep with me tonight and every night for the rest of my life." Then she stood on her toes and kissed him on the lips. She felt a need growing inside her from that moment; the fire in her loins had burned hot during the evening celebrations and meal.

During their time together over the past months, they had become closer. It had been three months before their first kiss. She remembered it vividly despite there being many more. Once four months ago, he had placed his hands upon her buttocks during a passionate kiss. Another time, he had fondled her breast, but they had never ventured further than that.

She had seen him naked in an accidental bathroom encounter. She wasn't sure if she had entered the bathroom daydreaming or if it was an unconscious action driven by her curiosity. He had finished showering and was towelling himself dry. Her gaze had drifted downwards, settling on his penis hanging between his powerful thighs. She had wondered how it would feel in her hand and body when he was aroused.

He had stared at her, unconcerned with his nakedness. She had felt her face blushing, her shyness overcoming her; she turned and almost ran from the bathroom.

Hiroki knew of her childhood experience and understood that an intimate relationship with her may not be possible. Sakura had never considered a close relationship possible with any man. However, tonight, she was ready. She had a desire, and she wanted him so bad it had consumed her thoughts throughout dinner.

Sakura rinsed her mouth with water and put her toothbrush away. She looked in the mirror. She liked the woman she saw smiling back at her. She stepped back so she could see how she looked in her nightgown. It was a gift from Megumi. The fabric was incredibly sheer. It weighed nothing and hid nothing. Her naked body beneath the material was visible, the darkness of her areolae prominent, her hardened nipples pressing against the fabric.

Her chest tattoo, a dagger and five ribbons were visible, symbolising her slaying of the men who changed her life. Her panties had felt like gossamer in her hands, and she had taken great care when putting them on to avoid puncturing the delicate fabric with a fingernail. She was delighted Megumi had provided such a seductive present for her wedding night. She had nothing nearly as beautiful or sexy as this outfit. She turned to the door. Outside, in the bedroom, Hiroki was waiting.

Sakura took a deep breath, sighed, opened the door, and entered the bedroom. Hiroki was sitting in bed, his hands on the blanket, fingers interlaced, resting in his lap. He looked more nervous than she felt, making her smile, a smile that beamed at him. She watched him stare as she slowly walked towards the bed. His mouth gaped; she was enjoying the effect she was having on him. Then, confidently, she slipped under the covers, turned to him and placed her left hand on his chest against his pectoral muscle. Her leg rested against his leg, and she knew he was naked. Using her index finger, she gently closed his mouth and kissed him. Next, she pressed her tongue between his lips, which he parted to allow her better access, and she explored his tongue, his teeth and the roof of his mouth as she slowly slid her left hand down his body.

She felt the eight muscles protecting his abdomen and continued to his groin. Using just two fingers, she lightly touched the glands of his penis. He had a full erection, it was hard, and she felt its length. Her fingers continued their journey until she had his testicles in her hand and gently squeezed them.

He gasped!

She was ready!

She pulled down her panties while he lifted her nightie over her head. Then she straddled him, held both his arms above his head against the pillow so he couldn't touch her and readied herself to take him. He was so hard that it was easy for her to position herself perfectly upon him. She felt the tip of his penis enter her then she stopped.

She wanted to savour the moment she saw the desire in his eyes, the beads of sweat on his brow. He was breathing heavily, heavier than her. She kissed him as she slowly pushed down onto his manhood, taking him into her warm embrace.

She slowly rocked her pelvis against him, entirely focused on the act of lovemaking, burying him deep within her. This was their first night, the consummation of their marriage, and she had never been happier.

***

After their lovemaking, they had laid in an embrace, Sakura resting her head on his chest, and both had fallen into a deep, dreamless sleep.

Now she was awake!

Something had awoken her. She looked over at Hiroki, who was also awake.

He gestured for her to leave the bed and stand against the wall, the hinge side of the bedroom door. Silently they both got out of bed, their senses on high alert. She listened but couldn't hear anything. They took up their positions by the door, Hiroki standing on the side where the door would open away from him, allowing him to attack whoever was there.

They stood for a minute, the time passing slowly, and then the decorative door handle started moving slowly downwards. Whoever was on the other side of the door wasn't rushing. When the latch had been completely released, the door opened silently. A big, black hand moved out of the darkness and wrapped around the side of the door, slowly opening it further.

She studied the hand. Even in the room's darkness, she could see it was heavily tattooed. It was positioned on the door above her head. She thought whoever was on the other side must be a giant of a man. When the door was three-quarters ajar, another monstrous hand appeared holding a Taurus TX22 equipped with a silencer. It looked like a toy in the big man's hand.

Sakura knew the mafia used this weapon for in-close hit jobs. Even with a silencer attached, the .22 rounds can easily penetrate the human forehead from three metres. This calibre is preferred as the smaller charge is almost silent with a silencer attached. Also, due to its low velocity the round cannot exit the skull; instead, the bullet ricochets inside the head until it loses momentum. This results in the brain being reduced to a jelly-like state, causing instant death for the owner.

She saw a big black head, the size of a bowling ball ducking under the door frame entering the room, gang tattoos adorned the skull and face. As the big man entered the room, Hiroki struck with a powerful upper cut to his elbow targeting the joint were the ulna and humerus join. Sakura could hear the bones splintering in the big man's arm, the gun flew from his hand, and he screamed in pain.

He turned and grabbed Hiroki by the throat, lifting him off the ground using his undamaged left hand. Hiroki's eyes bulged as he struggled in the big man's grip. Sakura attacked from behind delivering a barrage of punches to the man's kidneys. It took six blows before he finally arched his back, dropped Hiroki and turned to face her.

She ran towards the bed searching for the gun, she saw it in the moonlight, grabbed it, turned and fired three rounds, two in the chest and one in the forehead. The bullet to the forehead, just flattened, it failed to penetrate the thick bone. The chest shots had been more successful, the left side of his face lost nerve control and slid down, giving the appearance it had melted. He kept moving towards Sakura, just metres from her, she fired a round into his eye, he slowed, then crumbled to his knees and fell forward, dead.

Sakura ran to Hiroki, turned him onto his back and gave a sigh of relief when she saw he was breathing. She saw black bruising appearing on his neck. She kissed him.

Then, she heard three loud gunshots, her mind instantly recognising they had been fired from an un-silenced 9mm.

Sakura realised this was not a random break and enter.
This was a professional hit.
They had been found!
There were more of them.
She hoped the others were ok.

Innocent Lives

Sakura Bianchi Book 3

In this pulse-pounding conclusion to the Sakura Bianchi trilogy, loyalty, resilience, and the unbreakable bonds of friendship will be tested like never before. Can Sakura finally escape the clutches of the Yakuza and find the peace she so desperately craves? Or will her relentless pursuit of justice ultimately lead to her destruction.

The opening chapter follows.

Red Agate Resort
Sedona Arizona USA

Sakura's Wedding Night

1

The almost imperceptible click of the door's electronic lock disengaging was enough to wake Yumi.

Nine months of training with Sakura's team had enhanced her senses and improved her fighting skills. She rolled over in the luxurious bed towards the sound. Moonlight passed through the thin privacy curtains, providing a dim, ghostly light. The large room was open, with a sofa separating the bedroom from the lounge area. A sliver of light outlined the door as it slowly opened. Whoever was entering her room, uninvited, was being cautious and silent.

She reached under the pillow. Her hand touched the cool steel of her custom-made knife, its design similar to a World War 1 trench knife. A knuckle-duster metal guard protected the grip. Her fingers found their way through the four finger holes and located the grip's non-slip silk braiding. Sakura had commissioned the artisan, Yoshida Yoshihara, Japan's foremost swordsmith, who had taken six weeks to create the beautiful knife. Using the finest Japanese Katana steel, each layer was folded and beaten into the desired shape. The blade was six inches long, a diamond shape when viewed from the tip, and was razor sharp. It could be used to slice, stab, or bash.

The intruder entered the room, his silhouette illuminated from behind by the hallway light. Yumi could see he was short in stature with a stocky physique. Slowly, he closed the door, leaving it slightly ajar. Darkness engulfed him, the moonlight couldn't penetrate that deeply into the room. Yumi sensed rather than saw him walk silently but determinedly towards her bed.

She turned onto her back simulating a momentary wake-up. She discreetly moved her left arm from under the covers, emitting a delicate snore to feign returning to sleep. Through squinted eyes, she observed the intruder briefly halt before continuing their deadly journey towards her.

Seconds passed, but it felt like minutes as he cautiously approached her. When he was within two yards, he raised a handgun and pointed it at her head.

Just a little more please, mister, come closer.

He moved closer.

Before he could fire, Yumi grabbed the wrist holding the gun and forced it upwards and away from her. Simultaneously, she struck him under the chin with the knuckle-duster grip. She had practiced daily with this knife, perfecting the ten different moves for which the trench knife design was famous. Her strike was precise, and she heard and felt his jawbone shatter from the knuckle-duster's four pyramid-shaped points. His head jerked back, and he let out a scream, but she silenced it when she ruthlessly dragged the razor-sharp blade across his throat, cutting the jugular and carotid arteries. She pushed him away, and he fell to the floor, bleeding out.

———

Sakura was awake! Something had awoken her. She looked over at Hiroki and saw he was also awake.

He gestured for her to leave the bed and stand against the wall, hinge side of the bedroom door. Silently, they both got out of bed, their senses on high alert. She listened but couldn't hear anything. They took up their positions by the door, Hiroki standing on the side where the door would open away from him, allowing him to attack whoever was there.

They stood waiting, the time passing slowly. Eventually, the bedroom's decorative door handle slowly started moving downwards. Whoever was on the other side of the door wasn't rushing. When the latch had been fully released, the door opened silently. A big, black hand wrapped around the side of the door, slowly extending it. Despite the darkness in the room, she could see that the hand was heavily tattooed. It was positioned on the door above her head.

Whoever is on the other side must be a giant of a man.

When the door was three-quarters open, another monstrous hand appeared, holding a Taurus TX 22 equipped with a silencer. It looked like a toy in the big man's hand.

Sakura knew that the mafia preferred the smaller 22-calibre because it was the quietest handgun with a silencer attached. It is their choice for in-close hit jobs. Due to the low velocity of the round, it doesn't exit the skull. Instead, the bullet ricochets inside the head until it loses momentum. This results in the brain being reduced to a jelly-like state, causing instant death for the owner.

She saw a big black head, the size of a bowling ball, ducking under the door frame and entering the room. Gang tattoos adorned the skull and face. As the big man passed through the door, Hiroki struck with a powerful uppercut to his elbow, targeting the joint where the ulna and humerus join. Sakura could hear the bones splintering in the big man's arm. The gun flew from his hand and he screamed in pain.

He turned and grabbed Hiroki by the throat, lifting him off the ground using his undamaged left hand. Hiroki's eyes bulged as he struggled in the big man's grip. Sakura attacked from behind, delivering a barrage of punches to the man's kidneys. It took six blows before he finally arched his back, dropped Hiroki, and turned to face her.

She ran towards the bed, searching for the gun. She saw it in the moonlight, grabbed it, turned and fired three rounds, two in the chest and one in the forehead. Because of the thick bone of the giant's massive skull, the bullet flattened against his forehead instead of penetrating. The chest shots had been more successful. The left side of his face lost nerve control and slid down, giving the appearance it had melted. But he kept moving towards Sakura. When he was only yards from her, she fired a round into his eye. He slowed, then crumbled to his knees and fell forward, dead.

Sakura ran to Hiroki, turned him onto his back, and gave a sigh of relief when she saw he was breathing. Black and yellow bruising was already appearing on his neck. She kissed him.

Then, three loud gunshots caught her attention, and she realised this was not a random break and enter.

This was a professional hit.

They had been found!

There were more of them.

She hoped the others were ok.

———

Megumi woke, remembering it was Sakura's wedding night, and they had stayed in a motel. The room was in total darkness. Kai had closed the rubber-backed curtains before seducing her. He enjoyed exploring her body in the dark, using his fingers, lips, and tongue. His practiced touch produced feather-like sensations along her torso, legs and most delicate parts. Her orgasm had been body shuddering. Kai could do that to her. The faint scent of their lovemaking still lingered on the sheets.

So, what had woken her?

Megumi rolled over to face the hotel room door and watched it slowly open. She reached under her pillow, felt the synthetic grip of her Glock43, and closed her hand around it. The weapon's familiarity calmed the drumming in her chest. Blood pulsated at her temples as her body prepared for fight or flight.

Sensing Kai was also awake, she whispered to him, "Intruder! Move on three." The door opened further and a hand illuminated by the hotel corridor reached into the room, searching for the light switch.

"Three."

Both Kai and Megumi launched from the bed when the light came on. The man burst into the room, stopped and took a professional shooting stance. His head moving left to right, searching for them in the now brightly lit room.

Kai tumbled forward over the end of the bed and onto the floor, adopting an evasive zigzag pattern as he rolled towards the bathroom. Megumi rolled off the side of the bed onto the floor, away from the intruder, simultaneously chambering a round and taking a kneeling position.

Kai had captured the hitman's attention, who was able to fire two shots before Megumi sent an armour-piercing 9mm round through the intruder's right temple. The left side of his face exploded outwards and sailed three yards across the room. Its journey was halted by the wall with a SPLOTT sound.

It took a moment for the man's brain to register that he was dead. Finally, he slowly collapsed to his knees, then toppled forward. His body reached the floor before the left side of his head. Megumi watched as the detached face slid slowly down the wall, leaving a gruesome red trail, the combination of brain matter and blood proving to be quite the adhesive.

———

Situated in the Sedona desert, USA, the Red Agate Resort boasts a straightforward design. The entrance to the reception is in the centre of the single-level building, with two wings extending to the east and west. The lavishly appointed honeymoon suite was at the end of the western corridor. Sakura's grandfather, Hirutu, had booked the entire motel for five days to ensure only the bridal party and the hotel owners were there. The western wing also accommodated her family and friends.

Sakura ran from the bedroom into the living area and opened the door to the hotel corridor, scanning the area for risks. Yumi's room was on the left with the door slightly opened. Two gunmen carrying Uzi semi-automatic machine guns were guarding reception at the far end of the corridor. One man raised his Uzi and fired a brief burst at her as she dove into Yumi's room.

A cloud of dust partially filled the room as the machine gun rounds broke plaster away from the door frame and adjacent wall. When the firing paused, Sakura slammed the door shut and hooked the door lock into place. She knew a hefty kick could breach it but it might buy them a few seconds.

Sakura turned and saw Yumi holding the knife she had given her on her 17th birthday, her nightdress drenched in blood.

"Are you hurt?"

"No. The blood is his." Yumi pointed towards the puddle surrounding the head of the man lying on the floor.

Yumi whispered, "What's happening?"

"Someone has discovered us!"

Sakura grabbed the intruder's handgun, gently pulled on the slide to confirm it was loaded and checked the magazine.

"Good, it's full. Nine rounds." She handed Yumi the handgun she had taken from the giant intruder, as it contained fewer rounds.

Pausing to evaluate their situation, she considered what she knew.

1. There are at least two gunmen with automatic weapons.

2. Hiroki is out of action.

3. Yumi is armed.

4. Kai and Megumi are in the adjacent room; their status is unknown.

5. Grandparents' status is unknown.

6. Tatsuo's and Takeo's status is unknown.

Fuck it, I'm going to kill these pricks!

"Wait here Yumi, there are at least two more killers out there." Sakura looked through the hotel door peephole. The area immediately in front of the room was clear. She lifted the latch, stood to the side, and opened the door.

Two rooms further along the corridor, Hirutu was wide awake. The automatic gunfire was unmistakable. He kissed Mirako tenderly and said, "Go to the bathroom and lock the door." Mirako obeyed immediately, as she had for the 38 years they had been married. She was a traditional Japanese wife and respected her husband's decisions unquestioned.

Hirutu searched for something he could use as a weapon, his eyes falling upon the wine opener. He freed the spiral corkscrew from the handle, positioned it between his second and third finger, and tightened his grip on the handle. It wasn't much of a weapon, but it would do. He stood with his back against the wall next to the door. Four rounds smashed into the door lock, followed by a kick, and the door flew open. A sudden burst of gunfire echoed through the doorway, followed by the entrance of a man who rushed into the room, unaware of Hirutu's presence. He paused, scanning the area, before Hirutu attacked him from behind, slamming the corkscrew into his right eye. Three inches of twisted steel penetrated his brain and a warm gush of fluid flowed over Hirutu's hand as he applied an armlock around the man's neck. He squeezed as hard as his old muscles allowed. The man struggled and tried to break Hirutu's deadly embrace until he finally went limp. Hirutu loosened his grip and the man fell to the floor.

––––––

Sakura squatted and peered around the edge of the doorway. One armed guard remained, firing into Kai and Megumi's room. Sakura aimed and fired two rounds, both finding their target. He fell to the ground. Megumi walked from the room, stood over the man, and fired a round into his skull. The two 22 calibre rounds had critically wounded him. The 9mm round finished the job. Sakura ran towards Megumi and hugged her. "Are you OK?"

"I'm uninjured, but Kai has taken a round to his thigh."

"Megumi, go to the owner's room, stop them ringing the police. Their bedroom is behind reception."

"On it!" Megumi fled towards reception. Sakura picked up the Uzi and released the magazine. Only six rounds remained in the 32-capacity magazine.

"Sakura, take this." Hirutu threw her the full magazine he had found on the man he had killed.

"Thanks. Can you please attend to Kai and Hiroki. Both have sustained injuries."

Sakura loaded the fresh magazine into the Uzi's pistol grip and slid the fire selector from automatic to semi-automatic. This setting would fire a round with every squeeze of the trigger. She had practiced with an Uzi on their home firing range and knew she was more accurate with semi-auto selected.

———

Diego's knee shook as he sat in the driver's seat of the modified Ford Transit van. The rear compartment was windowless and bare except for multiple anchor points for securing people. They used this van for human trafficking, kidnapping and hostage transport. He would turn 16 in a month. In the meantime, he was driving with a fake license. It was just three weeks ago he faced his initiation into MS-13, the ritual 'beat-in'. Eight men, the biggest and meanest in the gang, had 13 seconds to kick and bash the shit out of him. It had been brutal but necessary to prove his willingness to be a probationary member of the Westlake MS-13. He had spent five days in hospital and a further ten days in bed at home, but it was worth it. He would need to kill someone to become a full member and knew that was inevitable.

After enduring the initiation ritual, he earned the opportunity to join the mission, tasked with chauffeuring hostages to Las Vegas and delivering them to a triad boss. The MS 13 rarely collaborated with triads and he suspected there was a substantial payment for delivering the Asian couple.

It had taken all day to drive the almost 500 miles from his home turf of Westlake to Sedona. It was the first time he had been out of California and he was enjoying the majestic red rock landscapes of Arizona. This mission was an opportunity for him to progress within the ranks of the MS-13 organisation. He could start to make some real money and score better bitches for sure.

The black SUV parked before him had transported all his brothers. His passenger was a giant known as the Ice Man, the most famous assassin in California. They had only spoken intermittently during the journey; however, he had told Diego that he ran with the Crips before deciding freelance killing was a better option for him.

Diego knew that once you were a Crips gang member, it was for life. This man had to have been highly respected for them to permit him to resign. Perhaps, because he was a stone-cold killer, they had decided it was safer for all to let him leave the gang.

The Ice Man made him very uncomfortable.

He could detect the evil lurking within this man.

He was the scariest man he had ever met.

Diego's senses were on high alert, alarm bells ringing in his mind.

The initial excitement of the mission had transformed into fully blown skin-creeping anxiety.

No… if he was honest with himself, it wasn't anxiety.

He was shit scared.

They were to capture two Asians, one a petite woman and the other her male companion. They hadn't appeared dangerous in the photos he had seen, they just looked like ordinary people. Why was it necessary to have a team of seven, five of them heavily armed? He knew that the three who would search the motel rooms were considered the best fighters and assassins in the Los Angeles area.

Who are these people and what have they done to receive such attention and sizeable reward?

He lit a joint to calm his nerves. He would have enjoyed a line of coke but had used what he had on the drive. Once paid and back home, there would be plenty of money for sniff and bitches. He lowered the window and exhaled the rancid smoke. He heard shots, then automatic weapons. That wasn't good; it was supposed to be a quiet grab-and-go mission. He tossed the reefer, opened the glove box, and removed the Smith & Wesson revolver.

A naked woman ran from the building. At first, he thought she was running in fear away from the gunmen. Then he saw she was carrying an Uzi, her face set in a snarl as she ran towards them. She fired three rounds into the SUV in front and he saw the driver's head explode, the windows painted with blood. The woman hadn't even slowed. She had taken him out whilst running.

Fuck this, I'm out of here.

Diego started the ignition, selected reverse, and slammed his foot on the accelerator whilst pulling hard on the steering wheel. The wheels squealed as the van laid rubber from the tight turn.

It wasn't fast enough though.

The shooter disabled his vehicle by shooting out the four tyres and the windscreen. He reached across to grab the revolver, but it had slid off the seat onto the floor. As he reached down to grasp it, the passenger window blew out, and the barrel of the Uzi poked into the cabin.

"If you want to live, put your hands on your head."

Diego reached for the gun.

It was the last thing he would ever do.

About the author

Paul McDonald is the author of the Sakura Bianchi Series:
Book 1 Innocent Assassin
Book 2 Innocent Girls
Book 3 Innocent Lives

I am retired and living in Bundaberg Queensland, Australia, with my wife on our bushland property.

Acknowledgements

It takes courage to write a book and it requires the assistance of others to make it a good story. Being a self-publisher, I don't have the luxury of editors and proofreaders, so it can only be achieved with the help of friends and family.

I would like to thank the following people who have made this story what it is.
Thank you to: -

My wife Michelle, who's keen eye identified the most subtle errors when proofreading the final version.

Piers Chapple for undertaking the editing and proofreading of the manuscript, a skill I still need to improve.

Samantha Lang and Shelley Dickson for reading the first draft and identifying areas for improvement.

www.ingramcontent.com/pod-product-compliance
Lightning Source LLC
Chambersburg PA
CBHW051558030726
47592CB00001B/344